A Light in Babylon

Also by Carole C. Carlson

The Late Great Planet Earth (with Hal Lindsey)
Satan Is Alive and Well on Planet Earth (with Hal Lindsey)
Straw Houses in the Wind
In My Father's House (with Corrie ten Boom)
The Married Man (with Bob Vernon)
Woman (with Dale Evans Rogers)
Grandparents Can (with Dale Evans Rogers)
Established in Eden
The Terminal Generation (with Hal Lindsey)
Corrie ten Boom, Her Life and Faith
Say Yes to Your Potential (with Skip Ross)

Carole C. Carlson

A Light in Babylon

A Novel

Based on the Life of Daniel

WORD BOOKS
PUBLISHER
WACO, TEXAS

A DIVISION OF
WORD, INCORPORATED

A LIGHT IN BABYLON
A Novel Based on the Life of Daniel

Library of Congress Cataloging in Publication Data:

Carlson, Carole C.
A light in Babylon.

1. Daniel, the Prophet—Fiction. I. Title.
PS3553.A7319L5 1985 813'.54 85-9258
ISBN 0-8499-0452-8

Printed in the United States of America

567898 KP 987654321

Author's Note

Daniel was a real man; he lived at a time that was fraught with turmoil, national power plays, and political intrigue. He knew and experienced the emotions common to all human beings: love, fear, hate, and discouragement.

In writing this fictionalized version of a familiar Bible story, my greatest concern was that fact and fantasy would become so blurred that the reader would not be able to discern the difference. The biblical account is fact; anything beyond that is drawn from my imagination. As you search the Scriptures you will see that the account follows the Bible as accurately as I could make it.

Historical accuracy was my goal, but if there are some differences in the time element among various interpreters, I hope that you will acknowledge the over twenty-five-hundred-year gap between the prophet Daniel and the present century.

Getting to know Daniel has been a great adventure, a journey into a time of such importance that only the future will be able to testify to its full significance. Few men have made the impact on all generations that did this son of Judah, chosen for one of the most important missions to our generation.

May your journey into his world be a life-changing experience, as it has mine.

Carole C. Carlson

PART I

Into Captivity

"Hear, I pray you, all people, and behold

my sorrow: my virgins and my

young men are gone into captivity."

Lamentations 1:18, KJV

1

CRIES IN THE CITY

"STAND HERE, DANIEL . . . away from the wall. The very stones have ears."

Abiel looked cautiously around his beautiful Jerusalem courtyard. This garden was his escape from the pressures of court duties, the place where he could breathe the fragrance of the myrtle and balsam or drop crumbs to the gentle palm dove. But in these days the tranquility was deceptive. A man's home was no longer a safe refuge. Palace spies were everywhere, eager to report any conversation which hinted of disloyalty to King Jehoiakim.

Not that Abiel considered himself a traitor. He was a noble, with obedience to the reigning monarch bred and trained into him. Deception was not part of his nature. But there were higher loyalties than to a king, and they must take priority, even with lives at stake.

He snapped a twig from a green bay tree, pressing its spice-scented leaves to his nostrils. In the branches a pair of capricious goldfinches played a game of tag. Abiel sighed. He was a man whose rugged features beneath a thick, black chin beard belied his gentle nature. To him life was made for beauty, for love, for building and creating, not for greed and suspicion. He hated playing this game of subterfuge.

In his youth, Abiel had been straight and strong, like the son who stood tall beside him. But the years had given him a slight stoop and a squint to his eyes from examining many architectural plans in his assigned position as chief builder for the king. He was still a strong man, but his strength was in his convictions, his ability to work hard, and his simple but unswerving loyalty to the God of Abraham, Isaac, and Jacob.

Daniel stood waiting for his father to speak, eyes shining with anticipation. To be summoned from his studies in the middle of the day was no common occurrence; his father must have something important to discuss with him.

Although born into wealth and influence, Daniel had clearly not been softened by his background. Discipline was evident in his taut body and keen eyes. His knee-length tunic, made of fine linen, was girded at the waist with a simple hemp rope. In the sunlight, filtering through the ash-grey leaves of the gnarled olive tree, his curly hair glistened with health. And his bearing reflected a strong confidence unusual in one so young.

Abiel spoke in a quiet voice: "Daniel, to anyone who might be watching it must appear that we are speaking casually. I am going to send you on a simple errand, that's all. However, what I am about to tell you could mean life or death."

"I'm at your command, father." Daniel felt a thrill go through his body. Abiel was not one to exaggerate; this could not be a child's errand to fetch a tool from one of the carpenter's stalls—a task he was usually given. Being sent on an important assignment meant he was accepted as an adult. And it was about time! He was, after all, fifteen years old.

Abiel gripped the strong shoulder of his only son, the boy who had grown into a man too soon. How could he send this special one on such a perilous mission? And yet . . . who could carry this message? His servants were a cowering lot who feared the wrath of the king. He could not go himself, for his face and position were too well known in the streets of Jerusalem. Daniel, on the other hand, was a student who spent most of his time with his tutor, learning traditions and manners as befitted a young Jewish noble. In many ways he had been sheltered. He would probably not be recognized. . . .

I should have taught him more of politics . . . and women, Abiel thought. Is there ever a time when a father believes he has done a good job in raising his son? But there is no time for regrets. The Lord grants wisdom, and there comes a time when a father must let go.

"But beware, my son. Keep your eyes front and your feet swift. We have many enemies in Judah who seek vengeance upon true believers in Jehovah."

Abiel paused and walked over to the garden gate. Had he heard something? A lizard scurried through the bushes, rustling the leaves in its path. *How foolish,* he thought, *that I should find my chest becoming tight over the slightest sound.*

He looked at Daniel, realizing that his son needed an explanation. For the years he had raised him after his mother had died, he had always tried to be honest with him. "Daniel, I am an architect, a builder, not a manipulator. But these are days when men cannot hide from duty. I will obey Jehovah, not man."

"And I, too, father," Daniel said. He did not fully understand what his father wanted him to do, but the son of a Hebrew noble was taught to obey first and question later. And he knew there was danger. His father disagreed with the oppressive decrees of Jehoiakim. Abiel could be beheaded for treason if the king heard even a rumor of disloyalty.

"Your task, Daniel, is to warn my friend, Jeremiah. He is a man of courage, but he is in great danger. If he does not cease his prophecies about the downfall of Jerusalem, his life will be worth less than that of a sacrificial lamb. The king, may his wicked heart be changed, wants the prophet silenced—or tortured into submission."

King Jehoiakim was playing a treacherous game of pretense. On one hand he was a mere puppet of King Nebuchadnezzar, the ruler of Babylon, and yet he was conniving in secret with Babylon's rival, the Pharaoh of Egypt. He thought he could gain the favor of both without one knowing about the other.

Most Judeans were indifferent to royal politics. What did it matter whether Egypt or Babylon ruled? One tyrant was the same as another. But Jeremiah, reading the future, saw otherwise. He believed Nebuchadnezzar was an agent the Lord would use to punish Judah. And the prophet took every opportunity to proclaim his views, unpopular as they were.

"Be careful not to let others see you, my son, but you must try to save Jeremiah from his own rashness. Jehovah has given him the gift of prophecy, but his warnings about the downfall of Judah could bring his head on a platter to the king. Tell him that he must cease his speaking or he will lose his tongue."

One of the Nubian servants in their home was mute as the result of the king's wrath. Daniel knew his father's urgency was well founded.

"Hurry, Daniel . . . and may the angels surround you."

Abiel thought how blessed he was to have this boy for his own. *But, Lord, I know I don't possess him,* Abiel silently confessed. *He is your gift, the fruit of my loins and his mother's womb. O Jehovah, protect him from those who could harm him.*

Embracing his father quickly, Daniel left their peaceful garden, moved along the pebble paths to the iron gate surrounding the palace compound, and into the bustling streets. Once he was outside the cool walls surrounding the palace, the unrelenting Judean sun spilled its brilliance upon him, making his smooth skin glisten like polished marble.

"A coin . . . just one mite to feed my poor mother," pleaded a small boy, his unwashed hand tugging at Daniel's tunic.

Daniel smiled at the round-cheeked little beggar and tossed him a silver piece, hurrying on before he was besieged by a dozen teasing children.

Jerusalem. He loved the very sound of its name. As he walked the streets, he was aware of his surroundings, but his mind spun with more than the sights and sounds he encountered. This was the most holy of all places. It was here that King David had brought the Ark of the Covenant, transforming the city from a Canaanite sanctuary into a place sacred to God. It was here that David's son, Solomon, had built the great Temple, the house of the Lord, atop the holy mount.

Daniel breathed deeply of the smells that enveloped the streets. Could anything be greater than being young and living in times like these, no matter how perilous? He wanted to protect his city from the evil that was creeping through its gates. This was, after all, the very place where a prophet named Isaiah had said that the great King, the promised Messiah, would some day reign. The thought was too awesome for him fully to comprehend.

As he swerved to avoid a donkey, laden with a wobbly burden

of wheat and barley, he felt a hand upon his bare shoulder and turned to look into the seductive eyes of a street harlot.

"Come over here, you of the smooth skin; I have ripe wine to taste." Her lewd glance brought a flush to Daniel's cheeks.

He looked at his sandals and moved on quickly. A queasy feeling hit the bottom of his stomach. What would the Messiah think of His city if He were to come now?

Daniel was steeped in the knowledge of his spiritual ancestry. During long walks with his father he would hear the stories of their history. From ancient times, the Lord had promised Abraham: "I will bless those who bless you, and the one who curses you I will curse."

How could the people of Judah forget such a great heritage?

History had proved that Jehovah kept His promises. He had told Abraham that his people would be slaves for four hundred years in a land not their own. This had been fulfilled by bondage in Egypt, but then the Lord had saved Israel from the hands of the Egyptians by parting the Red Sea. Moses and all of his people had sung, "The Lord shall reign forever and ever." And yet, they had grumbled as they trudged through the wilderness and complained about all of the inconveniences.

How soon the people of Israel forgot Jehovah's blessings! Even when Moses was receiving the Law and the Commandments from the Lord on Mount Sinai, his people had been corrupting themselves by worshiping a golden calf.

As Daniel passed through the Street of the Bakers, his bare legs warmed by the heat from the ovens, his senses tempted by the aromas from the cakes of dough flattened on the stones, he noticed that an icon of Astarte, called the "Queen of Heaven" by the idol worshipers, was displayed in the stall. He remembered hearing that this heathen goddess had been admired by the Philistines and that Jezebel's priests had served her image. Daniel wanted to shout the cry of Moses: "Hear, O Israel! The Lord is our God, the Lord is One!"

With eyes of wisdom beyond his years, Daniel frequently allowed his mind to wander, questioning the trend of the times. His friends would say, "Daniel's staring into space again. Do you think he's practicing to be an astrologer?" Those jibes made Daniel bite his lips. He did not want to appear self-righteous, but he also wanted nothing to do with fortune-telling; he had watched with disgust the trancelike attitudes of the servants in the house of Abiel when they were communing with soothsayers. Still, he took the teasings good-naturedly, for he did not have a brooding disposition. Life was too full of unexpected joys to be concerned about the passing opinions or criticisms of his peers.

The sellers called out to him, "Bread? Fine bread for the royal feasts?"

It was not often that Daniel had the opportunity to leave the palace confines and go to the marketplace. In the hours of the morning before the noonday heat turned the city into a languorous slumber, he was usually in the classroom. He spent long hours learning his people's history and the songs of Zion from the sacred scrolls.

A shepherd passed him, prodding three reluctant sheep through the crowds; children scurried around the mire in the path, laughing as one of their playmates planted a bare foot in a fresh deposit.

On one side of the street, a potter was shaping an earthen vessel from a moist blob of clay. Daniel watched for a moment as the man crushed the jar back into a shapeless mass of mud and began over again. That was the sign of a craftsman who found a defect in the clay. Daniel smiled and nodded in admiration. He recognized a person who took pride in his work.

Next was a stall where a carpenter, using his rule and compass, was shaping a plow for the use of a farmer; behind him was a stack of low tables and stools—simple furniture he had made for a home.

The freedom of the marketplace was heady to Daniel. Here he could see the faces of the people, imagine the source of the goods they brought for sale or barter. The villages and farms outside the gates of Jerusalem belonged to the men and women he longed to know . . . the people who must look at the stars He created and the earth He blessed and love the Lord God Jehovah. Did the hills of Judea shelter them from the rottenness which was oozing through the city streets like a contamination from Sodom?

What were they like, these peasants of Judah who stamped the wine presses and tended the olive orchards? He wondered if Jehovah had chosen to have him born in the city, into the House of Abiel, for some foreordained destiny. Why couldn't he have been a shepherd or a fisherman?

Daniel shook his head as if to clear it of mental wandering. He had a job to do. If the king heard that Jeremiah was warning the people again about the downfall of Jerusalem, there could be more bloodshed. He began to run, weaving through the streets, trying to avoid the boys and girls who were playing their innocent games. His throat tightened as he looked at these laughing little ones. Would any of them be offered as human sacrifices in the Valley of Hinnom? How could Jehovah withhold judgment on a nation which slaughtered children?

As he raced through the narrow alleys, Daniel was not unnoticed. Among the swarthy skins of the Hebrews, it was unusual to find someone as light as he. His face was the color of smooth teak, not the mahogany of the desert people or country dwellers. Everything about him, from his fine tunic to his palm-bark and leather sandals, spoke of a young man of wealth. He seemed to be without any physical flaws, and some in the marketplace jeered at him with envy.

"Hail, noble one. Watch where you walk or you'll carry dung back to the palace." A youth of his own age, sitting cross-legged in front of a peddler's fruit cart, taunted him.

They mocked and picked up pebbles to throw at him. Daniel ignored their ridicule; nevertheless, he increased his speed. Then, as he veered around the sharp corner of a stone wall, he collided abruptly with a small, soft body, sending her sprawling on the cobblestones.

"Don't move— Let me help you— I'm sorry— Are you hurt?" As Daniel reached down to lift her, his hand touched the warm blood on her arm. His apologies were stopped by angry black eyes, squinting between heavy lashes which were fast becoming wet with tears.

"You broke my pendant! My father will be furious."

A gold chain dangled on the front of her heavily embroidered bodice, and the distinctive fragrance of roses permeated the rumpled girl as she clutched to find the broken vial of perfume which had been attached to her necklace.

"See what you've done?" she sniffed, "why don't you keep your eyes open?"

Daniel stared at her. From her clothes and the gold bracelets on her slim arms, it was clear she was not from the peasant class. Without sisters, he had very few encounters with girls of his age, but he thought that in his whole life he had never seen a girl like this. He remembered how he had felt his pulse pound when the priest had read the Song of Solomon on the eighth day of Passover. For a moment, the words, "like a lily among thorns" lingered in his mind.

"Are you going to stand there or help me up, now that you've ruined my day?"

Daniel lifted her to her feet and apologized, "Please forgive me. I was in such a rush, I didn't see you." He tried to brush the dirt from her blue linen tunic, but felt awkward in the attempt. He put his hands behind him.

"Do you have a companion with you?" he asked. A girl of her class did not travel the streets without a servant as a protector or an older woman for a chaperone. What was she doing in the marketplace alone?

"I did, but somehow we became separated; perhaps when I stopped to look at the cloth from Egypt she just kept going." Her tears began to flow. "My father will be so angry with me . . . he worries all the time."

Daniel couldn't decide what to do with her. She should not be left unprotected. On the other hand, he had his duty. Impulsively, he said, "If you are willing to come with me, I'll deliver my message and then see you home."

She shook the dust from her garments and examined her scraped elbow. Assured that nothing was hurt except her youthful dignity, she took a good look at this tall son of Judah. A smile played across her lips; she thought how fortunate she was to have an encounter with someone so handsome. He was awkward and quite shy in her presence. What difference would it make if she went with him? It could be an adventure. Whatever she did, it was inevitable that she would face the wrath of her father, so she might as well enjoy herself while she could. Besides, she didn't relish the idea of being in the streets alone.

"If you're not hurt, I must get on to warn Jeremiah." Daniel almost slapped his hand upon his own mouth. Was he forgetting his father's admonitions so soon? But those dark eyes confronting him were lacking in guile; instinctively he trusted her.

For the first time in his young life he began to realize that there were feelings experienced by a man that were unknown to a boy who had been sheltered so long in the household of Abiel. . . .

"I'll go with you."

"Then hurry." Daniel began to run down the narrow alley. Without a thought for her fine clothes, she gathered up her skirts and ran after him in the direction of Solomon's Temple.

The Temple was a special place to Daniel, who had grown up in the shadow of its sacred walls. For the formative years of his life he had lived under the rule of King Josiah, the one who had restored Temple worship, stirring the hearts of his people to return to the God of Abraham, Isaac, and Jacob.

When Daniel had been no higher than his father's thigh he would ask, in the manner of small boys everywhere, "Tell me the story about the great discovery, Father."

And Abiel would stop his work and put his arms around the son he loved so much, the one he felt in his heart had been chosen by the Lord to be used in some way yet undisclosed. King Josiah himself had said at the time of Daniel's circumcision, "May your house be blessed with the glory of the Lord and may your son be raised to obey His commandments."

"Now, let me see, Daniel, what story do you want to hear?" Abiel would ask.

"You know, father, about the time you were working to repair the Temple and . . ."

"Of course, of course . . . how could I forget?" Abiel's eyes would become thoughtful, relishing the memory. "I was in charge of the carpenters and masons for the royal building projects. King Josiah wanted only quality material for the Temple reconstruction, so I was told to buy the very best lumber and stone. Those were the days, son, when craftsmanship was expected. All the altars of Baal were to be destroyed and the graven images ground to dust. Now that was a job I assigned to myself!"

Abiel had relished the memory of shattering the idols. He would raise his heavily muscled arms and pretend to slam his great hammer down upon the despised stones.

Then, with a dramatic flourish, Abiel would lower his voice and wait for Daniel to urge him on.

"One day a most amazing treasure was found. The laborers had been working all morning and had stopped to eat some barley bread and milk. The Levites were playing music and the mood was joyous. Suddenly the High Priest, Hilkiah, gave a loud shout. It was such a startling sound in the quiet of the sanctuary that we all stopped to see if he had been injured in some way."

Daniel, who already knew the story by heart, would ask eagerly, "What did the High Priest find, father?"

And Abiel would pause and speak in a reverent tone. "He found a scroll, hidden by the dust of ages, that contained the Law of Jehovah, given to Moses!"

That proclamation had never failed to cause Daniel to tremble. His father would stand and raise his arms, the sleeves of his robe falling to form the image of an eagle, his face glowing at the memory of the priceless discovery. "We couldn't believe it at first. To think that the book of the Law would be buried beneath the stones of the temple!"

Daniel had been proud that his father was present at such a significant moment. It was as if Jehovah Himself had reached down to touch the hands of the workmen that day. *Does God really plan our simplest actions for His purpose?* Daniel wondered.

"The scroll was taken to Shaphan, the secretary to King Josiah," Abiel would continue, "and when the king heard what was written on it, he tore his clothes in terror. He said, 'These are the commands of the Lord God, and neither we nor our ancestors have followed them. What shall we do?'

"And so, my son," Abiel would say, "King Josiah sent the priest and other high officials, including this humble servant, to consult with Huldah, the prophetess. She told us that she had received this prophetic message from the Lord God of Israel:

" 'Tell the man who sent you to me'—that was King Josiah—'that I am going to destroy this city and its people, just as I stated in that book you read. For the people of Judah have thrown me aside and have worshiped other gods and have made me very angry; and my anger can't be stopped. But because you were sorry and concerned and humbled yourself before the Lord when you read the book and its warnings that this land would be cursed and become desolate, and because you have torn your clothing and wept before me in contrition, I will listen to your plea. *The death of this nation will not occur until after you die*—you will not see the evil which I will bring upon this place.'

"And that, son, is the message we took to King Josiah."

As a child, Daniel had spent long hours with his father, listening to the words of the prophets. At times, it seemed that God was using these men as great warning signals without offering any hope; there were so few who followed the laws of God for His chosen people.

"Daniel, if you learn nothing else from me during your lifetime, remember that Jehovah is loving, but He is also just, blessed be His name. He cannot tolerate His people continuing in disobedience to His commandments."

Daniel had never seemed to tire of listening to his father, even though the significance of his words was not always clear. "The Lord will punish His people, just as I punish you when you do wrong. But that doesn't mean that He doesn't love us, nor does it mean that I don't love you."

Daniel had known the sting of his father's love. A branch from the fig tree had been frequently applied to his knuckles when he strayed from his lessons or neglected to come home at an appointed time.

But there had been other realities more difficult for Daniel to fathom. When his mother died, he had thought God must be very unjust. She had been so beautiful, with soft brown eyes that sparkled with happiness as she instructed the servant girls in the tasks of the household—loving her family to the exclusion of all palace pleasures. Lavish jewels and silken robes had been hers, but such possessions had never obsessed her. Then one day she had developed a fever and her face had become unnaturally flushed, the merry eyes were glazed. Within a few days she had fallen silent, and Daniel's world had seemed to collapse.

He and his father had left Jerusalem for a time and wandered in the Judean hills, building a campfire and pitching a tent under the brilliant stars of Israel. They needed to escape from their daily activities and reflect upon the unfathomable will of Jehovah.

"Look at the stars, son. Does Jehovah care any less for us, His children, than He cares for the orderly way in which they travel across the skies?"

When they drew their cloaks to shield themselves from the chilling desert night, Daniel had heard his father weep—and realized that deep emotion was not the sole possession of women. When the time had come for them to return to the duties in the court, Abiel told him something Daniel would never forget:

"My son, I have heard from the scrolls of the prophet Isaiah some words of great encouragement. He said, 'O Israel, how can you say that the Lord doesn't see your troubles and isn't being fair? . . . He gives power to the tired and worn out, and strength to the weak. Even the youths shall be exhausted, and the young men will all give up. But they that wait upon the Lord shall renew their strength. They shall mount up with wings like eagles; they shall run and not be weary; they shall walk and not faint.' "

"But why did my mother have to die?" Daniel had asked.

"I don't know the answers, Daniel, to many of the great trials of life, but I do know that God made me, and He chose you to be my son. He has His reasons for our lives. We only need to be sensitive to what He tells us to do."

Those words of his father's emerged now from Daniel's memory as he neared the Temple, followed by the surprisingly swift-footed girl. "Run and not be weary," echoed with each step.

As they approached the Temple area, Daniel wondered how he would ever find Jeremiah and warn him. Every day the prophet stood upon the Temple steps and spoke to those who gathered in the inner courtyard. He must be stopped.

"We'll wait in the courtyard until I see him," he whispered to the girl, "and then I'll speak to him in private before he begins to talk. Please stay close to me." He started toward the gate that separated the teeming outer court from the inner court of the Temple.

The girl grabbed his tunic. "Are you going in there? . . ."

"Of course."

"But I . . . can't . . ."

A wave of irritation passed over Daniel. He had forgotten women weren't allowed in the inner court. "Why did I allow her to come?" he thought. Then he looked at her pleading dark eyes and the irritation disappeared.

"You can stand at the gate," he said. "I will go in and do what I came to do. If anyone bothers you, I will be where I can reach you quickly."

She looked at him doubtfully. "I would rather stay with you." But seeing his resolute face she agreed, and the two of them started toward the gate.

Through the gate in the wall surrounding the inner court, or priests' court, Solomon's Temple loomed, dwarfing the people and animals in the court with its size and grandeur. In front of the Temple, stood two objects which were intimately connected with worship. One was the altar of burnt offering, where flame and smoke rose from the roasting of the sacrifices. The other was the "molten sea" or mammoth bowl made of bronze and containing an immense reservoir of twelve thousand gallons of water used for ceremonial washing by the temple priests.

The two young people stood to the side, keeping out of the way of the drovers who were herding sheep and oxen into the courtyard. The place was a din of sounds from scores of human and animal voices.

The sun reflected from the limestone, mined out of the great quarries of King Solomon, that comprised the outer walls of the Temple. The stones were so large that, if one were stood on end, two large men could stand behind it and not be seen. The Temple itself was built on a nine-foot-high platform, which was reached by ten steps.

Daniel watched those steps carefully through the gate. It was there that Jeremiah would be preaching.

At the top of the steps were the great cedar wood doors from Lebanon, inlaid with gold and flanked by towering bronze pillars, which were made from copper brought from the mines of Solomon, south of the Dead Sea. The Temple was a building of lavish beauty, as well as the place where God manifested His presence by the Shekinah glory. Only the priests entered the Holy Place, which was the dwelling place of God.

"There he is, little one," Daniel said, motioning to the grey-bearded man who was walking toward the Temple steps. "Stay here, I shall go and speak to him."

"I'm coming with you," the girl said, reluctant to be left with all the bleating lambs that were being led to slaughter.

"No— You can't— Stay here—" He squeezed her hand and left her standing by the gate as he hurried toward Jeremiah. He stopped the old man at the foot of the steps. Jeremiah had seen the youth approaching him, and concern showed in his troubled eyes. It was one thing to preach before these crowds that mocked and taunted him, but a boy like this didn't have to become involved. Why was the son of Abiel hurrying toward him with such urgency?

"What is it, my boy? Don't you see this is no place for you?"

"My father, Abiel, sent me, sir." Daniel lowered his voice and looked around. Was anyone listening? One man standing by the corner of the Temple seemed to be eyeing them suspiciously. "I was told to warn you that the king has his spies watching you, and that if you say anything more which displeases him, you may be flogged . . . or worse."

Jeremiah did not look like a threat to anyone. He was a man of simple tastes, at heart a gentle person. He wore a shabby cloak, with full sleeves from his thin shoulders to his elbows. His sandals were frayed and held together with rope. Under his arm he carried a plain clay jar.

This ordinary man cried for the people and the land he loved, and he longed for their repentance. Did everyone think he searched for trouble? He followed the voice of the Lord, who told him what to say. Many times the words put into his heart and expressed with his mouth were as startling to him as they were to his listeners. How could a mere youth, or even a mighty king of Judah silence the words of Jehovah?

Jeremiah set down his jar on the first step leading to the Temple and then looked up at the great structure. His pale grey eyes squinted as the sun reflected from the brilliant white stones. How could he be silent about what he knew? He looked at Daniel—young, vigorous—and thought that as long as there were youths like this there might be hope for the country.

"I must speak as God directs me, my boy. Most people of Judah believe that as long as the Temple stands in Jerusalem the city will never be taken by an enemy. God has told me otherwise. This city is doomed."

"How does God speak to you, sir?" Daniel asked quietly. "Do you hear His voice as Moses did from a burning bush? Does He visit you in the form of an angel?"

Daniel searched the piercing eyes of the prophet for answers to his probing questions. He longed to understand the complexities of the inner spiritual life. Hadn't his father told him that the reforms under King Josiah had brought about a great surge of religious fervor in the land? And yet he knew that today the revival was all but forgotten; the moral state of the nation was worse than ever.

"When Jehovah speaks it is clear, no matter what means He uses. But my boy," Jeremiah said, answering Daniel's thoughts, "man will never be able to lead a righteous life by having rules and laws laid upon him. All reform begins in the hearts and minds of people."

Jeremiah looked with compassion at the strong youth. His good friend, Abiel, had raised this boy well. "Return to your father, boy, and tell him that God will honor his concern for me. But you must take the girl and leave, for she should not be in this place, and your life may be in danger if you are seen here with me. Jehovah has other work for you to do in the future."

Daniel realized with a start that the girl had followed him into the courtyard and was standing close, her face turned up to Jeremiah, completely absorbed by his words. He looked around wildly at the crowd, but in the confusion of the courtyard no one seemed to notice the tiny feminine figure.

"We must find someone to take you home, little one," Daniel told her. "I am staying, but this is no place for you."

"No," she answered, "as long as you don't leave me alone I'll be safe."

Daniel felt himself grow a bit with those words. His academic and athletic life had not placed him in contact with young women, except the servant girls in the household. These were the foolish young women who were always making horoscopes and trying to read the future in the stars. Somehow he knew this girl would not be like that. She reminded him of his mother.

"Stay close to me, little one." There was no indication that she would do anything else.

"My name is not little one. It's Deborah."

The two young people moved outside, pressing their backs against the stones of the wall surrounding the courtyard. Through the gap they could see that a few were beginning to gather around Jeremiah.

The old man climbed the steps and stood facing the great inner courtyard. He began to speak, his voice resonant and authoritative over the voices of the crowd.

"Judah, listen . . . I bring you a message from the Lord of Hosts, the God of Israel: 'don't be fooled by those who lie to you and say that since the Temple of the Lord is here, God will never let Jerusalem be destroyed. You may remain under these conditions only: If you stop your wicked thoughts and deeds, and are fair to others, and stop exploiting orphans, widows, and foreigners. And stop your murdering. And stop worshiping idols as you do now to your hurt. Then, and only then, will I let you stay in this land.' "

"Who are you to know what God says? Are you a high priest or the king himself?" A swarthy man with a knife girded in his belt shouted at Jeremiah and spat on the ground in front of him.

More began to gather, laughing and pointing their fingers at Jeremiah. They had not come to listen, but to condemn. Life in Jerusalem was not easy for these people. Taxes were severe and it was common knowledge that public monies were supporting King Jehoiakim's extravagant way of living. However, the pleasures of the city were abundant. Prostitutes could be had for a loaf of bread, and strong wine was available to dull the senses when life became too oppressive. What did it matter that every jot and tittle of the Law was not obeyed? After all, the Temple was standing and the priests still presented sacrifices for their sins.

Jeremiah ignored those who jeered, and he continued speaking. His detractors were silenced, listening sullenly to words that condemned them with whipping impact.

"You think because the Temple is here, you will never suffer? Don't fool yourselves! Do you really think that you can steal, murder, commit adultery, lie, and worship Baal and all of those new gods of yours, and then come here and stand before Jehovah in His Temple and chant, 'We are saved!'?"

The crowd began to get restless. Jeremiah was continually telling them that the Lord had given him these warnings. Who was he to meddle in their private lives?

Jeremiah found it difficult to keep his voice steady. He loved this land, but these people were worse than wayward children in their wicked ways. Why wouldn't they listen?

"God has told me that He will destroy this Temple because of the evil you have done—and that He will send you into exile."

"Blasphemy!" shouted someone from the crowd. "Tell the priests, for this man says the Temple will be destroyed."

"Report him to the king. He has ways of handling treason. He'll turn his body into pulp for the buzzards."

Jeremiah raised his arms for silence. The hecklers quieted momentarily. "The Lord has said, 'I will end the happy singing and laughter in the streets of Jerusalem and in the cities of Judah, and the joyous voices of the bridegrooms and brides. For the land shall lie in desolation.' "

He picked up the clay jar from the step beside him and dashed it to the ground in front of the crowd: it broke into a hundred pieces at the feet of the listeners. The crowd became quiet. Jeremiah's voice rose, "This is a message to you from the Lord of Hosts: As this jar lies shattered, so I will shatter the people of Jerusalem; and as this jar cannot be mended, neither can they."

As the prophet continued with his awesome words, Daniel and Deborah remained close to the gate, away from the crowd that grew increasingly impatient and rowdy with each dolorous prediction. They saw several men at the edge of the crowd pick up rocks and aim toward the prophet. Then someone emerged from the corner of the Temple and whispered into Jeremiah's ear. Within seconds the two men drew their cloaks around them and disappeared from view before anyone knew where they went.

For a moment, there was a curious silence. People looked at each other, not knowing what to say. Deborah whispered, "Daniel, did you see that? Jeremiah seemed to have some kind of invisible protection. No one in the crowd came near him."

Daniel stared at the Temple steps, incredulous as the others. "I remember my father saying that when Jeremiah was very young, the Lord said to him, 'Don't be afraid of the people, for I, the Lord, will be with you and see you through.' I believe, Deborah, when Jehovah chooses one of His children to do His work, He sends guardian angels to protect him."

Daniel's heart was tossed in two directions. He was burdened by the prophecy of destruction of Jerusalem and exile, and yet he was experiencing the first surge of a new emotion.

Daniel and Deborah. The names seemed to fit together. He looked down at her soft hair, her clear skin that had been shielded from the harsh sun and dry heat of the region, and felt very protective. He could be strong enough to withstand any hardships which might come upon this land, but he did not want to see this lovely child-woman suffer.

Daniel moved away from the gate. "Come, Deborah, I must go

to my father and tell him what the prophet has said. I've done my duty in warning him, and the Lord has seen fit to guard him from his enemies."

Daniel pondered as they pushed their way through the Temple crowds. He knew his God was just, but he did not understand all of His ways. Would he ever grow old enough, as old as Jeremiah, and learn more of the Lord God of Israel? The times were so unsettled. Could Jeremiah really read the future?

Deborah voiced what he was thinking. "Do you think he is a true prophet of the Lord?"

Was this a woman who could think, as well as look beautiful? Daniel answered, "The Lord told Moses that the true test of a prophet is that everything he says must come true. I don't believe Jeremiah has made up all these predictions. But my father tells me that the priests think he is a charlatan and that many in the court wish to silence him with a sword. He is in great danger if he continues."

"But what do you think?"

Daniel looked at the Temple. Solomon had built it with riches beyond comprehension. Within the Holy of Holies was the Ark of the Covenant, containing the Law of Moses. Who would dare destroy such a sacred place? And yet, Daniel replied, "I would not have come to warn him if I didn't believe in him. Jeremiah has said that the Lord appointed him as a spokesman to the world."

Daniel lowered his voice, but spoke with conviction. "I believe Jeremiah is one of God's chosen prophets. Unless Judah returns to the Lord God, what Jeremiah says will happen. The people of Israel will be severely punished."

"You're as gloomy as Jeremiah. God has said we are His chosen people," Deborah replied. "Why should the good people be punished with the bad?"

"Prophets are not always popular," Daniel answered, knowing that his response was not what Deborah wanted to hear. He was beginning to realize that he was not making a good impression.

"You speak thoughts I don't understand," Deborah said peevishly. "Why think about the future when there are so many pleasures today? I must find my companion and go home or I will be in more trouble than even Jeremiah could predict."

"Wait, you mustn't go alone. I'll see you home."

"Take me to the Street of the Merchants and leave me. I will go to my house from there."

Deborah realized with sudden nervousness just how bold she had been to be in a public place without a chaperone. And with a young man . . . at the Temple! She was not a child, but a woman of marriageable age. This was one adventure she would have to keep a secret, even from her sister.

Daniel followed Deborah from the Temple courtyard back to the Street of Merchants. He walked discreetly behind her, and didn't speak. The streets were not as crowded, for the people were beginning to return to their homes for the evening worship. Peddlers who had brought their fruit and vegetables to the marketplace were strapping what they had not sold onto the backs of the donkeys and leaving the city.

Finally Deborah stopped and turned to Daniel. This had been an afternoon she would remember. And if her father found out, he would not let her forget it! "Goodbye, Daniel. I know my way home." And she ran away down the street.

Daniel watched her until she was out of sight. "Lord," he prayed, "let me see her again."

As Daniel returned to report the outcome of his mission to Abiel, the dour words of Jeremiah seemed to fade into the background. The day had brought this unexpected encounter, leading in an unknown direction. Wandering past the merchants' stalls, dodging the carts filled with leeks and onions, Daniel's handsome face shone with the glow of a youth experiencing his first love. Through his mind ran the words of the proverb he had studied in his classes. Now the words seemed to have a new resonance and meaning:

> There are three things which are too wonderful for me;
> Four which I do not understand:
> The way of an eagle in the sky,
> The way of a serpent on a rock,
> The way of a ship in the middle of the sea,
> And the way of a man with a maid.*

He had accomplished his assignment and no one was harmed. His heart contained the strangest excitement. Even the mournful predictions of Jeremiah could not make him depressed. Life was exciting!

Father God, he prayed silently. *Will I ever know the way of a man with a maid?*

---

* Proverbs 30:18–19, NASB.

2

NO LONGER A BOY

"DO WE THINK we are free? We're slaves . . . slaves to the king! To work for an unjust cause is like having an iron yoke around your neck." Abiel sunk onto his couch, his strong face etched with exhaustion. Daniel unlaced his father's sandals and began to massage his feet to ease the tension in his body. Being the royal supervisor of King Jehoiakim's workmen was a demanding job.

"He is puffed up with his own grandeur," Abiel complained to his son. Who else could he confide in, when the whims of this new ruler could bring imprisonment or torture?

Abiel had built his life on belief in his fellowmen; he did not question their truthfulness. Now betrayal was everywhere. His best surveyor had his right hand amputated with the axe of the king's guard when he mildly criticized the regime. Men viewed other men with suspicion. Abiel recalled the recent words of Jeremiah: "Their tongue is a deadly arrow . . . with his mouth one speaks peace to his neighbor, but inwardly he sets an ambush for him."*

Abiel began to relax as Daniel gently kneaded the soles of his feet. It was good to have his son at his side. More than anything else, he wanted Daniel to have a life of fulfillment in service to Jehovah. But was happiness possible today? Why was the joy of

* Jeremiah 9:8, NASB.

the Lord hidden? Why must this pall of distrust contaminate Judah?

"You, my boy, are the brightest spot in my day."

Daniel winced at being called a boy. His feet could fit in his father's sandals and he could lift an ephah of grain with one arm. He was as tall as Abiel, ready to take his place in the kingdom as a leader of men. He longed to prove his manhood, to know a woman as his father had known his mother. "With respect, my father," said Daniel, fixing his eyes upon the troubled man, "I will always be your child, but I am now a man."

Abiel took a long drink from a jug, fingering the delicate design on its surface. Made by a true craftsman, no doubt . . . an art in which there was little pride in these days of careless workmanship. Daniel no longer a boy? He was right. Few boys—men—had such keen knowledge of the prophets and the Law. Daniel's agile mind had absorbed the proverbs and the psalms; frequently he could be found surrounded by younger children, telling them tales of their rich history. His ability as a storyteller could make his rapt listeners visualize the parting of the Red Sea or envision the walls of Jericho crumbling as the trumpets sounded.

Abiel examined his son, his heart swelling with pride, knowing that Daniel's keen mind and acute memory set him apart as a youth blessed with the gift of wisdom. Surely he would be capable of conducting a king's business someday. *May he serve a monarch who is worthy,* Abiel prayed.

"Yes, Daniel, you are a man. I've been too selfish to notice. It is now time to choose a woman for you, for it is not good for a man to live alone."

A flush spread across Daniel's face. He had not expected this announcement from his father.

What was it like to live with a woman? Daniel wondered. Not the ordinary tasks of a home, but to . . . well . . . to live with her? For all of his bold claim of being an adult, Daniel knew he was naïve in the ways of love. He wanted to ask his father, and the time of intimate questioning seemed to be ripe. "Father, do you remember the story of Jacob and Rachel? He saw her and loved her immediately. When you sent me to warn Jeremiah, I met a girl and . . . well . . . I can't forget her. I awaken at night and feel the softness of her arm. I dream about her and toss in my bed."

Abiel sat up straight, his weariness forgotten. "Have you forgotten, Daniel? It is your parents who arrange a betrothal. With your mother in the heavenly places, that responsibility is mine. Put this one out of your mind, Daniel. You must be wed to one of your own class."

"But, father, you don't know her." Daniel knew he was coming close to disobedience and must be cautious about his attitude.

"Enough!"

Daniel lowered his eyes so the hurt was hidden. Did his father think Deborah was one of the street harlots? Could he not understand his longing to see her again?

I will accept the one he chooses, Daniel thought, *but I do not have to love her.*

In the weeks that followed Daniel thought of Deborah in the fleeting moments when he was not absorbed in his studies. In order to train for a position as master builder, he was examining the intricacies of Hezekiah's tunnel. Two hundred years before Daniel's birth, Jerusalem had been besieged by the armies of Sennacherib, the king of Assyria. However, foreseeing this threat, King Hezekiah had ordered his men to tunnel a conduit from the waters of the Gihon Spring through the rocky hill Ophel into the Pool of Siloam, in order to supply the city with water and at the same time cut off the enemy's supply. Once, when Daniel went to examine the south end of the tunnel, he thought he glimpsed the small figure of Deborah dipping a jug into the pool and drawing water. He hurried to see her face, but when he reached the reservoir she was gone. It was difficult for him to concentrate on his studies that day.

Four of the brightest scholars in the court of nobles had been assigned the project of drawing an architectural design of Hezekiah's tunnel. The students marvelled that men could dig through solid rock from opposite ends and still be able to meet in the center. The young Hebrews—Hananiah, Mishael, Azariah, and Daniel—were becoming fast friends during their intense training.

The young men with their diverse personalities complemented each other. Hananiah was a scholar who spent hours writing his thoughts on scrolls. He aspired to be a sopher, or scribe, and to prepare and issue decrees as Jehoshaphat, the recorder, had done for King David and King Solomon. Azariah was the consistent optimist, refusing to allow defeating thoughts to enter his conversation. ("Azariah was born with a smile on his face," Daniel once commented.) Mishael was made for laughter. He was a harmless prankster, and whenever the thongs of sandals were tied in knots or a lizard found in a sleeping pallet, Mishael was usually the culprit.

They were a team, and enjoyed the challenge of working together. They felt no rivalry among them, and they could sense the moods of the others.

"Your mind is not on our assignment, Daniel," Hananiah said. "Is the little bee buzzing in your head?"

Daniel grimaced. During their walk from the palace area through the Kidron Valley, Daniel had told his friends about his encounter with Deborah, whose Hebrew name meant "bee." Now it was obvious to him that he was going to bear the brunt of some teasing. But how could they know what it was like to be in love? Even his own father, who knew him better than anyone except Jehovah Himself, had chosen to ignore his recent vagueness, his absent looks.

"Forget what I told you," Daniel replied. "If any of us are to be betrothed, it will not be our choice. Now, let us begin measuring the tunnel. It is more important for our minds to be filled with knowledge than with fantasy."

Mishael and Azariah exchanged amused glances, knowing that since the day of Jeremiah's speech their friend had had difficulty keeping his mind on the pursuit of knowledge. However, they did not challenge him. Although the Hebrew youths had grown up together, studied with the same tutors, and been prepared for similar positions in the court, it had long been Daniel to whom they looked for leadership. He was not easily provoked to anger, but he was known among his peers as standing firm in what he believed and able to challenge any adversary to a hard wrestling match. If he did not want to talk about Deborah, they were reluctant to pursue the subject any further.

Who could answer some of his questions? Daniel wondered as the four began their work. His father was too absorbed in the increasing tension of the times, constantly dwelling on the evil ways of his countrymen. Whenever Abiel was not at the Temple worshiping, he was meeting with his friends in serious discussions about the political and moral condition of the city.

That night, after the evening meal, Daniel left his quarters in the palace and ventured to the hiding place of Jeremiah. By this time the prophet's open warnings and dire predictions about the fall of Judah were making him a despised enemy of both king and people. But Daniel, like his father, believed in Jeremiah and respected him as a chosen vessel for the voice of God. Surely one as wise as he would be able to answer a young man's questions.

The prophet was living in a hut near the places of burial in the Kidron Valley east of the city. Daniel glanced behind him to be sure he was not being followed as he made his way outside the walls of Jerusalem. He found his way to Jeremiah's hovel by the directions given by a loyal friend, using the marks on the tombs for an eerie guide.

The entrance was hidden behind a dwarf date palm, just as Daniel had been told. He tapped lightly on the door, pressing his mouth close and saying, "It is Daniel, son of Abiel."

Jeremiah opened the door a crack, squinting in the dusk to see his young visitor.

"Shalom . . . come in, come in."

Daniel quickly kissed his fingers and placed them on the mezuzah on the doorpost. Then he stepped into the room, which was furnished with nothing more than a mat on the floor and a small brazier which provided the only heat and light. A pot of vegetables was stewing on the grate.

"To risk coming to see me you must have a good reason, my young friend," Jeremiah said. "Did my speech in the marketplace upset you?"

"I have some questions of a personal nature to ask you," Daniel answered. "My mind is confused and I don't know what to do."

"You are so young to be troubled," observed Jeremiah with compassion. "How I wish I was not always carrying such doleful news to the people I love."

Daniel sat down cross-legged in front of the fire and stared at the feeble flames before he spoke.

"I'm afraid, good Prophet, that my concerns are selfish. Will you tell me, is it wrong to want to marry for love? My father is consulting with his friends to choose a woman for me, but I have seen the one I wish."

Jeremiah sat back against a shabby cushion and fingered his grey beard. "Do you love the Lord God with all your heart and mind, Daniel?"

"More than life itself," Daniel answered.

"Then don't be troubled. The Lord will do His will in your life. As for me, He has said, 'You shall not take a wife for yourself nor have sons or daughters in this place.'* I have accepted His will for my life, and I know that He has a plan for yours. I believe, Daniel, that you are going to be used mightily by the Lord. Whether this includes a woman and family, I do not know."

As Daniel looked into the wise eyes of this great man he felt a quickening in his veins, followed by a surge of self-doubt. Was Jeremiah right? Could the Lord of the universe really use him, a motherless son of Judah? He felt less the man he claimed to be and more a child again. "But holy Prophet, I am just a youth."

Daniel was startled by Jeremiah's deep laughter, which filled the little room with its rolling music. When his unsuspected mirth had subsided, the prophet said, "Daniel, I said the same thing to the Lord: 'But I do not know how to speak, because I am only a youth.' And He said to me, 'Everywhere I send you, you shall go, and all that I command you, you shall speak.'** And so it will be with you, Daniel. He chooses the most unlikely ones of us to do His work. Are you ready?"

"I don't know. I am willing to do the Lord's work, but I don't know what it is I am to do."

Jeremiah looked at Daniel and sighed. He would never have a son, but if he could . . . "Daniel, you are ready."

For the next few weeks Daniel spent long hours in prayer and study. He refrained from speaking of Deborah to his father, who was not open to discussion of the subject.

One evening, as Daniel put down his stylus and set aside the clay tablet on which he was copying figures, his father entered their home with an unusual exuberance. "Enough studies for a while, Daniel. We have been invited to a wedding feast. Prepare your finest garments . . . this will be a time for rejoicing! The young people have been betrothed for a year. Yes, it's a good match."

It was good to hear some lightness in Abiel's voice; he indulged himself in so few pleasures.

The festivities were to be held in the house of Barak, a member of the Royal Guard and, it was said, a strong believer in Jehovah. He would, naturally, be a friend of his father's, Daniel thought.

---

* Jeremiah 16:2, NASB.
** Jeremiah 1:7, NASB.

Their political and religious views would be sympathetic; a person needed to be very careful of his choice of confidants these days.

"Also, my son, I happen to know that Barak has beautiful daughters," Abiel said with a wink. "He has kept them well protected until they are of marriageable age."

"I suppose it is fortunate for the bridegroom that they are beautiful," Daniel said indifferently. "It would be more pleasant to be wedded to someone whose face was not ugly beneath her veil."

On the day of the wedding, Daniel and Abiel entered the house of Barak, first having their feet washed by a grinning servant and their heads anointed with oil. It was evident that their host was honoring each guest lavishly. "The perfume is from Egypt, I believe," Abiel whispered to Daniel. "Barak will spend a king's fortune for this feast."

It was obvious from the food spread on the low tables that the father of the bride had spared no expense. There were long bowls filled with cucumbers, onions, beans, and leeks, lavishly seasoned with olive oil. Dates, figs, and pomegranates spilled over carved trays, and many jugs of wine were being passed to the guests.

The charred odor of meat roasting on a spit brought saliva to their mouths. Such extravagance . . . but then, it was Barak's money. And everyone knew that this fare had been blessed by the priests and properly prepared according to Mosaic Law.

Daniel and Abiel were greeted effusively by their host and shown to a place at the table. "I am honored to have you in my house," said Barak, kissing the right and then the left cheeks of his friend and the son of his friend. "May I give you a cup of water before the feast?"

The formalities over, Daniel sat down on a cushion next to his father, enjoying his place with the older men. He looked at the bridegroom, reclining on a red pillow at the head of the table, and wondered how he felt . . . he was so elegant and reserved. Such rich robes! They were scented with frankincense and myrrh, and the girdle around his waist was made of pure silk. How would it feel to be dressed in such fine clothes? If the Lord chose, Daniel thought, he would be a bridegroom some day.

"When will we see the bride?" he asked his father.

"In due time. Women take long getting ready. This is a day she will always remember. She must look her best."

They settled back to eat and enjoy the music from the psaltery, harp, and lyre. Servants brought trays of food in such profusion that the guests began to loosen the girdles around their waists. A minstrel wandered back and forth among the tables, singing the songs King Solomon had written for generations of lovers. Israel was made for singing; without music, their souls could not find expression. Daniel listened attentively to the words that had never meant much to him before now:

> By night on my bed I sought him whom my soul loveth: I sought him, but I found him not. I will rise now, and go about the city in the streets, and in the broad ways I will seek him whom my soul loveth.*

Abiel wiped the meat juice from his mouth with the back of his hand and stole a sidelong glance at Daniel. When one listens so intently to love songs, there is more reason than liking the music. How long could he keep him by his side?

Barak stood and clapped his hands for attention, his round face glowing with pleasure. "My friends, behold my daughter, Rachel."

The door was opened and two small girls, their hair festooned with ribbons, danced in, throwing saffron flowers before the litter being carried by two servants. The bride wore a tunic of fine silk from Egypt and an outer cloak of deep violet. Her arms were covered with gold bracelets and her face was discreetly hidden by a sheer veil. The litter was lowered and she stepped out to join her bridegroom under a canopy of palm branches decorated with yellow crocus and grape hyacinth.

The wedding guests began to sing and to toast the bride and bridegroom.

"May the Lord send his angels to guard you."

"May your wife be like a fruitful vine within your house."

"May your children be like olive plants around your table."

"Praise the Lord, O Jerusalem. Praise your God, O Zion."

Barak's wife took a timbrel in her hand and began to dance. Soon many of the men and women joined her in dancing around the canopy, while the young couple sat viewing the party.

"Barak is a wealthy man, indeed," Abiel said as an aside to his son. "Some say he gave his daughter a dowry that would buy a king's crown."

---

* Song of Solomon 2:1–2, KJV.

Daniel did not hear a word his father said. From the time the bride had arrived, he had eyes for no one but the small, black-haired girl who followed behind the wedding procession. It was she . . . the girl from that unforgettable day. She had spied him immediately among the wedding guests and had given him an impish grin beneath her soft veil.

Deborah, Deborah . . . Daniel thought he could compete with the court singer at that moment. The Lord had answered his prayers. She was more beautiful than he remembered. Her hair was braided with gold and pearls; her gown was dyed a pale saffron, like the crocuses scattered beneath her feet.

"Father . . . look . . . remember the girl I told you about? There she is . . . that's Deborah."

Abiel looked at his son and saw the glow on his face, heard the excitement in his voice. He remembered the sensation he had felt when he first met his beloved Narah. Yes, he understood.

But what could youth know of love? One did not love upon just a brief encounter. Love was pain and joy; it must grow when the sun is gentle and when it rises like a scorching wind. Love should be strong to survive. He wanted his son to know the greatest love, Abiel thought, just as he had known his Narah—blessed be her name.

"So . . . that is the one. You may not remember, but you played with her when she was a small child. She is the second daughter of Barak."

"Would it be proper for me to speak to her now?"

"We will speak later about these matters, Daniel. There is a time for everything. Now, eat."

It was not easy to concentrate on the remainder of the feast while Deborah was watching him. After the bride and bridegroom were toasted by their fathers, relatives, and friends, they left to be alone in a room which had been arranged to be their bridal chamber. There they were to physically consummate their marriage while the guests continued with the party.

Barak kept the happy mood alive by proposing a game. "Listen, my friends, we will examine our knowledge. If I declare a winner in this test of wits he will receive . . . what should I choose? . . . Ah yes, he shall have his pick of my fine camels."

Barak placed his hands on his hips and grinned, flushed with his generosity and, perhaps, from a bit too much wine. "We will pose a riddle or a question, and then you will all have to state an answer. I will judge the worth of your wisdom." Barak laughed at his own self-importance. But he was, after all, the host at this feast.

Barak stood before his guests, pulled at his long beard, and addressed the men who had tired of the dancing and singing and once more reclined at the feast table. He looked at his friends with pride. It was good to have this time of rejoicing; there was not enough laughter in Jerusalem these days.

"First riddle: Why has it been said that before a rooster approaches a hen, he promises her: 'Come to me and I shall give you a gown of many colors.' But afterwards he says, 'May I lose the comb on my head if I have the means to buy such a thing'?"

"Barak, my host," answered Daniel quickly, "Solomon said, 'Bread obtained by falsehood is sweet to a man, but afterward his mouth will be filled with gravel.' "

Barak looked down at Daniel and said, "I have heard you are a scholar, my boy . . . your answer was fair."

Daniel looked slightly irked; he wondered when people would stop calling him a boy. His father rubbed his nose vigorously to hide his amusement.

"Next question: It is the custom in our land to plant a cedar tree when a boy is born and to plant a pine when a girl is born. When they are married, a canopy is made of branches woven from both trees. What is the reason?"

Daniel spoke again before anyone else could answer. "Solomon said in his Song of Songs that 'his banner over me is love.' The canopy is the banner of Jehovah's love for the couple who are wed."

The older men could not reply as fast as Daniel. But the prospect of a camel from Barak's stable spurred some of them to clear their throats and pay more attention. How did this son of Abiel become so wise at such a young age?

Barak sat down heavily, spreading his legs in front of him and folding his hands on his ample stomach.

"Enough!" Barak burped loudly. "The others are no match for you, son of Abiel. You are now the happy owner of one of Barak's camels."

That night Daniel asked his father's permission to arrange a meeting with Deborah. Abiel spoke to Barak, and the fathers agreed to grant their approval. There was very little reluctance in either of them.

When the week-long wedding festivities were over, Daniel sent a servant with a message to Deborah to meet him at the Pool of Siloam on the sixth hour of the following day. When the appointed time arrived, he waited anxiously for her and she soon arrived, followed by a female servant.

Daniel was not sure what to say. "I saw you at your sister's wedding," was his feeble opening remark.

"Yes, I saw you, too." Deborah did not seem as bold as she had the day in the marketplace.

They talked for a while about ordinary topics, a conversation of banalities and trivia. How do a boy and girl get acquainted? They discovered that they both wanted to see the country outside Jerusalem, that locusts covered with honey were delicious to eat, and that the music of the harp was the most beautiful. Important discoveries.

They stood a pace apart, so that no indiscretion could be reported by the servant. Finally Daniel asked the question that had bothered him for weeks. "Deborah, have your father and mother made any arrangements for your betrothal?"

Her answer sent his heart singing with hope. It was, "Not yet."

When Barak and his wife had recovered from the wedding, Abiel returned to the home of his friend. He brought with him this time another friend to act as a deputy in beginning negotiations for Daniel and Deborah's betrothal. The purpose of the visit was no secret to Barak, for they had spoken of the possibility. Barak, also, had chosen his deputy, and before the discussions refreshments were offered to his visitors. However, according to custom, Abiel said, "I will not eat or drink until I have told my errand."

There followed a bit of arguing about the dowry, for Barak felt that the camel should be included and Abiel insisted, "That was won fairly by Daniel, and should not be part of the dowry. After all, your second daughter will be getting a young man of great wisdom, endowed with a handsome face and form." Abiel did not brag often, but this was different. Daniel deserved the best, didn't he?

"And you do not think my Deborah is the fairest of all maids?" Barak asked.

"Let us continue . . . we know they are both fortunate."

"So be it. My word is my covenant. Deborah shall be Daniel's betrothed." Barak looked at his wife, who was silent in the company of her effusive husband. She nodded her assent, as she always did. She hoped that she had raised Deborah to be as submissive to her husband, but she had her doubts. Their youngest daughter had been showing a feisty nature in recent months.

"And my word is my covenant, good friend," said Abiel, knowing that this was the desire of his son's heart. With that Barak signaled for the drinks to be brought in and the fathers and their deputies drank to seal the promises.

When Daniel heard the news, his shout could be heard throughout the house. In the home of Barak, a pretty dark-haired girl grabbed a timbrel and danced to her own singing. They arranged to meet in a tree-shaded garden in the Kidron Valley, but when the time came they found it difficult to speak. Their individual rejoicing turned to awkward embarrassment when they saw each other.

"It's good to see you again," Daniel said matter-of-factly, wondering why his mind had become so inept.

"I'm glad you were at the wedding; father said you answered his riddles very cleverly," Deborah chattered, knowing that her words sounded shallow.

Daniel looked intently at Deborah's grey-haired servant, who was watching them intensely. The old woman quickly averted her eyes and stared at the clouds. He moved closer to Deborah and took her small hand in his. *How can a touch cause such sensations in my body?* Daniel wondered. Deborah looked at the ground, suddenly too shy to say anything. All of the bravado she had exhibited when they first met had dissolved. Was it proper to feel this way? She raised her head and Daniel leaned down and touched his lips to hers. The servant cleared her throat and they drew apart quickly, flushed with the thrill of first love.

They must exhibit proper reserve, or they would not be allowed to meet alone. They spoke of inconsequential matters, getting to know each other better. What did it matter that war surrounded them and the city was corrupt? In this time together, everything seemed right.

And so Daniel and Deborah were betrothed. The covenant was made between their families with spoken words. It was another time for great rejoicing in the two houses, but nothing to compare with the excitement felt by the two young people.

The weeks that followed seemed so slow. A whole year must pass before the actual wedding. The young couple saw each other seldom, only when their fathers sat together to discuss the troubled times. Daniel listened closely to the opinions of his elders, but Deborah fidgeted with her weaving in the background, bored with the endless conversations about politics and wars.

"Have you heard, Barak, what the prophet Jeremiah is saying about Judah?" Abiel asked his friend, cautiously. He did not know how sympathetic Barak was to the teachings of the street-corner orator.

"Jeremiah is a fool. He is risking his life with his words of doom. But he is a brave fool. I do not have his courage, but I agree . . ." Barak, afraid to express an opinion about the ruling king in Judah, let his voice fade. A member of the Royal Guard had to be careful with his words. "However, I do not believe his gloomy words about our holy city. The royal line of David will continue until the promised Messiah appears on the throne, and the Temple will stand as a sign that Jehovah keeps His promises." Barak's wife nodded in the background.

Abiel shook his head. "I don't know. How long will God be patient with our people? I'm almost glad Narah did not live to see the harlots in our streets or the unwanted babies being left to die or men fondling each other."

Daniel glanced at Deborah. Bright spots of embarrassment flushed her cheeks. How he wanted to shield her from the degrading influences surrounding them. She was to be his bride, pure and virginal in body and mind. Solomon had said that house and wealth are an inheritance from fathers, but that a prudent wife is from the Lord. Yes, he thought, his Deborah would make a prudent wife.

Outside the walls of Jerusalem, across the hills and through the valleys, the stealthy advance of enemy troops came in the disguise of a merchant caravan. Beneath the animal skins which covered the carts were spears and torches, weapons of destruction, instead of food and goods from the lands to the north. They walked by night and in the daytime slept with their cloaks covering their faces.

While men of Judah sat after their day's work was done and

speculated about the future and women busied themselves with the chores of the present, the secret caravan drew nearer. This was a detachment of the Royal Guard of Babylon, assigned for special duty. They traveled through the land of Palestine, neither plundering nor disturbing the people. They were the hardened, disciplined soldiers of the new ruler of the strongest kingdom in the East, some of them seasoned veterans of the battle to overthrow Ninevah.

As they crossed the final stretch of the Judean wilderness, their swords were readied for conflict. Many of these men had fought the fierce Assyrians and conquered. Whatever their assignment would be when they reached the city, they were prepared. They had not been told the purpose of this mission, but that was unnecessary; whatever the king commanded, they would obey. They only knew their destination was near. Over the next ridge was the Kidron Valley, where they would make their final encampment, awaiting instructions to besiege the walls of the place called . . . the Holy City of Jerusalem.

3

ROAD TO EXILE

It was evening, and Daniel knelt in the small room his father had set aside for prayer and study. Through the open window he savored the fragrance of the green bay tree and the soft light from the stars over Jerusalem. He prayed out loud, his words rushing with youthful exuberance in praise to Jehovah. His heart was full of thanks. The time of harvest would soon begin; rumors of the threat from Babylon's new ruler had quieted; there was a calm in the air. But his greatest praise was given in anticipation of the wedding celebration that would soon join the houses of Abiel and Barak.

But suddenly the door of his prayer room shook with the pounding of a heavy fist. Words, harsh and guttural, in an unknown tongue, shouted from the corridor. Daniel heard a cry of terror from a voice that did not sound human. It was a shriek of pain like an animal being prepared for slaughter. He pulled the door toward him and caught Abiel as he was pushed over the threshold, the side of his head gushing blood onto his white tunic. With horror, Daniel stared at the place where his father's ear had been, then looked up to see the tiny round of flesh impaled upon the end of a sword.

"Don't try to fight them, Daniel," his father cried through his pain.

"Father, your ear . . . who . . . ?"

"From the land of Shinar . . . go . . ." Then Abiel, mercifully, lost consciousness. Daniel stooped to help him, but found his arms whipped behind him and heavy ropes wrapped around his wrists. His face exploded with the impact of metal on his jaw. Rough hands held him tightly and shoved him outside.

Daniel shouted, "Lord God, protect him," as he looked back at the figure of his father sprawled on the floor. Would he ever see him again, alive? He must keep his wits about him . . . . must think what to do. . . . As he was half pulled, half dragged along, he saw other men shouting the same unintelligible commands, pulling many of his friends, some of them with eyes swelling shut from beatings. There was Mishael's mother on her knees in front of one of the foreign soldiers, crying for him to release her son. Small brothers and sisters were wailing with fear; fathers were trying to shield their sons.

He fought panic that rose in him like an overwhelming tide. Then, in words unheard, a Voice seemed to say, "Do not fear, Daniel, for I am with you. You will receive My power in this evil day."

And Daniel, along with the choicest young people in the land, was taken captive by orders of Nebuchadnezzar, the king of Babylon.

Dazed, aching from their wounded bodies and confused minds, the captives were herded out the Gate of Ephraim, in the northeast sector of the city, into a field where they were ordered to stop for instructions.

"You are now captives of Babylonia. Our great king has commanded us to bring you into our land. You are honored to be the chosen ones." A sarcastic smile spread across the dark face of the guard. The only law of war was conquest, not compassion. And yet he had been instructed not to harm these miserable Judeans. No matter, a few weeks of travel would heal their bruises and toughen their muscles.

Daniel struggled to free his hands from the ropes, but found that he was rubbing his wrists raw. He saw his friends, Hananiah, Mishael, and Azariah, in the crowd. Why were only young people among the captives? What was the purpose of all this? Who would take care of his father? Would he ever see his home again? He dropped to his knees and cried, "Lord God Jehovah, help us!"

"Stand up, boy; your God cannot help you now." Daniel looked up into the Babylonian face that reflected not cruelty, but compassion. Was it possible to have a friend among the enemy?

"I am Arioch, captain of our great king's bodyguard. Soldier . . . come over here and remove the shackles from these prisoners."

Through eyes blurred with tears, Daniel examined his captor. His face was young and beardless. He looked not much older than Daniel—possibly in his early twenties. On his head was a helmet, closely fitting and rising like a cone to a sharp point, which could not contain a mass of flaming red hair. His tunic reached halfway down his thighs but left his arms bare. The short sleeves nearly burst with the hard muscles of an archer; the upper part of his body was covered by a breastplate of leather, skillfully sewn with small metal plates that allowed him freedom of movement, but strong protection. In contrast to the sandaled captives, he wore high boots, laced in front.

"My men have been too rash with some of you today. You will fare better from now on. Our orders are to bring you to our land without harming you. I apologize for your treatment."

"But why were your men so cruel to my father? What will happen to him?" Daniel pleaded.

"Don't you believe your God will take care of him? Isn't that what you asked in such a loud voice?" Arioch was curious about Daniel's prayer. How would this member of the Judean elite react when really tested? Would he be like the Assyrian slaves, cowering and pleading for mercy like blatting sheep? Would he deny the power of his one God then, and see the wisdom of worshiping many gods?

Daniel rubbed his throbbing face and stared at Arioch. It had taken this heathen to calm his heart. Surely the Lord God Jehovah who brought His people into this Promised Land would guard His faithful children wherever they were. "You are right, noble Arioch. My father is in the hands of the One who made him. May I beg your mercy for the others? Many are hurt and bleeding and their wounds should be bound."

Arioch nodded a quick assent, anxious to continue his task. He must not waste time verbally sparring with this youth, although the mental stimulus might be refreshing after the dull minds of those under his command. Why did Nebuchadnezzar give him this tiresome duty, anyhow? He suspected that jealousy in the court had resulted in his assignment to come to this uncultured city, temporarily banished from the sophistication of Babylonian society.

"You . . . guard . . . take your hands off that girl," Arioch shouted in a commanding tone. He would tolerate no breach of his orders. "Now listen to this, soldiers of Babylon. By command of our mighty king, you are to treat these prisoners with respect. They are to be brought into the Land of Shinar in good health and without physical abuse. Any guard reported disobeying these orders will have his eyes removed with a red-hot sword. Is that clear?"

The only sound was the low moaning of the wounded captives and the braying of the donkeys awaiting their burdens. The soldiers released their bone-crunching holds and stood at attention before Arioch. They knew the quick retaliation for disobedience in their ranks, and they valued their eyesight.

"Form lines, two by two, and follow the lead pack animal. We will alternate groups of four with a donkey and our supplies. I will decide if any captive may ride. We have a journey of sixty days. We will join a camel caravan in Damascus. Until then, you walk."

Arioch gave his commands with precision. He had been well trained in the Chaldean school for guards.

I must keep my wits about me, Daniel thought. *If this is the path the Lord has chosen for me to follow, He will walk with me. If it is true that these Chaldeans have been ordered not to harm us, there must be a reason He wants us in Babylon. Oh Lord, I'm not brave. My father is injured . . . I don't know how Deborah is . . . what will they do?*

Daniel squinted his bloodshot eyes and searched the faces of the captives. He saw Mishael, his face devoid of his usual grin, and called to him. "Mishael, Jehovah be with you."

Mishael wiped the blood from his mouth and waved at Daniel. He attempted to smile through swollen lips. "Daniel . . . stay with me," he shouted above the voices. "Ask the guard to put us together."

Daniel received a prod in his side and felt the knob on the end of a wooden staff pushing him in the direction of his friend. Arioch, like a shepherd with his flock, was lining up his young charges in pairs and signaling for the line to get moving. The Chaldeans adjusted the packs on the donkeys, securing the thick felt saddles and testing the tightness of the ropes going under the beasts' bellies. The storage bins of grain had been looted in Jerusalem and other provisions hastily assembled for the caravan. Each animal had a driver beside it, constantly cajoling and whipping the recalcitrant creatures.

"Thank you, noble Arioch," Daniel shouted as Mishael took his place beside him. It would be easier to bear this terrible separation from home if they were together.

And so they began to walk. How could they have anticipated a fate such as this? God had promised them this land, and for many years Judah had withstood the onslaught of her enemies. The fierce Assyrians had seized control of the northern kingdom of Israel and driven the people into exile; many of them had crossed the great Euphrates River and shuffled into oblivion. But Jerusalem . . . Jerusalem had withstood the onslaught of the Assyrians under King Hezekiah, encouraged by his prophet Isaiah, who urged him to resist. Yes, Daniel knew his history. How could this be happening to them?

The sad procession headed north. Daniel did not turn to look at the walls of his beloved city. His bruised jaw throbbed painfully, but the agony in his heart was worse. Was this part of Jeremiah's prophecy about the downfall of Jerusalem? What had happened to the old prophet? Mishael walked beside him; for miles not a word passed between them. The donkeys brayed, the guards muttered, but the captives trudged in silence. Each person was engrossed in his own sorrows, swallowed by fears of the unknown and worry for loved ones.

"Daniel."

"Yes, Mishael."

"Why do you think the king of Babylon wants us?"

Daniel trudged along the stony road for a time without answering. "Remember, Mishael, what we heard about the Assyrians? When they were conquering cities the king would order his troops to bring the youngest members of the royal line to his court as hostages . . . and then teach them the ways of Assyria so they could serve as governors once the remainder of the populace was conquered."

"But the Babylonians have conquered Assyria . . . you know yourself that Nineveh has fallen."

"The king of Babylon may be following the same pattern as the Assyrians. I believe he has determined to have Jerusalem and all of Judah."

The impact of those thoughts silenced the conversation of the young friends. They walked for several hours along winding roads beside fertile fields pregnant with ripening ears of corn and wheat. But no farmers could be seen. Evidently news of the enemy caravan had arrived and they were in hiding, perhaps viewing the sad procession from behind their sheaves of newly cut grain.

"Daniel, do you think the king of Babylon wants to train us in the ways of his kingdom?"

"We'll find out. We must stand together, whatever happens."

Arioch jumped from his chariot and raised his staff above his head, brandishing the carved eagle at the top in a commanding symbol. "Halt the caravan. We shall rest here for a few minutes!" Daniel, catching through sweat-blurred eyes the glint from the head of the bird, remembered his father's words of encouragement: "They shall mount up with wings like eagles; they shall run and not be weary; they shall walk and not faint."

"Hear this," Arioch shouted, "We will stay ten minutes in Ramah and then go on to Mizpah. This first day, we go as far as Bethel."

Daniel caught his breath. Bethel was only twelve miles north of his home, but sheltered as he had been within the walls of Jerusalem, he had never seen it. They were walking into his history book. Thousands of men of the tribe of Benjamin had been slain in this very area where they were resting. Bethel had been the earliest location for the Ark of the Covenant, and it had been between Ramah and Bethel that Deborah, the prophetess and judge, had sat under her palm tree and dispensed judgment to the sons of Israel. At Bethel golden calf idols had been placed and the people had worshiped them; Jeroboam had made sacrifices upon the altar to the calves and burned incense to them. Abiel had told him how King Josiah destroyed the heathen idols at Bethel and burned the altars where Baal was worshiped.

The captives sunk to the ground, talking very little, absorbed in their grief, confusion, and fear. Daniel stood, searching the prostrate forms for other friends. Then he saw her. At the head of the caravan, separated from male captives by a cart of provisions, was a small group of young women. And among them, leaning against a fig tree, he caught an unmistakable profile.

"Deborah!" he shouted. "Turn around . . . it's me . . . it's Daniel."

Immediately she saw him waving his arms, his face comforting her across the crowd. Her prayers had been answered. She had cried aloud to the Lord God Jehovah to be with her to quiet her trembling body, to give her some sign that He had not forsaken her to these barbarians. Surely the Lord had sent Daniel to protect her. She did not fear hardship, for her body was young and strong, but she saw the lust in the eyes of these Chaldeans and was terrified at the thought of being robbed of her virginity. She had heard the stories about the brutality of the Assyrians toward captive women. Rape was more to be feared than death.

"Daniel, Daniel," Deborah cried in relief and longing and began to run toward him.

"Stop, girl, you are not to leave your place." A Chaldean guard grabbed her arm, twisting it in his hard grip.

Arioch had seen the exchange between Daniel and Deborah and read the message immediately. These personal relationships tended to complicate his job. It would have been much easier to have been commanded to return with treasures of gold and jewels, but transporting all of these . . . children . . . and giving them firm but careful treatment was such a tedious task. But then, he thought, with some satisfaction, there were not many in the kingdom to whom Nebuchadnezzar could entrust such a job. It took someone with the ability to lead, someone with enough diplomacy to handle nobility as well as these churlish troops. *Yes,* Arioch agreed with himself, *I was a good choice.*

"You, Daniel, sit down." Arioch ordered. "And soldier . . . you are not to touch the captives, especially the women. Or I will have your tongue on the end of my spear."

"Please, noble Arioch, may I make a request?" Daniel asked. "May I walk with the girl? I will see to it that none of your soldiers touches her, or the others. You cannot keep watch on everyone, and I give you my word that you can trust me." Daniel paused, praying silently that the Lord would touch the heart of this foreign commander and grant his wish.

"Trust you? Why should I give you that honor? You are a captive and I am your enemy. Do masters trust their slaves? Do kings trust their subjects? Does any man trust another in these days?"

"My word is my bond. I give it to you in the name of Jehovah."

Arioch stared into the face of this Hebrew youth, holding his eyes steadily for almost a minute. This was a mannerism he had learned to make those of devious ways flinch before his unwavering gaze. Daniel held his head high, determined to meet the challenge of this unusual test. He saw in the young commander arrogance, yet admiration. And he thought he detected a need for friendship, for the camaraderie that every man desires to fill the void left by absence from home and family. Just as surely as Daniel had been uprooted, Arioch had been sent into an alien land on a mission that he seemed to find distasteful. As they stared at each other, they felt, somehow, that between them could grow a bond which would transcend the boundaries of country and culture.

"Yes, I trust you," Arioch spoke in a low tone so his troops did not hear—if they knew of his regard for this Hebrew they might think less of him as a leader. "You may walk with the girl, you of the unflinching eye. But do not think that because I have trusted you to protect her you have license to fondle her yourself. I am to bring unblemished young nobles and virginal maids to Babylon."

He paused, a wry smile playing across his face. "Why Daniel, you're blushing!" Arioch laughed at the Hebrew's embarrassment. Could it be that this handsome one had never known a woman? He, Arioch, could boast of many encounters since he had been the age of this one! And the girl was beautiful; had it not been for his orders he would have taken her himself . . .

"We are betrothed, Arioch, I will not go into her until our marriage is consecrated in the eyes of God."

"What a waste . . . but how fortunate for me that the gods have sent one such as you to assist me. Now, we shall go on. There will be time later for talk."

"And Mishael . . . may he walk behind me?"

"You have persistence, son of Judah. Take your friend to the front of the line . . . but don't press my good graces too far." Arioch was enjoying the authority given to him on this mission to make decisions. They may not be important ones, but if he proved worthy in small ways, the gods would surely favor him with greater responsibilities.

That night the caravan rested at Bethel. Upon the orders of Arioch—and to the disgust of his troops—tents were pitched for the women. Before Daniel returned to his place with the men, he talked to Deborah, trying to quiet her fears. Life, which once had seemed certain and secure, now was fraught with the unknown.

He stood a distance from her, knowing that he was under close scrutiny by the captain of the guards. Daniel never felt so manly, so protective. He looked down at Deborah, knowing that he must be father and mother to her, and feeling like neither. "We must not dwell on the circumstances, little one, but search for the opportunities. Look at the heavens. We are told that it was near here, between Bethel and Ai, that Father Abraham pitched his tent and built an altar for the worship of God. Perhaps it was on this very spot that Jacob spent the night with a stone for his pillow, and dreamed about the stairway reaching from earth to heaven, and heard the promise of God that he would inherit the land."

"I wish we had Jacob's ladder right now so we could climb out of this place," Deborah whispered.

"Jehovah has a reason that we are here."

"Daniel, do you really believe that? He brought us together, but now would He be so cruel as to keep us apart in a foreign land?"

Why must she ask the questions I dare not express? Daniel thought. How could he encourage her and his friends if he allowed his faith to waver?

"I trust Him, Deborah. When we are the weakest, He will show His strength in our weakness."

"Hold me, Daniel, I don't feel strong at all." Deborah slid her body closer to him, shaking with fear and inviting his arms. The spunky, independent attitude she had shown that first day in Jerusalem had been drained by exhaustion and fear. How Daniel longed to put his arms around her, to quiet her and stroke her hair, to kiss the bruised flesh where the print of cruel fingers had left their mark. He had felt love before—for his father, for the friends who shared his life . . . his former life . . . for the dog he had nurtured from puppyhood and now must be whining for him—but never love like this. Aching. Choking. He would die for her.

"I dare not touch you, Deborah. I have given my word. But I will love you with my eyes and hold you with my prayers. I will watch your tent from afar. Now go to sleep, my little one; we have many days' journey until we reach the land of Shinar."

The next day's the caravan moved on. It was not large, perhaps a total of seventy Judeans and an equal number of Babylonian soldiers. The captives were young and able to travel about thirty miles a day. From Bethel they wound their way north, sometimes startling the peasant farmers with their appearance and sending them scurrying from their fields. Daniel remembered how he had longed to know more of his countrymen, but now there was no chance. The Judeans were just goods to be transported, following the same trade route that many caravans of merchants had traveled between Egypt and Mesopotamia.

Mile by mile they walked. Daniel encouraged Deborah and the others with his stories of the places rich in their heritage. The land was a constantly changing picture. At times they saw fertile valleys, surrounded by vineyards and orchards; other times they threaded their way through rocky areas strewn with huge boulders. The donkeys scrambled and waddled under their burdens, and the captives groaned as their sandals stumbled in the hard places.

"This earth has felt the footsteps of our forefathers, Deborah. We are walking over holy land." Daniel felt a surge of pride in the Lord God Jehovah's covenant with Father Abraham. God had promised that He would bless those who blessed the children of the Promised Land and curse the ones who harmed them. Could this mean that these Babylonians would bring down the wrath of God if they harmed Judah or its sons and daughters? That was little consolation at the present time.

"Holy land it may be, but my feet hurt," complained Deborah.

Daniel's feet, too, were bruised and aching, but it was greater torture for him to see this beloved one suffer and be unable to touch her. He would gladly have hoisted her up on his back and carried her. But he knew he must be cautious with the privileges he had and appeal to Arioch at the proper time.

"Look, Deborah, those must be Mount Ebal and Mount Gerizim. We are at Shechem, where Joshua gathered all the tribes of Israel. Joshua wrote in the book of the law that the people promised to serve the Lord, the God of Israel, and forsake all foreign gods."

"People don't remember their promises," Deborah answered. "Perhaps none of this would be happening to us if the king of Judah had not started all the heathen worship."

Suddenly pain shot through Daniel's leg as the heavy boot of a soldier came down on his foot, penetrating the soft sandal with its crushing weight. "Oh, do pardon me, noble son of Judah," the guard sneered. "I seemed to walk too close." It was the guard who had been reprimanded by Arioch for touching Deborah. Revenge showed in his sardonic smile. Daniel realized that survival, both in body and spirit, must be the goal for this journey. He must draw upon all the patience of Job to meet the assaults of such enemies.

"God be with you," Daniel answered, choking back a moan of pain.

The guard hesitated for a moment, and then, with a shrug, walked ahead of the line. He had hoped to provoke Daniel into rebellion that would earn him a good lashing.

For a time, Daniel kept his observations to himself, resolving to bring Deborah up on the historic significance of these places at a time when they would be sitting in their own home . . . somewhere . . . retelling the story of their exile trip to their children.

Almost a week had passed from the time they took that last backward glance at Jerusalem. Days were long, with the agony of separation growing each mile. Gradually Arioch became more lenient with his orders, allowing the captives freedom to trudge together in larger groups. Hananiah and Azariah moved up to join Daniel and Mishael and Deborah at the head of the caravan. And gradually Daniel began again to pass the time by telling stories of their country's history.

Arioch raised no objections to Daniel's stories. What harm could they do, after all? He knew that the southern kingdom of Judah was doomed and soon would capitulate to the might of Babylon, just as her northern sister, Israel, had fallen to Assyria. It was only a matter of time before this land would be an ash heap, never to rise again to its former glory. But these choice youths—what a stroke of genius on the part of Nebuchadnezzar—would bring the best of their knowledge and their beauty to build a greater and more glorious Babylon.

Arioch did not tell these captives of Nebuchadnezzar's plans, however. He wanted them to believe that they would eventually be returned to their homeland; they would be more inclined to be cooperative if they thought their captivity was temporary. Besides, who knew what final purpose Nebuchadnezzar had in mind?

"Halt," commanded Arioch. "We will stop here, on the Plain of Jezreel." They were approaching Megiddo, the town that dominated the whole movement of trade, guarding the major routes across the Palestine bridge.

Daniel sat on a stone a spear's length from Deborah. "See, Deborah . . . Megiddo. More battles have been fought there than any spot in the world." He had longed to see this place, but not under these circumstances.

Deborah dropped to the ground and leaned back, her eyes closed and her head resting against a dusty bundle of goatskins. At the moment she was not very interested in battles. The soles of her feet were blistered and bleeding; her lustrous hair dulled by dust. But she held her tongue; after seeing the pain and compassion in Daniel's eyes she had vowed not to complain again. She must prove herself worthy of being his wife.

Daniel let his eyes sweep out across the great plain. Visions of the armies of kings of Israel, Egypt, and Assyria passed through his mind.

Suddenly the sensation he had experienced when he was taken captive flooded his being. He heard unspoken words, clearly communicated. Thoughts too deep to understand flowed through his mind, and a Voice said, "Hear Me, Daniel . . . in this valley will be a time in history such as never has been nor ever will be again."

As Daniel looked across the valley, he could almost see the carnage that had occurred there in the past. It had been called the great battlefield of Israel. As the main artery between Egypt and Assyria, it had been the scene of many wars for domination of the city of Megiddo and the routes it controlled. Only recently it had become the death scene for King Josiah, who had ruled in peace for many years but finally had gone to battle against an invading Egyptian Pharaoh.

A pang of longing shot through Daniel as he remembered the prophet Jeremiah, who had lamented the death of Josiah and with him the decline of the glory of Judah. Was Jehovah speaking to him in a voice as clear as He did to Jeremiah? Was He giving him prophecies?

Daniel shook his head to clear his mind. *I am too young, Lord, for such honor,* he said in his heart.

"Refresh yourself, Daniel." Arioch held out a goatskin of cool well water, wondering what thoughts were causing the awesome look in Daniel's eyes. This was no ordinary boy.

"Daniel, what do you see in the valley? You are staring so hard."

Deborah had a way of bringing him back to reality. But was

what he heard any less real than the brown-green earth beneath his feet or the cloudless sky above his head? Was the Voice a Person who was closer to his soul than any human being? It was a paradox.

After resting for a time, the caravan continued to wind across plains, and through the Galilean hills. With each mile, Daniel's spirits grew lighter. There were times when he had to remind himself that he was no more than a slave in bondage. The bruises on his face had begun to fade, and the pain of separation had faded to a dull ache. A feeling of anticipation invaded his soul. With God as his guide and Deborah beside him, how could he remain depressed?

"Look, Daniel, isn't it beautiful? Wouldn't it be wonderful to be able to bathe in those blue waters?" Deborah looked longingly from their resting place on a hill above the Sea of Galilee. She sighed, fingering her soiled robes and remembering the servants she had in Jerusalem. But Daniel viewed Galilee with different eyes. He remembered from his studies the words of the great prophet Isaiah. Didn't he speak of a great prince of peace, the promised Messiah, who would come from the line of David?

"Deborah, the Promised One will walk here by the way of the sea, through Galilee. Isaiah prophesied it."

"You are always so certain. How can we be sure of anything when we are at the mercy of our enemies and going to a foreign land?" Sometimes Deborah wished Daniel would look at the reality of their predicament.

Daniel found it difficult to answer Deborah. If he told her of the growing sense of purpose in his heart, of the silent Voice that gave him strength, she might think he was lacking in concern. For a while he would keep his thoughts to himself. He had studied Solomon's proverbs that spoke of having sound wisdom and discretion. This was a time for discretion.

Their route took them along the life line between the two great civilizations of the Euphrates and the Nile, the route trodden by patriarchs and merchants, soldiers and armies . . . And now the first little band of exiles. They caught their breath when they sighted the snow-capped peaks of Mount Hermon, but there was no time to stop and admire. They were prodded on, like the donkeys with their lumbering burdens, until they reached Damascus, the largest oasis at the edge of the Syrian desert.

With the last part of the journey in sight, the prisoners were assembled before Arioch and instructed about camel riding. The hilly country of Judah had not been suited to those valuable beasts, but now the caravan had reached the long stretch of arid desert. "We will be traveling by night most of the time. You will learn that the camel is your friend, as long as you sway to and fro with his body."

"Sounds as if we could get seasick in the desert," Mishael observed. He stared up at this new mode of transportation and spoke to the camel: "Jehovah must have had a sense of humor when he designed you, my bony friend. Say, Daniel, didn't you win one of these creatures in a game of wits at Barak's house?"

"I never collected my prize," Daniel laughed. "But if Job could manage three thousand camels, I guess you can handle one."

The desert trek was uncomfortable, but tolerable. Without the camels it would have been a death march; the dry bones of men and animals frequently marked their paths in that desolate part of the world. Days were spent huddled in the shade of the camels' bodies, and nights saw the caravan, single file, weaving its way across the moonlit sands. To hold off thirst and hunger, they found it was wise to refrain from talking.

The desert code of manners was not unkind. When the caravan approached the tents of the Bedouins, they were invited for coffee spiced with cardamom and ginger root, given food, and treated as guests. The unwritten rules of hospitality, passed from generation to generation, were strong in the desert tradition. For the young captives it was a time of remembering, and a time of increased apprehension. Stories of the cruelty of Nebuchadnezzar were whispered from captive to captive. On the other hand, the soldiers loved to brag about the grandeur of Babylon and to contrast their usual lavish lifestyle to this lowly task of guarding a group of Hebrew children.

One evening, after a scorching day in which no one spoke lest conversation increase thirst, Arioch announced that they would soon leave the desert and enter the land of Shinar. "You are fortunate, Judeans, to be approaching the mighty Euphrates. We will follow its shores south to Babylon. We have had good rains this year and the wheat is high. Our dates are sweet and our oranges juicy."

Mishael limped along the sandy path, swatting at the insects that swarmed around the animals. He nudged Daniel and said, "If he doesn't stop I'll be tempted to think that I'm eager to get there."

"You will soon see the greatest city in the world; you will view wonders such as you cannot imagine. Long after your little city of Jerusalem is a spot of dust in the middle of a forgotten land, Babylon will stand." Arioch leaned against his camel, his eyes gleaming with pride as he described his native city.

Daniel could not be quiet. "The Lord has promised our father Abraham that He will make of his descendants a great nation. He will not forsake us, even in Babylon."

Irritation pulled at the corners of Arioch's mouth. This youth troubled him. He had the boldness to challenge his captors, speaking words that could cost him his tongue. And yet he was a man of honor; he had kept his promise and not touched the girl. It must be very difficult for a young man betrothed to such a one to control his desires. *I am not sure I could do the same,* Arioch mused, his eyes resting appreciatively on Deborah. Even weeks of squinting at the desert sun had not dimmed the dark beauty of those black eyes . . .

"Daniel, son of Judah, you will soon be a son of Babylon. Our gods are many, and your own god—Jehovah as you call Him—is no match for ours. We shall see how splendors such as your eyes have never seen will make you forget your God and your Jerusalem."

Arioch stood with his legs apart, hands on hips, his hair dulled to tarnished copper by the desert dust. He surveyed his hostages with pride; they were submissive, but unharmed. Their bruises were healed, the young women untouched, although some of his troops were surly because of his restrictive orders. One of the enticements of foreign conquest was to take the women. But not this time.

The captain of the guard looked at Daniel, his prize captive. This Hebrew was a puzzling challenge. Arioch wanted somehow to master him, to break his spirit. But at the same time he wanted to talk with him, to understand his strength . . .

He shook his head and spat into the dust. These were idle fantasies. His task was to deliver these captives to the king, and it was almost complete. Let Nebuchadnezzar worry about this arrogant young nobleman from Jerusalem!

Arioch addressed all of the captives and guards, but his eyes were fastened on Daniel.

"Babylon is the city of gold. No foreign power can invade its walls. Babylon will stand forever.

"Praise Marduk!"

4

BABYLON THE GREAT

DESERT GAVE WAY to the valley of the great Euphrates. As the landscape changed, so did the mood of the young Hebrews and their restless captors. Tension mounted; emotions were becoming raw. For the exiles, Babylon meant facing the unknown in an alien land, but for the guards it meant home, a glittering oasis after dreary travels.

Deborah pressed a hand to her parched skin. How she longed for the gentle oil she had once been able to apply so extravagantly. She wondered if she would ever be pretty again.

"Daniel . . . I'm afraid. Will we be sent to a slave market? I'd rather die than have one of those barbarians touch me."

"God is with us. Trust Him, Deborah . . . He will not forsake us even in Babylon."

The bruises on his body had healed, but the ache in his heart was intense. He must not waver, for others looked to him for strength. Also, he was ever conscious of the watchfulness of Arioch. The ambitious young guard had granted him favors, and Daniel was grateful; however, he was wary of this man who saw omens at each turn in the road and demons in every mishap.

When someone had become ill during the march, Arioch had led incantations to expel the evil spirits. Fingering his gold amulet, he had stood over the sick one, lifted his face toward the sky, and commanded, "Let the evil demon leave; let the demons strike at each other. May the good spirit enter his body." His eyes had rolled and his voice had become guttural. With face contorted he had chanted, "Evil demon, malignant plague, the Spirit of Earth has driven you out of his body. May the favorable genie, the good giant, the benign spirit, come with the Spirit of Earth. Come, O god Marduk, god of fire, destroyer of enemies. Destroy the plague. . . . O brilliant, fertile fire, destroy this evil."

When Mishael had heard this chant he had whispered to Daniel, "Tell the fellow to eat some figs. He needs a good cathartic."

"Hush, Mishael, your jokes may land us in chains. Arioch is very serious about his gods." Daniel had chided, but he had been glad that the irrepressible humor of his friend had not been squelched. Laughter was good medicine for tired bodies.

From the unrelenting stretches of desert sand, the caravan moved into a fertile area which had been created by the Euphrates and Tigris rivers as they rushed down from the mountains of Armenia, laden with silt that would enrich the earth for crops and orchards. The land between the two rivers was called Mesopotamia. What a relief it was to see fields of ripe barley and wheat stretching for miles beside the road. The Hebrews watched as the farmers piled up the harvested grain, covering each stack with a reed mat for protection. Beneath a grove of tall date palms, fruit trees bent with the weight of their ripe produce.

Arioch ordered one of his men to buy some oranges for a few shekels, and apportion one to each guard and captive. The sweet, juicy fruit was a feast for parched throats.

As they traveled through the valley, the Chaldean emphasis on demons and witchcraft became more evident. Deborah forgot her grimy appearance and itching scalp as she stared at the houses they passed. "Look, Daniel," she whispered, "can you imagine having such an ugly statue outside your home?" She pointed to an image with the body of a bull, wings of an eagle, and the head of a fanged hyena. It stood guard at the door of a peasant's circular hut, defying the evil spirits to enter.

A feeling of oppression swept over Daniel, filling his inner being, suffocating him. He realized that this land was far deeper into occultic practices than Judah had been.

His thoughts were interrupted by a jab in his side. "Move along, noble dog, we will see the gates of Babylon before dark if we have to prod you like donkeys." The soldier who had stamped on Daniel's foot still took every opportunity to provoke him. When Arioch wasn't looking he would snarl threats and obscenities, and it seemed to infuriate him even more when Daniel made no attempt to retaliate, but responded with quiet smiles.

They continued their march in silence, watching with the curiosity of foreigners the different kinds of people they passed. The peasants did not turn to look at them. They were too close to slavery themselves to empathize with the plight of others.

Daniel, the architect's son, took special notice of the buildings along the way. Most of the houses were made of clay. He knew that finely chopped straw was used to reinforce the strength of the clay and wondered if he and his fellow captives were going to be used as laborers to make bricks by collecting straw from the fields, as the Pharaohs had forced the Israelite slaves to do.

Most of the houses were one story in height, although buildings with added stories began to appear as the caravan drew closer to Babylon. The poorer dwellings were undecorated except for whitewash on the outside walls and red-painted door frames; Arioch informed them that the color red frightened devils and barred the entrances against evil influences.

By noon on the last day of the trek the mood of the guards had changed from surly to exuberant. They were nearing their home, their mission a success. None of the Hebrews had died along the way. Only the weakest captives remained on the camels, the others found it a relief to feel the ground beneath their feet. "Faster, Hebrews," the guards shouted to the walkers along the column. Surely the gods would reward them for the successful completion of this troublesome assignment. What did the king want with a few dozen Hebrew . . . children? (One could hardly consider these beardless youths and small-breasted Judean girls adults.)

Arioch rode his white stallion the length of the columns, constantly surveying the caravan. He had bargained for the beautiful Arabian steed in return for his camel. After all, he thought, it would be important to ride into Babylon in a manner which was worthy of his position.

Arioch reined in alongside Daniel, who was walking his customary distance from Deborah. He dismounted and pushed back the damp red hair from his face. Along the river shore, the humidity was increasing, causing the caravan to slow its pace.

"You have obeyed well, Daniel, son of Judah. Not once have you touched the girl. I've been watching you."

"You had my word, noble Arioch."

Arioch gave him his unwavering stare, which was met with equal steadiness in Daniel's eyes. "Tell me, Daniel, why don't you curse me? Instead you call me 'noble.' "

"My God has placed you in authority over me."

"The gods have given you unusual wisdom for a boy," Arioch responded, although he was not much older than Daniel.

"I am a man, sir."

"After you are rested and well fed in Babylon, you will have your chance to prove that."

"As you say."

Arioch rode back to his position at the head of the column, and Daniel focused his attention on the network of canals that flowed beside their path. Traveling along the banks, the Hebrews watched the boats and barges laboring up and down the waterways.

"Judah could use irrigation like this," Azariah said to Daniel, pointing at the canal gates which regulated the water. If too much water went through, the embankments would wash away and the fields would flood; if too little water flowed, weeds and silt would choke the canals and the fields would not be irrigated. But the gates kept the water at a steady, controlled flow that turned the desert green.

Daniel's eyes became thoughtful, remembering the teaching of his childhood. "Perhaps, Azariah, this will happen someday in Judah. The prophet Isaiah said that the Lord promised, 'I will make a road through the wilderness of the world for my people to go home, and create rivers for them in the desert.' "

Surely these waterways were designed by men with great abilities, Daniel thought. In this land, as in his beloved Judah, the ability to turn the arid region into food-producing land was vital. These Chaldeans had wisdom, he conceded.

The Euphrates was shallow, and vessels moving along the waterways were sometimes propelled by poles, other times hauled by men on the banks who put their hands to heavy ropes and pulled the crafts along.

Some of the boats were wooden or reed rafts, buoyed up with inflated animal skins. They were filled with goods, since there were many building projects in the area and many cities in need of supplies. From Carchemish on the north to the Persian Gulf on the south, commerce choked the crowded canals.

Soon the caravan was trudging through the outskirts of Babylon, past cowsheds and sheepfolds, barns and granaries. Then a shout arose from one of the guards. "Look, now you can see it . . . the great ziggurat. We're almost there!"

The guards cheered as they moved closer to the immense brick walls of Babylon. The excitement of journey's end had given them renewed energy to march into the city with a flourish, not to drag in like a defeated army.

Before crossing a deep moat that surrounded the city walls, Arioch called a halt. "Don your helmets, soldiers of Babylon. Shoulder your spears and stand straight." He called one of his men to fasten him into a linen and leather tunic which he had saved for the entrance onto the Processional Way. One never knew who would see him at the head of guards and prisoners. Perhaps even the king himself might view him from a terrace of the palace. Or maybe one of the women who had waited impatiently for his return would be impressed by his appearance on the white stallion. He moistened his lips at the thought, and anticipation overcame his weariness.

As they drew closer, the walls of Babylon loomed in proportions that defied imagination. They rose a hundred feet into the air and were so thick that four chariots could be raced abreast atop them. At regular intervals along the wall were higher towers, so awesome in height that the people approaching the gates could barely see the soldiers that manned them.

Arioch, sitting erect on his prancing horse, led the column. Following him across the bridge that crossed the broad expanse of muddy waters was the little band of Babylonians and Judeans that had walked for almost two months to reach this destination.

Daniel looked at the defenses of this mighty city and thought how much stronger they were than Jerusalem's. It would take a clever invader to penetrate the moat and the fortress-like walls.

They entered a gateway where soldiers stood guard; a bronze door closed behind them with a rumbling clank. Ahead was a paved road flanked by white walls. Looking to the left they could see the tower they had viewed from a distance; its multicolored steps seemed to climb to the sky, dwarfing all other buildings in the city.

"Halt!" Arioch commanded. He stopped the procession to explain the meaning of the overwhelming temple tower they were passing. "This, people of Judah, is the great ziggurat of Babylon. It has eight platforms, each smaller than the other, reaching to a height of more than two hundred cubits. It is taller than the pyramids of Egypt and at its top stands the gold shrine which is sacred to our great god Marduk. At the very top of the tower is the sanctuary of Marduk. In it is a golden couch, where an unmarried woman is met and spends a night visited by a god. A sacred marriage is consummated with a mortal."

Arioch's eyes sought Deborah's to see her reaction to these words. Everything he had seen from the time he entered the city had brought fire to his loins, and his body ached to be satisfied. Perhaps she would be the one.

Deborah turned her head away, intuitively understanding the message in the eyes of the captain of the guard.

"You are seeing the mighty building linking heaven and earth. Mark it well in your minds."

"The Tower of Babel!" Daniel whispered to Mishael. "They will never reach heaven by climbing that."

Each terrace was painted a different color. "Like Joseph's coat," said Mishael, feeling very small beneath the shadow of these immense buildings. Nothing in Jerusalem, not even the Temple, was that big.

A few children started to gather around the caravan, searching for any small prizes they might receive. Daniel remembered the little beggars in Jerusalem and felt a wave of homesickness. But the memories of the past were soon crowded out by the glittering sights of Babylon.

On their right was another temple, its walls covered with blue enameled bricks that were carved with rows of golden bulls and dragons. As they passed between the ziggurat and the temple, Arioch called another halt. There were some in this entourage that he wanted to impress.

"We are before the Temple of Marduk." (Arioch closed his eyes and rubbed his amulet as he described the temple.) "There are over eight hundred talents of gold in its statues. Each year a thousand talents of incense are burned at the great festival. Praise Marduk!"

Raising his hand for attention, he commanded, "Attention, all citizens of Babylon, you will bow to the supreme god, to the King of Heaven and Earth!" The order was shouted through the ranks. The soldiers fell to their knees, prostrate on the pavement, their arms stretched in front, the pointed ends of their helmets brushing the stones.

But the Hebrews remained standing. Arioch glared at them and murmured under his breath, "They will bow, they will bow."

And so they entered into captivity; apprehensive, frightened, and wondering what the days, even the years would hold.

To Arioch there was no place like Babylon, city of his birth and education. It was a place of beauty as well as power. *Someday,* he thought, *I shall be ranked with the ruling nobles. It is my birthright,* he boasted to himself.

He loved the glittering palaces and temples, the wandering streets, the colorful bazaars. Where else could you find a city surrounded by five miles of walls, eighty feet thick? Surely no enemy was strong enough to conquer such a bastion!

Brandishing his staff and reining in his mount, Arioch shouted, "Attention, foreigners from Judah. We have entered our great city Babylon, gate of the gods. You are now walking on the Processional Way, the honored thoroughfare that bears our king and priests and gods in the New Year's Festival, when we celebrate the marriage of Marduk with the Earth Goddess, who will bring fertility to the soil and good harvest to our fields. We shall follow the Processional Way until it turns north toward the great Ishtar Gate. When you see glazed walls in front of you, we will be close to the palace area. There you will be assigned your quarters."

"He is doing a commendable job in trying to impress us," Hananiah said to Daniel.

"It seems to be his nature," Daniel commented.

The guards grumbled when Arioch said the captives would be taken to rooms in the royal compound. Why should Judeans be housed in an area reserved for more privileged citizens of the land of Shinar? Arioch sensed their discontent.

"These are my orders from the king, may his name be honored."

The murmuring stopped; any hint of disobedience to King Nebuchadnezzar could bring swift and severe punishment. If you valued your sight, your tongue, or your life, you obeyed without question.

The Processional Way was broad and paved with colored stones from Lebanon. Some of the stones were inscribed, "I, Nebuchadnezzar, king of Babylon, paved this road with mountainstone for the procession of Marduk."

Arioch's chest swelled with pride. The road they walked upon was elevated above the street level, giving it the importance of carrying the procession of kings and conquerors. Even the Babylonian name of this thoroughfare meant "the enemy shall not prevail."

Daniel looked as his friends. They were dirty; their clothes were torn and their hair matted. Their shabby appearance was in such contrast to the opulence of their surroundings that he felt like one of the beggars who sat at the Dung Gate in Jerusalem.

As the bedraggled entourage continued toward the palace area, crowds began to gather and watch. Many were curious about these captives. Even in their present state it was evident that they were young and exceedingly handsome. The men eyed the girls with great interest. "Such beauties," they murmured.

Some of the women on the street glanced at the Hebrew girls with indifference—they would make pretty slaves. But the unmarried girls and courtesans viewed them with disfavor. These soldiers were their men, and they had not anticipated that the loot they coveted after a foreign campaign would be in the form of competition for their bodily favors.

Arioch smiled and nodded at the citizens along the way. He wanted the people of Babylon to see that these Hebrews were not a broken war remnant, but a chosen group.

"Out of our way, scum." Arioch brandished his staff at a tax gatherer who was in the path of his horse. What a nuisance these fellows were . . . but necessary. They squatted before their red abacuses, sliding the ivory balls to determine what percentage of every business transaction must be paid to the king. For a price the tax gatherer would lower the amount of a sale, collect the king's tax, and pocket the difference. But then, thought Arioch, there are so few men of principle. Expediency is a rule most live by—live for your own pleasure and appease the gods with your offerings.

Daniel, Mishael, Hananiah, Azariah, Deborah, and the other captives walked in quiet awe. They had never seen such grandeur, never experienced such sensuality. Shrines and statues were everywhere—some on pedestals richly embossed with gold, others recessed in the sides of buildings, surrounded by offerings of fruit and flowers. Images of deities stared at them from every niche. How could the people keep them straight?

Hananiah, with his intellectual nature, wondered if they would receive Babylonian training. Would they be required to learn the names of all these gods? Azariah, the perpetual optimist, was certain that the Lord God had brought them into this land for a purpose. For all the hardships, the journey had been an adventure to him. Mishael looked on the light side. These gods staring at them from every direction were a sorry looking bunch. If they had to worship idols, they could have at least built some attractive ones. He crossed his eyes at one paunchy female nude statue. How ugly.

Daniel merely absorbed it all. Why were they here? He remembered the Voice who had told him not to fear, and he felt a sense of assurance, even as his feet walked toward the palace of the king, that there was an ordained purpose in this captivity.

The Processional Way turned left and headed north toward the royal palace. In the distance they could see the Ishtar Gate, the brilliant surface of its bricks shining like a sapphire against the paler blue sky.

Daniel saw Deborah stumble on the raised stones of the street, and started to reach for her. He longed to hold her, to assure her that everything would be all right. But they had come this far and he had not broken his promise. He must not touch her. "Jehovah be with you," he called.

They walked around two sides of a vast precinct surrounded by massive walls, then turned into a small gate. In front of them stood a building of such amazing design that they thought their eyes were playing tricks. Raised up on an immense foundation of arched vaults was a series of terraces which soared to a height of forty-seven cubits.

"And we thought Hezekiah's tunnel was an amazing structure," Hananiah said in awe.

The outside of this great structure was made of brick, faced with hewn stones. The terraces were covered with layers of earth and planted with exotic shrubs, ferns, and large trees.

Arioch explained that Nebuchadnezzar had built the masterpiece to please Amytis, one of his wives, who longed for the mountains and colors in her hilly Median homeland. They were called the Hanging Gardens of Babylon, a wonder throughout all the lands from Egypt to Assyria.

Arioch looked up at the cool gardens and thought of the fig tree he had brought from Jerusalem for the queen. He hoped that it had been watered and nurtured by the guard in charge.

His mind lingered over her name. Amytis. In the past few months he had almost forgotten the beautiful queen. The memory of their last meeting, of the invitation in her eyes, was disturbing to Arioch. He could ill afford any liaison with her. And yet . . . she had told him that she was so lonely . . . No, he must not think these thoughts. They were dangerous.

He breathed deeply of the fragrance from the citrus trees in bloom. At that very moment servants were stationed along the terraces, hoisting water in buckets to each level to irrigate the lush vegetation. Had Amytis been watching his homecoming from a vantage point along the way? He would have a vapor bath before he presented her gift.

Arioch ran his fingers through his unruly red hair. It felt like a dry desert bush. Before long, however, he would have his slave rub the finest oil into his scalp, killing those cursed parasites and leaving him with a head crowned by burnished copper. He would be prepared for those soft, caressing hands of the woman that Ishtar, the goddess of love, would send him.

His eyes searched the gardens above him. Was she there at this moment? In the small pouch he fastened beneath his tunic was a pendant containing a vial of perfume. It was a rather crude Judean piece, but a token of their conquest of these rebellious people. The queen loved trinkets; she would look upon the pendant with favor . . . And Arioch's mind wandered off once more upon dangerous paths.

After the barrenness of the desert and the squalor of the riverbank dwellings, the opulence which spread before the captives' eyes was dazzling. As they passed the Hanging Gardens and entered one of the five massive courtyards in the palace area, it became evident that the Hebrew captives were not being lead to dungeons, as they had expected.

"Attention, sons and daughters of Judah," Arioch ordered. (Until further orders, he was unsure how to address them. They were not ordinary hostages.) "My assignment is over . . . for now. If asked, I know you will report that you were well treated."

He looked directly at Daniel, who nodded quietly in agreement.

Deborah tried to move closer to Daniel. She realized that with the journey's end his protection might be taken from her. She looked up at the massive walls surrounding the palace and felt smaller than ever.

"Guards, you are dismissed. Do not deplete the city's wine vats tonight," Arioch said. He smiled at his admonishment. It was advice he would not take himself. The wine fermented from the trunk of the palm tree would be all his soldiers could afford. But as for him . . . he had saved a special vintage, aged from the black grapes of Phoenicia, for this night. He glanced toward Deborah . . . no, not yet. The time for her fulfillment was in the hands of the gods—praise Ishtar! It would be another who shared his glass—and his bed—tonight.

They had stopped in front of a massive bronze door decorated with a bas-relief of a king in his royal chariot. Looming above them were images of immense horses yoked to a war chariot, their harnesses decorated with tassels and bells. Over the figure of the king was a parasol, covered with what appeared to be embroidery.

The door groaned open to disclose a fat, perspiring man, his grinning face a contrast to the elegant surroundings.

"Welcome to Babylon," he said, tapping his fingers together like a child anticipating a sugar treat. "I am Ashpenaz, the chief of King Nebuchadnezzar's eunuchs, in charge of all palace personnel. *All* palace personnel." He paused, waiting for the importance of his position to register.

The fellow is so pompous! thought Arioch. But then, perhaps he needed to compensate somehow for his loss of manhood. He was harmless, after all, and unwavering in his loyalty to the king.

"Ah yes, you are a fine looking group," said Ashpenaz. "A little dirty, of course, but we will take care of that. Yes, yes, we'll take care of that."

"The chief eunuch does everything in excess," muttered Mishael.

"Keep your opinions to yourself," warned Azariah.

"And did Arioch treat you well? Yes, yes, one of you be the spokesman . . . you with the curly hair, yes you . . . speak, speak."

He waved his pudgy hand, resplendent with rings, at Daniel.

"The captain is a man of his word, sir," answered Daniel.

"Good, good, I shall tell the King that his mission to bring back young men and women of Judean nobility has been accomplished. Now I, Ashpenaz, will take charge. Yes, indeed.

"Now, children, to your rooms, to your rooms. The young women will follow Shamash, and the young men will go with Melzar."

Appearing from behind the massive form of the chief eunuch were the servants. Shamash wore a simple dress with one smooth shoulder bared. Melzar had a knee-length tunic caught at the waist by a belt. His hair was long and held back by a simple band. Both servants carried keys. They stared at their charges with curiosity; it was unusual for foreign hostages to be housed in palace chambers.

"Please, Ashpenaz, may I make a request?" Daniel knew he had ventured asking a favor before . . . what did he have to lose?

"Speak up, speak up."

"Will you ask your servant to assign me to quarters with my friends, Hananiah, Mishael, and Azariah?"

"Granted."

"Granted," echoed Mishael beneath his breath. Hananiah signaled him with a warning wink. One of these days Mishael might get them all into trouble with his inopportune humor.

Deborah stood with the women, her small body trembling uncontrollably. Daniel stepped toward her, knowing he had not broken his vow with Arioch during the entire trip. Now it didn't matter. Deborah rushed into his arms, sobbing softly, the tears making rivulets down her dusty cheeks.

"The Lord protect you, little one."

"Come, come now, we'll have none of that," Ashpenaz clucked, like a mother admonishing two children. He sighed. They were so beautiful, these two; he must consider a small offering to Marduk for them. He relished the thought of playing matchmaker. It was his vicarious pleasure.

The men and women were separated and led down different hallways—apprehensive and relieved at the same time. The halls leading to the men's rooms were flanked by smooth alabaster columns, the air soft with the fragrance of orange blossoms. They were shown to their quarters, where tubs of scented water had been brought in for their baths. Bowls of pears and grapes sat on low tables.

"Why?" asked Hananiah, as he looked around the room he had been assigned with Daniel.

"The Lord's ways are mysterious. Do you remember, Hananiah, when we were studying the words of the prophet Isaiah, how the Lord said, 'Don't be afraid, my chosen ones'?"

"It's not fear that I have, but curiosity," said Hananiah. "In spite of all the horror stories we have heard about Nebuchadnezzar, these are not exactly slave quarters. Here, have a grape."

"I believe we're on trial. If Nebuchadnezzar is going to try to conquer all of Judah, he may be using us as hostages. On the other hand, I'm not sure that King Jehoiakim cares enough about us to fight. Perhaps we have been brought here to teach the Chaldeans more of our culture and our God. But, why should we speculate? We'll soon find out."

In the next few days they were allowed to rest, given clean tunics and new sandals, and taken on daily tours of the area by Melzar. He was a likeable fellow, but fearful of every action he considered a bad omen. When Daniel coughed, Melzar told him the gods were punishing him for evil thoughts. Along the maze of crooked back streets outside the palace compound, they saw the crippled and blind, scorned by passers-by. "They are possessed by demons," Melzar told the Hebrews. "The exorcists have done their best, but . . ." and his voice would trail. Why should he bother to explain to these Judeans, who were of such simple minds that they worshiped only one God?

Melzar took the Hebrew youths on a tour of the Temple of Marduk. They stood, dwarfed by the walls of the sanctuary, and stared at the gold and alabaster pillars which supported immense cedar roof beams. The temple and the complex of buildings housing lesser gods covered an area of over sixty acres. As they trudged past all of the shrines, the sounds of the chanters provided a cacophony that drowned conversation and offended their eardrums. Even

Mishael couldn't find humor in the surroundings. Azariah tried to count the shrines to various gods that were evident everyplace, but lost track when he reached three hundred and four.

The temple prostitutes mingled with the group until they discovered that they had no money for their services, then they draped themselves at the bases of the part-animal, part-human deities to wait for more lucrative encounters.

"And you shall have no other gods before me," Daniel thought as he listened to the tour recital.

Marduk, the chief god, was depicted in many ways. ("I like the old man best as a warrior . . . the dragon bit is pretty repulsive," quipped Mishael.)

For Daniel and his friends, the tours they were given proved very revealing. Surely Nebuchadnezzar must be a man who was a builder as well as a destroyer. He plundered and enslaved, ordered the executions and torture of those who would not submit to him, and yet caused his underlings to praise his desire to establish a new society in the Land of Shinar. What kind of a complex personality must he be?

When Melzar returned with his foreign charges, Ashpenaz was waiting for them in the courtyard of their compound. "They were well-behaved and polite, superintendent."

"Good, good," nodded the chief eunuch, "now we will see how they like their new names."

Ashpenaz patted his ample stomach and unrolled a scroll. "Listen, to me, listen now, the gods have instructed us to bestow upon you good Chaldean names. You will be known from now on in this manner . . ."

"He'll have to repeat them or we'll never remember," observed Mishael.

Melzar, hearing the remark, wondered how long this fellow would keep his sense of humor in days to come.

Ashpenaz began to read the Hebrew names of the captives, and as each young man stepped forward, he gave him a new Babylonian name. For the young men this seemed like a first step toward stripping them of their God-honoring heritage. Daniel's Hebrew name meant "God is my judge"; Hananiah's, "gift of the Lord"; Mishael's, "He that is a strong God"; and Azariah's, "the help of the Lord." Every name described God's providential care.

"Hananiah, you shall be called Shadrach, the inspiration of the sun god. Mishael, you are now Meshach, for the goddess Shaca." (Mishael/Meshach winced at the thought of being named for a female deity.)

"Azariah, you are Abednego, servant of the shining fire. And for you, Daniel, your name is Belteshazzar, after our great god Bel, keeper of the hidden treasures. Now, to your rooms, to your rooms. Tomorrow you will begin your studies." Ashpenaz dismissed them with the wave of his hand. He was beginning to enjoy this assignment. These boys were well-bred, not street ruffians.

They went to their rooms, confused by these foreign ways and foreign names. But they were not being mistreated. Strange jailers, these Chaldeans.

The Hebrews were restricted to the palace area and to the compound where they had been assigned. Their rooms, sparsely furnished but not unpleasant, clustered around a garden courtyard. The young women had been taken to another part of the palace enclosure, their fate to Daniel and his friends unknown.

That evening a group of young Hebrew men gathered in Daniel and Hananiah's room to pray and talk about their future. Hananiah spoke: "Well, now that my name is Shadrach, I guess we better all get used to it. It seems to me," he said, looking at his friends crammed into the small area, "that one of the basic problems is to learn to fit in without being swallowed."

Opinions were divided. For some there was no compromise. One Hebrew, his arms crossed solidly in front of him, said, "We must not fit in; we must stand out! Any integration into this pagan culture will be a denial of the Lord God of Israel. If we allow ourselves to be called by these new names, we are denying our fathers and mothers."

Other captives, like Caleb (now called Rabshakeh) took a completely opposite view. He looked around the room, eyeing the pomegranates on a tray and the sleeping mats rolled up neatly in the corner. "We would do well to forget Zion. Just think of what we have seen today—gold beyond anything in Jerusalem . . . beauty unmatched in Israel and Judah. We're here. Let's accept their ways. If in our hearts we believe in the one God, we can worship in silence and be much happier."

"Let us wait for the Lord's guidance," said Daniel, feeling somehow that there should be a balance in these opposing ideas. No progress would be made in arguing. "The important thing is that we meet for worship and find strength in praying together. We don't know what tomorrow will bring. We have no priest or prophet with us. We must strengthen one another and stay close to our God through prayer."

"It is easy for you to talk, Daniel—or Belteshazzar. From the time we left Jerusalem you were favored by Arioch. Do you have some special method of getting in the good graces of our captors?" Rabshakeh's sarcasm chilled the air.

"We need to sleep, Rabshakeh," Daniel answered. "Remember that the Lord who brought His people out of bondage in Egypt will not forget them in Babylon. Shalom."

Rabshakeh dug his fingernails into his palms. Why did the Lord, if He still cared at all, seem to give Daniel such self-assurance? He hated his smug righteousness. "Perhaps, Belteshazzar, you would like to know what I heard was happening to the girls? Melzar hinted that the prettiest ones were being prepared to be sold at a public auction. Deborah should fetch a high price, don't you think?"

Without waiting for a reaction, Rabshakeh left the room to return to his own quarters. Daniel fell to his knees in silence.

The others left, too, embarrassed by the cruelty of Rabshakeh's words. Life in a foreign land was going to be hard enough without dissension among the exiles.

"Lord, I know you have not forsaken us. You have promised that you will be with us, and that we are your chosen ones, the seed of Abraham, descendants of King David. Oh Lord, don't let me forget. Give me assurance that the little one will be safe."

And so he prayed far into the night. He fell asleep with his head resting on the seat of a reed chair and awoke in the morning curled on the bare floor.

He was shaken awake by Shadrach. "Ashpenaz is at the door. He says we must perform our ablutions in the courtyard cisterns and change our clothes, because we are to see the king. Look, they have given us linen tunics that reach to our feet."

Nebuchadnezzar had commanded that the young men from Judah be brought to the throne room early in the day. They hurried to dress and gathered around a fountain in the courtyard. Rabshakeh stood with his eyes downcast, avoiding Daniel, Shadrach, Meshach, and Abednego. Whatever happened today, the course of cooperation or compromise might be determined.

"You, you over there, Belte . . . Bel . . . you with the curly hair," Asphenaz waddled over to Daniel, having recognized that many of the assembled youths looked upon him as their spokesman.

"We have decided that you should keep your Hebrew name. I find the Chaldean name given to you is too awkward to remember, especially when I shall be addressing you frequently." He paused and smiled, the dimples in his cheeks making deep crevices. It was so rewarding, he thought, to have the authority to grant small concessions.

"But don't think this means you will be given any special privileges—not at all, not at all. Look alert, everyone, you are about to meet the king. Would that all the earth's people would have this honor! Follow Melzar. He will lead you while I inform the king, may he live forever, that you are coming." Ashpenaz tapped his fingers together in excitement. These prisoners were so handsome . . . and the king liked beautiful things.

Melzar inspected each young man and determined that the group was fit to meet the king. "Come with me, I'll show you where your place is in line," he said.

Meshach poked Abednego and said, "Now I know what the prophet Isaiah meant by 'All we like sheep have gone astray.' "

They left the compound and marched toward the palace. As they neared the gate they heard music—an orchestra of such high intensity that the sounds of the awakening city were drowned. The entire procession of the exiles was stopped to await the signal of Melzar for them to proceed.

Everyone was placed in precise order, according to the protocol of the court. First came the musicians with their harps, flutes, dulcimers, psalteries, and mandolins, followed by drums and cymbals. Then the dancers followed, swaying and clapping to the rhythm of the percussion. Close behind were the magicians, sorcerers, and astrologers, chanting indistinguishable words and waving incense to chase away the evil spirits. Daniel and the other exiles were last.

They entered the palace through a massive bronze door flanked by statues of colossal winged bulls with men's heads, which stood guard as further deterrent against evil spirits. Along the halls, statues of various genies stood in alabaster splendor. One was a giant woman, eyes and navel studded with precious stones, holding out poppies in her extended hand. Meshach stifled a laugh by biting his lips.

As they entered the throne room, the chanting stopped and the musicians, mystics, nobles, and various officials of the court bowed in homage to the king. He sat upon a gilded throne, his hands resting on the arms of the massive chair. Next to him was his favorite queen, Amytis, her heart-shaped face viewing the masses before her with imperious aloofness. She appeared bored by all the ceremony.

Nebuchadnezzar's face was angular and intelligent, and the rigors of battle campaigns showed in his athletic body. His eyes were azure blue. (*Like the Sea of Galilee,* thought Daniel, with a tug of homesickness.) The king's hair was piled on top of his head in the shape of a fez; his beard was waved and dressed in horizontal rows of curls. He wore a long linen tunic, and over this another open tunic, fringed and richly embroidered. As they drew nearer to the throne, they could see the design, worked in varied hues of rose, lavender, and purple. It depicted winged genies grasping in each hand a lion, which in turn was biting the breast of a bull. The whole design was symmetrical, bordered with lotus buds and decorated with palmettes. All other tunics in the court looked drab beside the king's.

Nebuchadnezzar ran his fingers over the hilt of his sword. He felt the shape of the crouching lions on the scabbard and was reassured of his strength. Praise Marduk.

All the people became silent as Nebuchadnezzar raised his hand. It was then that Daniel noticed Arioch, standing to the left of the queen, his red hair brilliant against the woven tapestry backdrop. Was it his imagination, Daniel wondered, or did Arioch give him a reassuring nod?

"Babylonians. We pay homage to Marduk." The king's voice, clear and resonant, rang through the great hall.

"Oh Marduk," he prayed, "lord of all countries, heed my words. I have built a temple for you; grant that I may be able to be proud of its glory. Grant that I may reach old age here in Babylon and that my posterity may be numerous, that the kings of all the countries of the world may pay me tribute; grant that my descendants may rule over men until the end of time."

He ended the prayer and raised his sword over his head, an indication that he would make another statement. "Now, let me see the youths from Judah. Bring them forward."

No one in the crowd moved.

Amytis leaned forward, her beautiful face showing interest in the proceedings for the first time. Arioch was quick to observe the way in which her eyes swept Daniel.

"And now, my young nobles, are you curious about my reason for bringing you here?" Nebuchadnezzar loved the drama of his own suspense.

"You have been carefully chosen because of your former positions in my puppet kingdom of Judah. We need your strong bodies and keen minds in our country. You will be taught in our Hall of Knowledge and learn Babylonian wisdom, the Chaldean language, statecraft, and culture. You will have a three-year course, studying in small groups with our finest tutors. All of the privileges of our ruling class will be yours."

He paused to impress upon them the magnificence of his gesture. For a full minute he looked at the Hebrews standing before him. And he stared especially long at Daniel, noting how confident this young man appeared, even in this alien environment.

"In addition, you will be supplied the finest clothes, and the best food and wine from the royal kitchen. When your training is finished, you will be brought to me for your assignments in the kingdom. Ashpenaz, you have done well. You will, of course, see to it that my orders are followed."

Ashpenaz lowered his head in assent. He knew what it could mean not to obey Nebuchadnezzar.

The king and Amytis stepped down from their thrones, followed by their personal servants. Orchestra, dancers, and the entourage of advisors and wisemen followed behind, singing praises to the king and the gods in a din of voices and instruments.

Arioch moved quickly beside Daniel and said quietly, "Deborah is safe. I have arranged it." Then he slipped away, leaving Daniel to return to his quarters with the others.

Back in their quarters, Daniel called Shadrach, Meshach, Abednego, and Rabshakeh into his room for a hasty time of prayer and planning. They needed to agree about what they would say to the chief eunuch when he arrived.

Ashpenaz could not believe what he heard. "What do you mean, you won't eat the king's food nor drink his wine? Are you insane?" His voice quivered with rage. "Don't you know, Daniel, don't you know that you will become pale and thin compared with the other youths . . . and the king will behead me for neglecting my responsibilities? No, no, I will not hear of it!"

Daniel had made his decision before they had left the throne room. He would study in the Chaldean Hall of Knowledge without a murmur. He would accept the name of Belteshazzar, if necessary. But he knew in his heart that he could not eat food sacrificed to idols; the Law of Moses forbade it. There could be no compromise with the traditional Hebrew dietary laws. But how could he be faithful to God without having Ashpenaz punished?

"You're a fool, Daniel," Rabshakeh said. "All four of you are fools! Why didn't you just say you have very delicate stomachs, and rich food upsets them?" Anyhow, we're in Babylon now. Times are moving fast . . . and we can't live in the past."

"There are some things, Rabshakeh, that our laws and prophets do not openly condemn, but this is one. Do you remember what we were told about Joshua? He said, 'Choose whom you will serve.' You must choose, too."

Rabshakeh left, closing the door roughly. The remaining four young men were silent for a few moments. Then Daniel looked at his friends and lowered his head. "Lord," he prayed, "we need your wisdom. How can we obey you without harming others?"

Melzar knocked and, without waiting for a reply, walked in. "What is this I hear?" he asked, a nervous agitation in his voice.

"Melzar, will you trust us to an experiment?" The solution to this problem came to Daniel suddenly. "For a period of ten days, give Shadrach, Meshach, Abednego, and myself a diet of vegetables and water. Then at the end of that time, you can determine how we look in comparison to the others who eat the king's food."

"Do you realize what you are asking?"

"Yes, I am asking you to trust me."

Melzar looked at Daniel. What was there about him that inspired such confidence? He had never met anyone like him. Before he realized the brashness of his promise, he said, "You shall have vegetables and water."

At the end of the ten days, the Judean youths gathered before Ashpenaz. "You are now to be assigned to your studies. I must say, yes indeed, that you all look very healthy. Daniel, you and your three friends have fared well on the royal food, after all. Yes indeed, you look better than the rest."

"Ashpenaz," whispered Melzar, "come over here. I have something to tell you." They drew away from the youths so none could hear.

"I think Ashpenaz lost some color in his face," observed Shadrach.

Ashpenaz turned to his four Hebrew charges and cleared his throat. "Now, young men," he said, nervously tapping his fingers on his belly, "you will begin your studies tomorrow. I hope you all will follow the curriculum. And you will follow the rules of your teachers. Exactly, do you understand?

"The king has given me his orders and, if the evil spirits stay away from me, I shall be on hand when he hears your final examinations. The king, may he live forever, is very, very particular about his commands. And I have become fond of your heads . . . as well as my own."

And so began one of the most intense indoctrination programs ever conceived in the minds of men—designed to turn God's people into willing servants of the Babylonian cults.

5

DREAM OF DESTINY

HIS HEAVY TIARA rested next to the sweetmeats on a low table beside the couch. Nebuchadnezzar shook his hair loose with relief. Spreading his lean frame on the silk cushions, he held out his hand and, at just a suggestion from his fingers, a servant handed him an ivory goblet, filled with aged wine from the grapes of Medea. When her father had brought Amytis to him, he had also transported many jugs filled with the "fruit of the gods" for the king's storehouses.

"Amytis, are you awake?" Nebuchadnezzar reached out to touch his queen, who seemed so remote, although she rested only an arm's length away. Was she pretending? So many times he would approach her and her indifference, or resignation, would make it like touching one of the stone statues of Babylon. She had built a fortress around herself as impregnable as the massive walls surrounding the city.

She did not stir. A person does not sleep without some movement. If that was her trick, he could outlast the ruse. She would have to get up eventually.

The mighty king of Babylon settled back on the pillows, musing over his strategy with this provocative wife of his. Why did he bother to consider the methods of winning her? He could have her any time he pleased; she was, after all, his personal possession. And yet, to have her willingly, totally, would be more of a triumph than invading an enemy camp with force.

He was Nebuchadnezzar, the conqueror—Nebuchadnezzar, the architect and builder, the greatest king the world had ever known. Hadn't he just returned from the battle of Carcemish, where the mighty armies of Egypt had fallen before his onslaught? He had not considered the dark-eyed beauties in the land to the north. There was a time for war, and a time for love. And the time for love was in Babylon.

What did she want from him? He had brought her bracelets studded with agate in exotic colors, robes with embroidery more lavish than a peacock's feathers, and plants to blend their fragrance and beauty into the hanging gardens.

Ungrateful, that's what she was. How could she be indifferent to the riches that he could offer?

"Amytis, wake up . . . if you are really asleep," he roared. Suddenly the sight of her immobile figure, unresponsive to his desires, infuriated him. He waved the hovering servants to leave and moved to her couch. She opened her eyes and smiled, knowing this was the part she must play as the submissive wife of the great king.

When they were finished, Nebuchadnezzar leaned back with a sigh. He would need to offer more prayers to the gods for wisdom in handling this woman. Perhaps they were born under the wrong stars. Maybe he should get rid of her. There were hundreds of others who would crawl to the top of the highest ziggurat to be in her place.

Amytis bit into a plum and wiped the juice from her lips with the edge of her tunic. The fruit was sweet and reminded her of the trees behind her father's house in the hills of Medea. What did the king know of such simple pleasures? His life was that of a god. He was not like mortal men, with feelings and needs. What was she to him, anyhow, but another treasure wrested from a foreign land? She was an adornment, a tapestry, a golden vase to be displayed and admired.

But there were others who cared for her, who risked their lives for a simple flirtation. What harm was there in that? She fingered the pendant containing the vial of perfume that Arioch had brought her from Jerusalem. It was nothing compared to the jewels the king gave her, but there was an element of danger in that simple gift that provided some zest in her boring life.

And now there were those handsome youths who came from Judah. One in particular. It would be intriguing to meet him. Amytis smiled at the daring of her imagination.

"You smile, Amytis. Are you satisfied?" Nebuchadnezzar was never sure about the moods of his elusive wife. If only he knew what she was thinking. But then, what did it matter? Surely the gods did not intend for a woman to have a mind.

"If you say so, my king," she answered.

Satisfied? How could he understand what satisfaction meant to her? She might be satisfied if she had a child, a baby to nurse and caress. A child would need her, at least for several years. She would feel useful, needed, truly loved by someone. She had gone to the temple every morning for months and sacrificed to Marduk. She had prayed to Ishtar, the goddess of fertility. Why was her womb empty? Was this one wish the king could not fulfill?

"Amytis, you may have anything you want on earth. I will see that you have it. Do you understand?"

"Yes, my king."

"Well . . . what will it be?"

"I want a child."

Nebuchadnezzar's blue eyes softened. Perhaps she was human, after all. A child? Of course, a son—a boy who would be trained in the Babylonian University. A noble who would continue his work of building and would not have to go to war, for by the time he was grown all the known world would be under the rule of Babylon.

"And we shall have a child," Nebuchadnezzar decreed, as if his heir would suddenly appear, carried on a golden throne by four strong eunuchs. "It is no coincidence, Amytis, that I ordered Arioch to choose the choicest Hebrew girl to be your personal handmaiden. The gods are good. Praise Marduk. You will need someone who is able to assist you while you are carrying the child."

Amytis brightened at the thought of a companion from among the recent exiles. She knew how lonely it was to be transported to a new country. Perhaps someone, for the first time since she had been taken from the house of her father and brought to Babylon, would need her. But still a nagging doubt stayed in her mind. Was Nebuchadnezzar capable of fathering her child? Nothing had happened up to now. And she had heard that sometimes a man and a woman could mate but be unable to produce offspring.

Nebuchadnezzar reached under his couch and pulled out his sword. He hit a brass cymbal with the broadside of the scabbard, causing the room to reverberate with the crashing sound. Immediately Ashpenaz waddled in, flustered over the insistency of the summons.

"Ashpenaz, you must have been close to the door to come so soon," Nebuchadnezzar remarked with a grin. The chief eunuch was his one constant amusement. It was a game to see his round cheeks flush with embarrassment.

"Yes, yes, your Majesty . . . I mean no, your Majesty. Oh dear, what may I do for you, your Majesty?"

"Summon Arioch and have him bring the Hebrew girl he has chosen for the queen. Oh, and Ashpenaz, you did well by the young Hebrews . . . they all look excellent. It's amazing what being fed the royal food for a while can do. Excellent—curse you, Ashpenaz, now you have me saying it! Anyhow . . . have you assigned them to their studies?"

"Oh yes, your Majesty. They have begun classes . . . and about their food . . ." Ashpenaz had decided that now, while the king was in such a good mood, was the time to tell him about Daniel and his three friends.

"Their food . . . of course . . . give them whatever they wish. They must be healthy. I do not want pale, thin leaders. When we bring more of their countrymen into Babylon they must see that we have treated them well. That way they will be more cooperative in becoming a part of our great kingdom."

Ashpenaz bowed and backed out of the room. He did not want any more conversation about food. Whatever the young Hebrews didn't eat, he would have extra rations for himself. Yes, yes, that was it! What a brilliant thought, he congratulated himself.

Daniel was in his room, sitting beside the window which faced the west. He was grateful for that window, because it meant he could look toward Jerusalem as he prayed. "Lord Jehovah, thank you for those servants of the king whose hearts you have touched to help us. Give them your special blessings and open their eyes to your truths."

Daniel paused, thinking of the ruler who had brought them here—that strange, troubled man whose brilliance had fashioned this city but whose ambitions rode over the bodies of people and nations. Nebuchadnezzar puzzled him. Something seemed to tell Daniel that this king was more of a tool than a tyrant, an instrument to be used by the Lord for His purpose. "And Lord," he continued praying, "watch over the king and give him your wisdom to rule."

In the evening, after their studies and personal prayer time, the Hebrew friends gathered in one of their small rooms and talked. Like university students everywhere, they argued about issues, compared notes on their classes, and speculated about their future. Shadrach was intrigued and stimulated by the extent of their education. "My head is bursting! Never could I have imagined that the wisdom of this land was so vast!"

"The language of the Chaldeans is extremely difficult to learn," Meshach said. "I don't understand why we don't concentrate on Aramaic. That is what is spoken in diplomatic circles."

"That leaves you out," laughed Abednego. "You may be in training for court jester, but a diplomat you're not!"

Just then the door to Daniel's room swung open and Ashpenaz plodded in unannounced. He was panting, as he usually did from the excess weight he carried, and smiled like a happy cherub at the students.

"Welcome, noble Ashpenaz," said Meshach, with a sweeping bow. "We have been waiting for your royal visit."

"I take it back," muttered Abednego. "You *are* a diplomat."

"Ah yes," beamed Ashpenaz, oblivious to the innuendo, "you must be studying the methods of our diplomacy. Very important, very important. Now, let me give you some news."

"You have word from Deborah?" Daniel asked eagerly.

"Let's see, now . . . yes, I do." Ashpenaz paused. He enjoyed his privilege of knowing inside information about the court. (Granted, sometimes that knowledge was obtained by his keen ear applied to the crack in a door.) "Deborah has been given to Queen Amytis as her personal handmaiden. An honor, indeed, yes indeed."

"And may I see her, Ashpenaz?" Daniel asked.

"You are a bold one. First you ask for special food, now special privileges. Next thing I know you'll be in the king's court yourself," Ashpenaz commented.

"My friend, our Lord God is King. We are already members of His court," Daniel responded with a smile.

"Oh my, my, there you go again," Ashpenaz wiped his hands on his sleeves in frustration. "Will you never stop talking about your God? You will get yourselves into severe trouble someday, mark my words. Just pay attention to your studies and forget your Hebrew God."

"We'll take the first part of your advice, Ashpenaz, but not the last," replied Shadrach. There was no need to consult the others; they had all agreed on their roles as students in Babylon: obedience, but not conformity.

"I must say, you four are easier to work with than some of the others . . . who refuse to learn anything we want to teach them and have anything to do with Babylonians. Some of the new visitors being brought in will not even speak to us. They tell us that our enticements are more dangerous than the Pharaoh's whip and torture."

"Then there are more Judeans being brought into the city?" Daniel asked eagerly.

"Of course, of course. Why else do you think Nebuchadnezzar, long may he live, wants you four to learn so much? You are needed in the court of the wisemen. You will be able to help your people more by cooperation than by isolation—contrary to what some others believe." Ashpenaz reached for a fried sesame cake which the youths had ignored on a tray. It was good to visit their rooms; there were so many delicacies they left uneaten.

"But aren't we being trained in order to return to Jerusalem?" Abednego asked with new concern.

Ashpenaz did not seem to know how to answer. "See here, young men, I only know that the orders of the king are for your present studies. It is not for me to question his future decrees." He quickly changed the subject. "Now, I shall speak with Arioch tomorrow and have him arrange a short meeting with Deborah. But, please, not too many more favors. There is a limit to what I can ask."

Ashpenaz pushed himself up from the stool, took another sweet from the tray, and started toward the door. These young men were so pleasant. He enjoyed visiting them; they were not like so many of the members of the court, always vying for position, looking for ways to gain favor. If Daniel wanted something, he made his request simple and forthright. They were so . . . how could he express it? . . . so likeable. Ah, if only he could have had sons, he would wish them to be like these boys.

"May Marduk . . . oh dear, I forgot . . . may whoever your God is bless you."

Classes seemed longer than usual the next few days. Why was it taking Ashpenaz so long to arrange a meeting with Deborah?

The schedule left very little time for personal concerns. Every daytime hour was filled with intense learning. The Hebrew students were astounded at the intellectual advancements of this heathen nation, and they found the challenge stimulating.

Early in their studies at the Hall of Knowledge they made a pact to meet and pray every night, if possible.

"If we remember the words of the Law and the prophets and repeat them to each other, it won't matter how much our minds are crammed with Babylonian wisdom," Daniel said.

"I remember a proverb of Solomon," Shadrach answered: " 'The Lord gives wisdom; from His mouth come knowledge and understanding; He stores up sound wisdom for the upright.' "* Shadrach's keen intellect was sharpened by an ability to recall from memory the words of the holy men of Israel—words his father had made him repeat over and over as a small child. Now he was grateful for those drills he had once thought were so tedious.

That proverb became a watchword for the young Hebrews as they were indoctrinated with the moral stories of Babylonian wisdom. Again and again they would repeat to each other, sometimes by merely mouthing the words behind the backs of their Babylonian teachers, "The Lord gives wisdom . . ."

They needed the support those words from Proverbs gave them, because at times the teachers seemed so right; there was such a fine line between the wisdom of man and the wisdom of the God of Israel. Some of the Babylonian students would argue with the Hebrews, "What difference does it make whether we worship many gods or you worship just one God? The principles are the same."

Daniel's answers were patient but firm. "The question is not just one of principles; it is one of results. Our God is a god of miracles. He led our people in the wilderness for forty years and brought

* Proverbs 2:6, NASB.

them into the land He promised. He parted the sea and caused the enemies to drown, while our people walked across on dry land. He gave to Moses, our forefather, commandments for us to live by, and He spoke to Moses from a burning bush. He has given us prophets who foretell the future and wisemen to teach us how to live for today."

"We have our prophets and wisemen, too. Our gods do miracles when we bring them enough sacrifices."

"The Lord God Jehovah is not a god made with human hands. He cannot be bribed to follow the wishes of His children. Our God is worthy because He is unchanging. He was in the beginning and will be throughout eternity. In Him is justice and honor."

"If you cannot see him, how do you know he exists?" asked the young Chaldean scholars.

"Because we have seen the results of His works."

The Babylonian questioners laughed at Daniel's answer. "One of the results is that you were taken prisoners by our soldiers. Is that the justice of your Jehovah?"

"We do not know why we are here, but we do know there is a reason."

The discussions about the heathen gods and the Lord God of Israel were endless. Daniel, however, was respected by his adversaries for his unwavering belief and clear answers.

Several days after Daniel made his request to Ashpenaz for a meeting with Deborah, he was summoned from class one day and told, "The captain of the king's guard wishes to speak with you."

Daniel's usual composure was shattered. He dropped the tablet he had been studying, stubbed his toe on the clawed foot of a stool, and collided with his teacher. "Excuse me, I'm sorry," he muttered.

"Poor Daniel," whispered Meshach to Shadrach, "no one is able to fluster him as much as the little bee. Her sting is sharp."

In the corridor, Arioch was waiting, running his hand through his burnished hair as if he were polishing a piece of copper. His clean-shaven face made him look younger than his twenty-one years. He leaned against a marble column and watched Daniel in the unwavering manner which was his habit.

"I greet you in the name of Ea, god of wisdom and knowledge," Arioch said with a slight wave of his eagle-topped staff. "May you learn from the god whose eyes are bright the skills of divination and magic."

"The Lord gives wisdom," answered Daniel, remembering almost automatically the words of encouragement agreed upon by his friends. "Please, noble Arioch, have you brought me news of Deborah?"

"Oh, yes, there was a reason for me to see you, wasn't there? You will be pleased to know that I rescued the beautiful Deborah from being sent into the service of Mannashi, the wife of the chief soothsayer. She is a shrew with a terrible temper. However, I used my influence, knowing that Queen Amytis was in need of a personal handmaiden, and suggested Deborah's services . . . with my personal recommendation, of course." Arioch paused to observe Daniel's reaction.

"I am very grateful, Arioch, for your kindness. God bless you."

Arioch cupped his chin in his hand and stared at Daniel. He rubbed his gold amulet and considered the paradox of Daniel. He was a captive in a strange land, separated from his home and family, denied even the sight of the girl he loved. And yet Daniel had blessed him, Arioch, one who was favored by the king (and queen), a privileged member of the inner court circle. It was perplexing.

"I have heard from Ashpenaz that you and your three friends are doing exceptionally well in the Hall of Knowledge—is that so?"

"We have been trained to apply ourselves to our studies."

"Excellent. I shall tell the king that my hostages are becoming a part of our culture."

Daniel hesitated, praying silently for tact and wisdom. "We are prepared, noble Arioch, to serve Babylon and pay tribute to Nebuchadnezzar. However, if there is a time when cooperation might violate our commitment to the God of our fathers, then our loyalty is to the word of the Lord God Jehovah."

"For your sake, Daniel, may you never be put to the test."

Arioch had never met another man—he could no longer call him a boy—who had the strength of this one. If he had been born in Babylon he would consider him a rival. However, with his foreign background there was little danger that Daniel could threaten Arioch's position as a favorite of the court.

In a sudden burst of generosity, Arioch continued, "I shall arrange for you to see Deborah. You will be excused from your classes tomorrow at sundown. Come to the first tier of the hanging gardens. I shall bring Deborah there."

There was jubilance in the classroom that day! The Chaldean teacher was baffled by the incessant sound of a bee, which seemed to come from the direction of Meshach's chair. Four young men from Judea stifled their laughter and diligently applied their styluses to the cuneiform tablets.

The air was heavy with the scent of orange blossoms budding in profusion in the famous gardens. Arioch approached Daniel, who was pacing beside a shrine to Hea, a god who had the body of a fish and the head of a man. According to the Babylonian teachers, this scaly deity was the god of agriculture. But by now Daniel had become indifferent to all the shrines and statues. The only thing he saw was Deborah.

Oblivious to Arioch, Daniel stared at her. She had changed. Her hair was glossy and fell in loose curls to her shoulders. Her eyes were shaded on the lower lids with turquoise, and her lips were brightened by red ochre. Her tunic was embroidered with threads more elaborate than those on her sister's wedding tunic. If she had been beautiful before, now she was regal.

Arioch looked at them and felt a twinge of jealousy. But why should he? He could have almost any woman in Babylon. Should he deny Daniel such a small pleasure?

"You may have some time alone. I'll return when the sun has set behind the Tower." Arioch left quickly, feeling beneficent about his part in this rendezvous. Why, then, was he envious? They had nothing, and he had been blessed by Marduk with one of the most honored positions in the kingdom. He shook the feeling from his mind as he paced out of the garden.

Deborah stood still, suddenly shy with this one who had been so familiar. Daniel touched her hair, now so clean and fragrant. Gently, he lifted her face and brushed her lips with his. For weeks he had lived this moment in his imagination.

"You are more beautiful than ever, little one."

Deborah drew his hand from her face and pulled him down on the marble bench beneath an orange tree. There was so much to say, and so little time.

"The king and queen have treated me well. I am to serve Queen

Amytis as her personal handmaiden and assist her during her pregnancy, when she conceives."

Deborah lowered her eyes, embarrassed that she had been so outspoken. Her mother had taught her that refined girls did not speak of such things until they were married. But in Babylon it was so different. There was nothing sacred about personal relationships between men and women. It was the chief topic of conversation among the women in the court.

"And do they treat you well?" Daniel asked.

"Oh, yes. I have many privileges. It's not at all what I expected. Although I am a captive myself, the queen has given me Assyrian maids to draw my bath and prepare my food."

"Prepare your food?" She must have known the stand he made when it came to eating food dedicated to idols.

"Oh, Daniel, it's such a small thing. We have to survive in this foreign land."

"Jehovah has brought us here, and we can best serve Him by obeying our masters, as long as we place God and His laws first."

Deborah knew what he meant. Daniel would never tell her directly not to eat the Babylonian food. He was not like the Prophet Jeremiah who thundered and condemned. But she knew Daniel was displeased with her.

She pulled her hand away from his and looked down at her small fingers, laden with the new rings she had been given by the king. Tears began to well in her dark eyes; she looked away to keep from crying. She had loved him for so long, but now there was something wrong. He was such a strong reminder of Zion, of all the things she had held sacred: the word of the Law, the voices of the prophets, the pride her mother and father had had in her. Those things were past. She would never see Jerusalem again. To keep her sanity she must adapt to the new ways.

"Every night we meet for prayers and memory work. We shall pray for your strength, my little one. It will not be easy for you, without the companionship of others who follow Jehovah." Daniel wiped the tear that was beginning to trickle down her cheek. He remembered the furrow her tears had made on her dust-covered face after weeks in the desert. Now the tears were colored with the paint from her eyelids.

Then the torrent was loosed. She collapsed in his arms, sobbing like a child who has been whipped. "Daniel, I don't deserve you. You are so strong and so wise, and I'm so weak." She leaned her head against his chest and cried, giving vent to the frustration of the past weeks, releasing the tension of her mind and spirit. She felt so hypocritical. She was a Judean, a believer in the Lord God Jehovah, a daughter of the House of Barak, and here she was looking, talking, and—yes—eating like a Babylonian!

"Hush, be still, my little one, the Lord forgives us."

"But we have no Temple . . . no place for a sacrifice for our sins."

"We have made our own altar. We do not have to have the Temple. God has appointed us to be both priests and prophets in a foreign land. When the time is right, we shall request that you be allowed to participate in our worship. A rope is strong when it is interwoven with many strands of hemp."

"But how can we meet? I don't believe the king would allow it."

"The Lord has softened the hearts of some Babylonians to grant our requests. Remember when we parted I said, 'The Lord protect you'?"

"Yes," she said quietly, like an obedient child.

"And He will."

They sat for a time, not speaking. Deborah relaxed, trying not to think about her confused emotions, but instead to enjoy the warmth of the moment. She could pretend that she was home again. Safe. Protected. She wanted to wash her lips and eyelids—to run through the streets of Jerusalem or sit by the fire and work on her embroidery. Would she ever see Judah again? Or would it be sacked and destroyed, as she had overheard the king boasting?

Daniel took her hand and pressed it to his lips. Her skin was fragrant with the perfume of roses and softened with aromatic oil. She was no longer the frightened little girl in the desert, but she was still his beloved. They didn't notice that they were no longer alone.

Arioch cleared his throat. "I hate to interrupt this pastoral scene, but the sun is low and Daniel must return to his quarters." *Why did I get involved in this liaison, anyhow?* Arioch thought. *From the time I first set my eyes on this Daniel he has haunted me.*

Daniel held both of Deborah's hands and looked into her eyes. "The Lord protect you," he said.

"And you, Daniel." She turned and walked away quickly without looking back.

Daniel laughed as he recalled a similar scene that had occurred at the Street of Merchants. "I was remembering the first time we met," he told Arioch. "She ran away without looking back that time, too."

"That is good advice, especially for you, Daniel."

"I will not look back, noble Arioch, for the past cannot be changed. But I will never forget what I learned from the Law and the prophets. Those are stored in my heart."

"Power and the intellect are the only things that survive in the real world. Things of the heart were made for dreamers, and dreams are for the astrologers and sorcerers to interpret." Arioch was uneasy, even as he made that statement. The man of war, the captain of the king's guard, was experiencing an inner warfare. What was so disquieting about this Hebrew youth?

"Enough!" he suddenly snapped. "It is time for you to return to your quarters."

"I am your grateful servant, Arioch. Thank you for allowing me to be with Deborah."

"Of course," Arioch said gruffly.

"Shalom," said Daniel, knowing that peace was what Arioch most needed . . . peace in his heart.

Daniel returned to the classroom, determined to study and show that a man of God could strive for excellence even in a foreign setting.

In the following years, Daniel, Shadrach, Meshach, and Abednego applied themselves with diligence to their learning. Every waking moment was spent in studying architecture, language, diplomacy, and literature. Their keen minds absorbed the knowledge of the advanced wisdom of the Babylonian empire.

"Most outstanding students, most outstanding," Ashpenaz would report to the king. He visited their rooms frequently, even staying sometimes for their prayer sessions.

One evening, Daniel told Ashpenaz, "You are going to live a long life, and serve more than one king, my friend."

"How do you know that?" Ashpenaz stammered. This Daniel made such definite statements. "Do you have some way of looking into the future, like the king's astrologers?"

Meshach examined Daniel closely. For some time, it had become evident to these three friends that Daniel had been developing a genius for visions and interpretation of dreams. "Do you realize what Ashpenaz is asking, Daniel? We have been discussing what has been happening to you lately,"—Meshach nodded in the direction of Shadrach and Abednego—"and we believe that the Lord has given you a special gift, just as he did Joseph of old."

Daniel sat with his head bowed, quietly praying. When he raised his eyes there was a glow in them, an acknowledgment that he knew he had been chosen for something special.

Sometimes at night he would awaken from a sound sleep, knowing that there was a Presence in his room. He would experience a Light surrounding his pallet, penetrating his eyelids, which were squeezed tight with awe. He knew it was the Lord; in the now familiar Voice he would clearly hear a prophecy.

"But, Lord, how can this be? I am young . . . without a priest or the Temple. Why have you chosen me?"

"You have obeyed me. I shall never leave you or forsake you."

"Did you say he has a special gift?" asked Ashpenaz, "My, my, I shall certainly tell the king. He may want to use you for one of his wisemen. In fact, he could use all of you!" He waved his arm to include Daniel's friends. "You are certainly smarter than most of the fools . . . or dear me, please don't tell anyone I said that . . ."

Daniel did not want his friends to think he was singled out for any special honors by the Lord. "I know Jehovah has given me a special gift at times. Sometimes it frightens me."

"Daniel, you surprise me," said Shadrach. "Do you remember when we were memorizing the psalms of King David? He said over and over that we have nothing to fear when the Lord is our defender."

"You're right, Shadrach. And we need each other to be reminders of such things."

And so they studied, prayed, and worked together for three years. At the end of their training, Ashpenaz took them before the king for their oral examinations. They were asked questions in the language of the Chaldeans and in Hebrew about many subjects. The king was pleased and awarded Ashpenaz a new ring for his watchfulness over their training. Daniel, Shadrach, Meshach, and Abednego were chosen to be among the king's advisors.

"Frankly, Ashpenaz," the king confided to his chief eunuch, "these Hebrew youths are ten times better than all the magicians and wisemen in the realm. They will be valuable for the future of Babylon."

The four young men remained in their student's quarters, but began to be called upon frequently as advisors in the court. All of them were told that important assignments were awaiting them.

Arioch found excuses to visit Daniel as much as possible. Many times he interrupted him as he was facing toward Jerusalem, praying with his eyes shut. Arioch would watch for a while, curious about the quietness of Daniel's worship. In the Temple of Marduk there was loud chanting. How did these Hebrews expect their God to hear them if they didn't shout? Strange religion. However, Arioch thought, they certainly did have a calmness about them. Would that the king might have some of that assurance. He was becoming more and more agitated every day. It was as if a demon were dwelling within him, gnawing at his insides.

"I've come to take you to Deborah," Arioch would sometimes say. This was something he could have assigned to one of his underlings, but the task gave him pleasure. He wondered how long this romance would last, with such lengthy separations. It was like watching a story unfold, and he was the reader of the manuscript.

Each time she met Daniel in the gardens, Deborah would be full of news about the king and queen. She chattered about court gossip, the newest fashions, and the trips she had taken.

"Did you know that I went to the summer palace with Queen Amytis? We rode on the royal barge along the Euphrates, with a huge canopy over us."

"Remember, little one, the custom in our land—the canopy made from the branches of a cedar tree and a pine tree? It would have been our wedding canopy to show that Jehovah's banner over us is love."

"It was a quaint custom," she said. "We had so many traditions in the old country, didn't we?"

"Those are the traditions of our forefathers, Deborah. They can be taken to any country."

Deborah twirled the new bracelet on her arm. It was difficult these days to be with Daniel. He was so . . . convicting. It was like sitting in her father's home in Judah, listening to him intone the words of the Law and the prophets. She was young. She had been told, frequently by Arioch, that she was very beautiful. She wondered if she should tell Daniel that she had accused Arioch of having an affair with the queen. Hadn't she seen her very own pendant, the one her father had given her, around the queen's neck? Who could have brought that to Amytis but someone who had taken it as loot from Jerusalem? When she had confronted Arioch, he had laughed, admitting or denying nothing, and the next time he saw her he had brought this golden bracelet. A bribe, perhaps? At any rate, she loved the queen, and would never bring her more trouble than she now had.

"Daniel," she said, remembering the latest news she wanted to tell him, "I am very worried about King Nebuchadnezzar, long may he live."

She is becoming more indoctrinated each day, Daniel thought.

"Why are you worried?"

"He was so loving to Queen Amytis when I first became her handmaiden. He told me I was to talk to her often, because she was lonely. Whenever he went out to inspect his building projects or was gone with his troops to other lands, he would give specific instructions about caring for the queen. In spite of what others say, he was really a kind, gentle man. But he has changed. Terribly."

Daniel leaned forward, listening carefully. In recent days he had been receiving unusual visions about the king. He had tried to put them out of his mind, but they were persistent.

"How has he changed?"

"He is restless and irritable. He shouts at his servants and mumbles obscenities at the queen; her eyes are always red from weeping. Sometimes he paces the floor of his room all night, only falling asleep with exhaustion as the sun breaks over the Tower. He spends hours on his knees in front of the statue of Bel-Marduk. He seems possessed by many demons."

"And he may be. This land abounds in them."

"Pray for him, will you, Daniel?"

"We will pray together." And Daniel took her hand and she lowered her head in obedience.

Arioch discovered them in this manner. *Such wasted time with a beautiful woman,* he thought.

"You will return to your quarters now," he stated. "Deborah, hurry to the queen. She is greatly distressed and needs you."

Nebuchadnezzar paced the floor of the throne room. His lean body had grown skeletal; food had lost its appeal. He looked at the ceiling, its thick cedar beams a result of efforts to rebuild after the great flood of the Euphrates caused the foundations of the palace to collapse. Was any man a greater builder of holy places than he? Every brick had his name inscribed on it. Every door of cedar and bronze was designed by him. He was a genius.

Suddenly his voice reverberated through the empty room—a scream of frustration like that of an animal caught in the iron claws of a trap. "Bel-Marduk, Ea, Ishtar, hear your great priest, Nebuchadnezzar. Give me sleep. Take away these dreams. What is the purpose of this torture?"

The only sound was the beating of his fists on the golden throne.

He pulled his sword from its scabbard, felt the keen edge of the blade, and held it to his wrist. With a moan, he recoiled from the thought and hit the brass cymbal once . . . twice . . . and with vicious blows, over and over again.

Servants, guards, everyone within range, rushed into the throne room, ignoring all court protocol. Ashpenaz followed, red-faced and puffing. They all stopped, not knowing what to say to their king, who stood before them wild-eyed and continuing to brandish his sword against the cymbal. The noise was shattering.

Amytis was the first to dare approach him. She spoke quietly, fearing this mood which she had seen building for weeks. "My king, what do you want?"

He stared at her. In the past he had wanted her more than riches or conquered lands. Now he just wanted peace within himself.

"I want all the magicians, the soothsayers . . . the sorcerers and astrologers. Bring me the wisemen of the kingdom!" he shouted.

He collapsed on his throne. Amytis knelt in front of him and laid her hand on his. These past few weeks her feelings for him had begun to change. For the first time, she felt that he needed her, and she longed to ease his terrible pain.

"Ashpenaz is already calling all the wisemen in, my lord."

Nebuchadnezzar murmured so that only she could hear, "Amytis, stay with me. Don't leave me alone."

Magicians, soothsayers, sorcerers, astrologers—all the wisemen in the city—hurried to the throne room. The hall was filled with the smell of incense. A din of chanting began as they assembled before the king, fingering their amulets and muttering their prayers.

Nebuchadnezzar pulled himself up, with Amytis standing close beside him. He looked at the gathering of his wisemen and said in an expressionless voice:

"I have had a terrible nightmare. In fact, night after night I have this same dream. I can't remember what it was. Tell me, for I fear some tragedy awaits me."

The wisemen looked at each other, wondering who would speak first. Finally a white-haired, bearded elder in the front spoke up. "King, may you live forever, tell us the dream, and then we can tell you what it means."

"You idiots! I tell you, the dream is gone—I can't remember it. If you won't tell me what it was and what it means, I'll have you torn limb from limb . . . and your houses made into heaps of rubble!"

The wisemen shifted from one foot to another. They knew this was no idle threat.

"On the other hand," Nebuchadnezzar continued, "if you tell me what the dream was and what it means, I will give you many wonderful gifts and honors. Now . . . begin."

He sat down on his throne, leaning forward with his elbows on his knees and his chin cupped in his hands, waiting.

The old soothsayer repeated. "O King, how can we tell you what the dream means unless you tell us what it was?"

"You are fools! I see your trick! You are trying to stall for time!" Nebuchadnezzar's voice became shrill. "You want to wait until the calamity that the dream foretells befalls me. If you don't tell me the dream, you certainly can't expect me to believe your interpretation!"

"But, King, there isn't a man alive who can tell others what they have dreamed. And there isn't a king in all the world who would ask such a thing! No one except the gods can tell you your dream, and they are not here to help."

"Out . . . out . . . leave me, you liars and charlatans! Arioch . . . where is Arioch?" he roared.

From the back of the room, where he had been watching this scene, Arioch walked with long strides. He feared that the king had lost his mind. But even in the midst of this insane scene, it did not escape his eyes that Amytis was standing close to her husband.

"Here I am, your Majesty. At your service," Arioch said.

"Kill them all. Execute all the wisemen of Babylon; have their homes and all of their possessions burned."

"But, King . . ."

"At once . . . at once, do you hear!" Nebuchadnezzar turned and stalked out of the throne room, followed by the queen.

The wisemen held up their long robes and ran, only to be barred at the great bronze door by Arioch's guards—trapped in the room of golden splendor.

Arioch knew he must delay for a time, if for no other reason than to determine the method of execution. He had heard the king's angry words with a heavy heart. It was his duty as the head of the guards to carry out commands. But how could he carry out this one? There were so many wisemen—even Daniel and his Hebrew friends were listed on the staff of advisors. How could he kill them all? Surely the king had gone stark, raving mad!

When Daniel heard of the order, he sat down on the single reed chair in his room and asked, "But why is the king so angry?"

Arioch told him about the dream, and of the king's impossible request.

"I shall see the king."

"He is in no mood to see anyone. You'll be wasting your breath."

"Take me to him."

When the king heard that Daniel was waiting to see him, he had him shown in immediately. The Hebrew was young, but he had more brains than most of the bearded ones who had no sense. They were frauds.

Daniel was taken to the private quarters of the king. He found Nebuchadnezzar reclining on a couch, his eyes hollow with sleeplessness. The queen sat by his side, stroking his head with a perfumed cloth.

"What do you have to say?" the king asked wearily.

Daniel looked at the king of the mighty empire and felt compassion for him. He thought about the mighty Solomon with all his wisdom, his building projects, his maidens and treasures . . . who yet, at the height of his greatness, had written, "Behold, all was vanity and a striving after wind, and there was nothing to be gained under the sun." Daniel stood with his feet apart and his hands behind him—a scholar, a strong athlete, and at that moment under the death penalty.

"Your Majesty, I am told that you have been having nightmares, and that your court wisemen cannot tell you your dream or its meaning."

"Fools, every one of them . . . fools."

"I have come to ask a stay of execution for them . . . and for myself and Shadrach, Meshach, and Abednego."

"Why should I grant this request?" Nebuchadnezzar examined Daniel carefully. The boldness of this captive was amazing . . . and even refreshing, after all of the sniveling cowards who vied for his favors.

"Give me a little time," Daniel replied. "And I will tell you the dream and what it means."

"You shall have the time. Now leave, but be quick about returning. I must be able to sleep or I shall go mad!"

That night Daniel and his close friends fell on their knees and asked the Lord to show them his mercy by telling them the secret of the dream. They prayed until sleep overcame their bodies, and they fell upon their pallets in exhaustion.

Before the dawn came, Daniel stirred on his pillow without opening his eyes. A vision appeared to him and the Voice was heard, audible only to his ears: "Go to the king, whom I have chosen as my light to the gentiles, and tell him his dream and the interpretation."

Daniel leaped out of bed and called his companions. As they stumbled into his room he said in a rush, "Blessed be the name of God forever and ever, for He alone has all wisdom and all power. World events are under His control. He removes kings and sets others on their thrones. He gives wise men their wisdom and scholars their intelligence."

The words came out in a torrent. Daniel was not conscious of his eloquence. His friends stood, their eyes glistening with tears, realizing that they were hearing wisdom from Jehovah through the voice of His servant. "He reveals profound mysteries beyond man's understanding," Daniel continued. "He knows all hidden things, for He is light, and darkness is no obstacle to Him. I thank and praise you, O God of my fathers, for you have given me wisdom and glowing health, and now, even this vision of the king's dream, and the understanding of what it means."

"Daniel, Daniel . . . you must hurry to Arioch. The scaffolds are being made ready for mass executions," said Shadrach.

Daniel kissed them on the cheeks in the Babylonian fashion and hurried to find Arioch. Although the hour was early, he found the captain pacing his room, delaying the king's command as long as possible.

"Take me to the king, Arioch; I will tell him what he wants to know."

Within minutes, the captain of the king's guard was boldly knocking on the bedroom door of Nebuchadnezzar . . . a breach of protocol which under ordinary circumstances he would not have dared.

"It is I, your Majesty . . . Arioch. I've found one of the Hebrew captives who will tell you your dream!"

The door swung open and Nebuchadnezzar himself ushered them in. Amytis was sitting beside the bed in her nightclothes, a basin of scented water on the stand. She had been wringing out a cloth to apply to the king's feverish head. He wanted no one else to wait upon him.

"Daniel, is this true? Can you tell me what my dream was and what it means?"

"Yes, your Majesty, I can." Daniel's brown eyes were steady and serious.

Arioch drew back against the wall, allowing Daniel to stand alone before the monarch. In all of his years of service, he had never heard anyone speak to Nebuchadnezzar with such authority.

Daniel stood tall and straight, respecting, but not bowing to the king of Babylon. In his mind echoed the words of Jeremiah: "I believe, Daniel, that you are going to be used mightily by the Lord."

"Your Majesty, no wise man, astrologer, magician, or wizard can tell the king of your dream and its meaning. But there is a God in heaven who reveals secrets, and He has told you in your dream what will happen in the future."

Nebuchadnezzar sat in rapt attention.

"You dreamed of coming events. He who reveals secrets was speaking to you. But remember, it's not because I am wiser than any living person that I know this secret of your dream, for God showed it to me for your benefit.

"O king, you saw a huge and powerful statue of a man, shining brilliantly, frightening and terrible. The head of the statue was made of purest gold, its chest and arms were of silver, its belly and thighs of brass, its legs of iron, its feet part iron and part clay.

"But as you watched, a Rock was cut from the mountainside by supernatural means. It came hurtling toward the statue and crushed the feet of iron and clay, smashing them to bits. Then the whole statue collapsed into a heap of iron, clay, brass, silver, and gold; its pieces were crushed as small as chaff, and the wind blew them all away. But the Rock that knocked the statue down became a great mountain that covered the whole earth."

"Yes, yes, that was the dream. Now I remember." Nebuchadnezzar spoke in a monotone, his attitude almost trancelike. Amytis moved to his side and put her arms around his shoulders like a mother protecting a child. Arioch stood transfixed.

"Now for the meaning of the dream. Your Majesty, you are a king over many kings, for the God of heaven has given you your kingdom, power, strength, and glory. You rule the farthest provinces, and even animals and birds are under your control, as God decreed. You are that head of gold."

The king nodded his head, assenting to this statement. Surely that was true.

"But after your kingdom has come to an end, another world power will arise to take your place. This empire will be inferior to yours. And after that kingdom has fallen, yet a third great power—represented by the bronze belly of the statue—will rise to rule the world. Following it, the fourth kingdom will be strong as iron—smashing, bruising, and conquering. The feet and toes you saw—part iron and part clay—show that later on, this kingdom will be divided. Some parts of it will be as strong as iron, and some as weak as clay. This mixture of iron with clay also shows that these kingdoms will try to strengthen themselves by forming alliances with each other through intermarriage of their rulers; but this will not succeed, for iron and clay don't mix."

"The image you saw, Daniel—gold, silver, brass, iron, and part iron and clay—it becomes weaker and weaker from top to bottom. What will happen when the Rock smashes it to bits?" Nebuchadnezzar leaned forward, his brow furrowed and his eyes piercing Daniel.

"During the reigns of the last kings, the God of heaven will set up a kingdom that will never be destroyed; no one will ever conquer it. It will shatter all other kingdoms into nothingness. . . . That is the meaning of the Rock cut from the mountain without human hands—the Rock that crushed to powder all the iron and brass, the clay, the silver, and the gold."

Daniel stopped and drew a long breath. "Thus the great God has shown what will happen in the future, and this interpretation of your dream is as sure and certain as my description of it."

There was complete silence in the room. Amytis felt the tight muscles on the back of the king's neck relax. She did not understand all that the Hebrew said, but she hoped that it would bring her husband peace. He had needed her, and she now knew she could love him.

Before his astounded wife and captain of the guards, the mighty king of Babylon fell on the ground before Daniel in an act of worship. He said, "I shall command my people to offer sacrifices and burn sweet incense before you."

Daniel was embarrassed that Nebuchadnezzar was on his knees. He shook his head in dismay. "Please, your Majesty, don't bow to me. It is Jehovah, the God of Abraham, Isaac, and Jacob who is the Revealer of mysteries."

"Truly, O Daniel," the king said, "your God is the God of gods, Ruler of kings, because He has told you this secret."

The king ordered Arioch to see that Daniel was given rooms in the palace, and he appointed him chief magistrate of the court, ruler over the whole province of Babylon, and chief of all the wisemen.

At Daniel's request, the king granted that Shadrach, Meshach, and Abednego would be Daniel's assistants.

The awesomeness of the vision he had been given was slow to develop in Daniel's consciousness. He wanted to share it with someone . . . but who would understand? He would write it down before he forgot one detail. How grateful he was for his studies in Aramaic. He must record that God had revealed to him the four different empires that would run their course before the kingdom of God was established and the promised Messiah would come to bring judgment upon all peoples and nations.

The Lord was mighty! He had not forsaken them, even in Babylon. And He had used a pagan king to reveal the future of all mankind.

But if Jehovah had given such far-reaching prophecies, Daniel wondered, why had He not revealed to him the simplest of truths?

Dare he make such an insignificant request? King David had pleaded with the Lord many times. He had recorded in his psalms these words: "For wherever I am, though far away at the ends of the earth, I will cry to you for help." Could he, Daniel, do any less?

"Lord, I don't know why you are using me to interpret these dreams of things to come. But may I ask a simple thing? It is not for a vision or anything profound. Forgive me for asking for such a small favor. But, please, Lord, what is my future . . . with Deborah?"

6

TRIAL BY FAITH

AMYTIS LAY on her couch, her once-slender figure swollen beneath the folds of a soft robe. Her rings cut the flesh; she dipped her hand in the gold-inlaid basin beside her and pulled on the tight bands, trying to pry them from her fingers. In the corner of the vast bedchamber, a single harpist was playing softly. Deborah sat beside her mistress, trying to cool her with a large fan made of peacock plumes, but the humid heat languished throughout the palace, adding to the restless waiting.

Deborah's arm was getting tired; she must have been fanning for hours. Her slight body was bone weary; the years of easy palace living had drained her of stamina, and for weeks she had found but little time to sleep. Why did this baby take so long to come? The Lord certainly chose a tedious method for bringing children into the world. All of life seemed to be waiting . . . waiting. The past few months had seemed so long, particularly since the king had charged her with the responsibility of keeping Amytis occupied during his absence.

"I know I can trust you, Deborah," he had said when he left. He needed assurance that his favorite wife would be carefully watched. "And when I return you shall have a special reward."

(Yes, Nebuchadnezzar had thought, it was time he allowed his chief wiseman finally to have this choice woman.)

Deborah took her duties seriously, but right now she was running out of diversionary ideas. "I've heard that a cargo just arrived from India," she chattered, knowing that the queen was always interested in new fabrics or perfumes. "Would you like to see what the merchants have brought? I'll ask Ashpenaz to bring some in," she continued without waiting for an answer. These days Amytis left most of her decisions to her handmaiden.

The queen licked her dry lips and choked out her words. "Deborah . . . my time has almost come . . . will it hurt?" Amytis felt the child within her kick—hard. It would not be long now.

Deborah adjusted her tunic and looked at her sandals. What did she know of such things? She was a virgin, and the mysteries of birth were unknown to her. Surely the queen knew more than she did.

Amytis groaned, rolling on her side and pressing her hand to her back.

"I'll call the midwife," Deborah said.

"No, no, not yet. I just want you to stay here. Talk to me." Amytis settled back on her cushion; the pain had subsided.

For more than eight years Deborah had served the queen of Babylonia, fixing her hair, attending to her clothes, traveling with her to the summer palace. She had become more than a maidservant; she was a confidante, a close friend. Deborah had adapted to the Chaldean lifestyle and enjoyed the luxury of her position. Judah seemed so far away. And Daniel . . . he had been given so many important jobs in the kingdom that they seldom saw each other. He had entreated the king many times to allow them to marry, but Nebuchadnezzar would say, "Wait a little while longer, Daniel. Amytis needs your little Judean beauty, and I need you. Be patient for a time. After my next campaign, you may approach me again on this subject."

Daniel had waited and toiled, administering the many details of his important position. The king had appointed him governor over the entire province of Babylon. His architectural background had given him the needed skills for supervising the repair of the old royal canal, built two thousand years earlier by Hammurabi. Daniel's loyal assistants, Shadrach, Meshach, and Abednego, had also assumed roles of influence in the kingdom. They knew now that the training they had received in the Hall of Knowledge was to enable them to help captives from Judah meld into this land and its manners. However, they had never ceased to hope that someday they would return to build a stronger Holy City of Jerusalem.

Nebuchadnezzar had left the land of the Chaldeans and led his finest troops in a march back to Judah. Arioch, now a seasoned veteran of this route over which he had brought his Hebrew youths, had accompanied the king as his second in command. They had been gone less than two months when merchant caravans had brought back the message that King Jehoiakim was dead and his son had succeeded him to the throne.

Who would return from Jerusalem this time? There were long, painful days of waiting in Babylon.

Amytis moved from one side to another, trying to find some comfortable position. Her pains were becoming harder and more frequent now. "Deborah, talk to me. When do they say the king will return?"

Deborah tossed her black hair back from her face; damp tendrils clung to her cheeks. It was so hot. But then, how much more difficult it must be for the queen. "He will be back soon, my Queen. And you will have a beautiful child for him to see."

"A son," she sighed. "He wants a son."

Amytis had begun to realize in the past nine months that love was more than wanting something from someone else . . . love was wanting to give to someone. She wanted to give Nebuchadnezzar a son. She wanted to give him her love.

"Do you know what it is to love a man?" Amytis asked Deborah. She saw her sudden flush. "Oh, I don't mean that way. I mean to love a man so much you would do anything to make him happy?"

"I think so." The words came before the thoughts. Deborah remembered what her mother had told her one time: "You are like a bee, never settling for long over the sweetness of one flower, but always darting on to see if another holds more nectar."

Of course she loved Daniel. She had loved him for nine years. But she was getting old. Life was passing her by. Why was the Lord God keeping them apart?

Amytis let out a loud scream and Deborah dropped the fan. "Don't move; I'll call the midwives." *How foolish,* she thought. Amytis was in no position to move.

"Deborah . . . wait . . . come close." Amytis, her heart-shaped face distorted in pain, signaled for Deborah to bend down.

She whispered, "If I should die, I want you to know that the baby is . . ." and she stopped, her delicate face contorted in pain. A sound came out of her mouth that pierced the room with its agonizing intensity.

For a moment, Deborah was immobile. She wanted to run, to escape this act of vulgarity that turned beauty into misshapen ugliness. She had been shielded from the process of childbirth as a girl in Judah; when her mother had borne her younger brother she had been sent away. She had no idea what to do at such a time.

Deborah reached for the hand of her mistress and was held tight in the grip of her fist. "Get the midwife," she shouted to the walls. How she wanted to get out of there!

In moments, the faithful Ashpenaz puffed into the room, his jowls flushed and perspiring, pushing two women before him. They wore tunics with short sleeves and no decorations; their arms were draped with white cloths. Deborah thought they looked like servants returning from the river with newly laundered clothes.

The midwives pushed between Deborah and the bed upon which the queen writhed, crying for someone to "do something!"

Ashpenaz took Deborah by the arm and led her to the door. "Come, little one . . . come, come, now . . . we'll wait outside. What a pity the king is in Judah." The chief eunuch shook his head. His calling was to serve the king in every way, but he did not like the role of waiting for his child to be born. What if Amytis should die? Nebuchadnezzar might vent his wrath on him!

Deborah, grateful for the reprieve, went to the gardens and sank down beneath a willow tree. Its shade was a caress upon her flushed skin. She pressed her face against the cool grass, thankful that she was not called upon to assist Amytis at this time. She remembered how her mother had said, "The Lord cursed woman when she disobeyed and told her that in her pain she would bring forth children. It is our heritage."

"I hate it," Deborah said, digging her fingernails into the soft earth. "I hate the curse. Why didn't the Lord give it to men?"

It was there that Daniel found her asleep, curled beneath the tree, its parasol branches shielding her from the heat of the day. He sat down next to her, admiring her glossy black hair against the paleness of her skin. She looked no older than she had when they had collided in the streets of Jerusalem. How long ago that seemed! Three years at the university, and then five years of learning the intricacies of language, court procedures, and province administration had prepared him for these times when Nebuchadnezzar was absent. But his duties had kept him away so much of the time from Deborah.

It pained him that she was so seldom allowed to join the nightly prayer sessions held by their little core of believers. Those meetings were their strength in this land of temptation.

Deborah moaned and turned in her sleep. *How beautiful she is,* Daniel thought. It had been so long since he had held her in his arms. He remembered a phrase from the Song of Songs: "This is my beloved and this my friend, O daughter of Jerusalem."*

Why was the Lord keeping them apart?

There were so many "whys" in his life. Since the interpretation of Nebuchadnezzar's dream, there had been times when he seemed to be transported out of the reality of this world and into another dimension in time. Alone, during his prayer time, he would hear the Voice saying, "Listen, my son, you are to be my revealer of things present and things to come."

Sometimes there was nothing more, and he would be left empty, wondering. At other times he had visions which were vividly real, but which he could not understand.

Daniel leaned against the trunk of the willow, welcoming this rare moment of relaxation. He had grown into an imposing man, his strength evident in his muscular body and lean frame. He wore the robes of royalty with dignity, not flaunting his status, but accepting it as a gift. When he walked the streets of Babylon, he was admired for the pleasant greetings he gave to noble and commoner alike. "Shalom," he would say in Hebrew, and then "peace be to you" in Aramaic. Women of the court whispered about him, wondering why he had no concubines. The soothsayers despised him as a foreigner, but reluctantly admired him because of his wisdom.

He was a strange alien—a captive from a foreign land who was responsible for affairs of state, a man who seemed impervious to graft in the city of gold. The responsibilities given him were awesome for a man of only twenty-four years. While Nebuchadnezzar and Arioch were in Judah, Daniel was in charge of the affairs of state,

* Song of Solomon 5:16, NASB.

trusted by the king to rule the vast community in his absence. He was also chief magistrate of the court, which meant that major decisions of the palace household were under his supervision.

Daniel settled down, resting against the tree trunk to wait for Deborah to awaken. *How ironic,* he thought; *in this rare moment when we could be alone, she sleeps.*

"Lord, guard the little one," he prayed. "Make your Presence real to her. It is so hard for her to hear your voice in the halls of the idolaters."

Daniel smiled to himself, remembering the proverb Abiel had taught him as a small boy: "In all your ways acknowledge Him, and He shall direct your paths."* And what strange paths He has designed for us, Daniel mused—from the streets of Jerusalem to the palaces of Babylon.

"But why, Lord, do you keep us together in this land, but keep us apart as man and woman?"

Deborah stirred and opened her eyes. The sun had melted behind the high stone walls, casting its fading glow upon the garden. Daniel lifted her gently to her feet and leaned down to brush some blades of grass from her cheek. Standing full height, she reached the middle of his chest.

"Daniel, have you been here long?" she said sleepily.

"Long enough to know that you are the most beautiful thing in Babylon." He leaned down and brushed his lips across her forehead.

Deborah put her hands upon his arms, feeling again the strength in his taut body and experiencing the security and safety she had always felt with him. He was unchanging, like the protection of her father; like the home she had left so long ago. Whenever circumstances began to shake her world, Daniel was always there . . . steady, comforting.

She stood on tiptoe and raised her face to his.

"Stop! . . . oh dear, I don't mean stop that . . . oh my, what do I mean?" Ashpenaz burst in like a well-fed pigeon, fluttering nervously and wiping his sweaty palms on the front of his tunic.

"The queen, is she . . . ?"

Ashpenaz stood still, regaining his composure and attempting a formal announcement: "Her Majesty, Queen Amytis, has given birth to a child, praise Marduk, and is resting quietly. She has requested

---

* Proverbs 3:6, NASB.

your presence in the royal chamber." He glanced at Daniel. "I mean, Deborah's presence. Her Majesty does not want men present at this time." (Ashpenaz had long before ceased to think of himself as a man.)

"And the baby?" Daniel asked.

"Oh yes, yes . . . the baby is a girl, praise Ishtar." Ashpenaz paused, trying to think of a redeeming aspect to this unfortunate happening. "She will become the mother of a future king of Babylon."

He waddled across the pebbled path and into the side door of the palace, muttering, "Yes, of course, that is what I shall tell King Nebuchadnezzar. . . . Marduk has destined this child to be the mother of a great king to carry on the glory of Babylon. He will be pleased." Ashpenaz raised his eyes skyward. "O gods of Babylon, may the king be pleased with a daughter."

Deborah gave Daniel a quick kiss, which landed awkwardly on his chin, and rushed out of the garden and into the bedchamber. The room had cooled in the early evening, and Deborah realized how long she had slept. Had Daniel been sitting beside her all that time? She rushed to the side of the queen, noticing that the slave girls were busy whisking away bloody rags and wiping the marble floor around the bed. She fought a churning in her stomach.

But then she saw the baby. Nestled against the breast of Amytis, one little hand resting on her bare skin, was a tiny, wrinkled creature. Deborah leaned over to look more closely, and Amytis slowly opened her eyes—an act which seemed to take great physical effort. "Isn't she beautiful?" she said weakly, lifting her hand to stroke the smooth cheek. "I prayed for the good genies to surround her. See, Deborah, the demons of pain have left the room."

As Amytis fell asleep in exhaustion, Deborah cautiously picked up the baby and was overcome by an unknown emotion. Perhaps to have a child was not so frightful after all. She remembered another thing her mother had said: "Children are a gift of the Lord."

Deborah looked at the red-faced little bundle in her arms and whispered, "May the Lord bless you, little princess." And for the first time she longed to have a child of her own.

As foretold by the Hebrew prophets, the Holy City of Jerusalem was moving inexorably toward its own destruction. For many years Jeremiah had been warning his people to change their evil ways, to repent and return to the God of their fathers. He was rewarded for his preaching by being imprisoned again and again, or by being put in stocks in a dungeon.

Only a few believed him, and even his staunch allies, such as Abiel and Barak, began to see him as an embarrassment. Finally, by royal command of King Jehoiakim, Jeremiah was forced to cease speaking in public. But, in open defiance of the king, he dictated his sermons and had them read aloud. Furious, the king of Judah confiscated the scroll of Jeremiah's sermons, cut it into small pieces, and flung the pieces on a charcoal fire. Jeremiah's arrest was ordered, and the prophet fled to safety beyond the king's jurisdiction.

But King Jehoiakim was writing his own doom. As a puppet of Babylon, he had sworn that he would not pay allegiance to the rival Egypt, yet he was conniving in secret with the Pharaoh. When Nebuchadnezzar heard of this treachery, he took action. He ordered his troops to lay siege to Jerusalem, surrounding the city with the mighty Babylonian army so that no supplies could reach the populace.

Jehoiakim, the foolish puppet king, met a mysterious death before the surrender of his capital. Some said that he was murdered and his body thrown into the streets of the city. The prophet he hated, Jeremiah, had predicted such an evil end for him.

Nebuchadnezzar himself organized the columns of prisoners, since the chief of his guards, Arioch, had been injured in a skirmish with a Judean soldier. A sword had pierced his thigh, and the resulting loss of blood had weakened him to the extent that he made the return to his homeland on a stretcher.

Nebuchadnezzar ordered his men to take all the treasures from the Temple and the royal palace. "See to it that nothing is destroyed . . . any man who hides or defaces any of the artifacts will be chained and whipped."

Even as the king of Babylon surveyed, from his gold-encrusted chariot, the dejected Judeans gathered in silent defeat, his mind wandered back to Babylon, to the son he would soon behold. This baby would be trained in all the arts and physical sports of challenge. He would be a visionary, like his father, building the glory of Babylon to greater heights. He would. . . .

Anticipating his triumphal return to Babylon, Nebuchadnezzar urged his guards to get the long march underway. He was ready to view his heir. And as for his beautiful Amytis, the mother of his son, he relished the thought of personally presenting her with jewels from the treasury of Solomon. His excitement mounting, Nebuchadnezzar signaled to his charioteer, and they clattered off across the plain, followed by the crowd of exiles.

And so the sad journey began, with the new king of Judah, Jehoiachin, his wives, the queen mother, seven thousand of the best troops, and one thousand craftsmen and smiths, along with the ablest men, women, and children of the kingdom, walking to Babylon. They were bound with cords and overcome with depression. What had happened to their Promised Land? How could they make a sin offering without the Temple?

Unrecognized at this grim time was a priest who walked among the deported people. Shuffling along with the thousands of exiles, carrying his entire possessions upon his back, was a man the Lord God had chosen for a special mission. His name was Ezekiel.

When the king returned from Judah and heard the news of the birth he roared, "A girl! How could it be? O Marduk, why did you let this happen? I prayed for a son. Where were the wisemen? Couldn't they do something?" He paced the floor in front of the queen's chambers, wanting to quiet his anger before seeing Amytis.

Ashpenaz listened to his master curse every known deity in a useless tirade before interrupting him. The servants and staff had learned long ago not to cross the king when he was in one of his moods. After venting his feelings, he was usually penitent, especially where the queen was concerned.

"O King, may you live forever," Ashpenaz began. "Marduk has destined this child to be the mother of a great king . . . to carry on the great work you have done in Babylon." The chief eunuch paused, praying that this idea would placate Nebuchadnezzar.

Nebuchadnezzar stopped his pacing; the thought had great appeal! His angular face, darkened by the insistent desert sun in spite of the protection of the royal canopy on his chariot, softened at the idea Ashpenaz presented. He pushed open the carved bronze door leading to the queen's chambers, determined to show Amytis he did not blame her for the sex of his child.

He removed his fighting sword from its scabbard and placed it on the floor before leaning over to kiss the queen. He looked at her for a moment before awakening her. It seemed to him that her face was softer, sweeter, than when he left. And suddenly he realized that it made no difference to him about the baby. Amytis was safe.

Deborah sat close by, holding the baby on her lap. She lowered her eyes while the king whispered to Amytis; somehow she felt she was intruding upon an act of intimacy. She waited for him to ask about the baby and wondered if he would want to hold her; somehow the thought of Nebuchadnezzar holding a little baby seemed funny. She looked down at the tiny one in her arms, running her fingers over the soft copper-colored hair, her thoughts troubled. The color was so unusual . . . But probably it would be said that the gods made the sun to shine upon her . . . in this country every happening had some sort of an omen attached to it.

When Amytis awakened, Nebuchadnezzar took her hand gently in his and kissed it. A few weeks before this warrior had led his mighty army against Jerusalem, ordering his troops to take the city without regard for the citizenry or respect for the women and children. But now he was the gentle husband, viewing a human life from a different perspective, because it was his child.

As Amytis opened her eyes and saw the king leaning over her, she felt the weariness and anxiety of the past few months leave. If he returned from his battles ahead of the troops, as she had been told, it must be true evidence of his love for her. But how would he react to the baby?

"Have you seen . . . our daughter?" she asked cautiously.

"She looks like she will be a fiery one. We shall call her Nitocris, 'mother of the great king.'"

Amytis relaxed. The king was not displeased.

"But I can only stay a moment for now; there are preparations that must be made. We are bringing ten thousand captives into Babylon, and many valuable treasures from Jerusalem. There is much work to be done." The king called to Ashpenaz and told him to summon Daniel immediately.

When Deborah heard this news she placed the baby in its silk-lined basket and approached the king boldly. "Please, your Majesty, will you tell me about the captives? I have not heard news of my family in over eight years."

"In due time, Deborah," he said, his usual impatience returning. "You are to see that my wife and daughter are well cared for. There will be time enough to learn of the fate of your countrymen. They will be in Babylon a long time. Your Jerusalem will never be the same. Judah is my puppet state and I shall determine its destiny."

Nebuchadnezzar, now once more the conqueror, tossed the loose fold of his tunic over one shoulder, thrust his sword back in its scabbard, and walked out of the room, leaving the two women agape at this astounding announcement. Amytis sat in shocked silence, but Deborah broke into sobs. "Lord God Jehovah," she cried in anguish, "have you forsaken your people?"

There was much work to be done in Babylon to prepare the city for the great influx of people. Shelter must be assigned, food supplied, work supervised in order to make the able-bodied Hebrew men productive as fast as possible. It was a gigantic undertaking, but Nebuchadnezzar was undaunted by the immensity of the task. He called Daniel to his quarters, knowing that this young man was one of the most capable in his entire kingdom. He had been well-trained, after all, at the king's own direction. No matter that Daniel still worshiped his one God. His God seemed to give him extraordinary vision, and that is what the King of Babylon needed!

"Sit down, Daniel, we have much to discuss." Nebuchadnezzar indicated a chair next to his and signaled for a servant to bring them some wine.

Daniel placed a hand over his goblet. He needed a keen mind and clear head at a time like this. For hours after hearing about the surrender of Jerusalem he had been on his knees in prayer for his people. It had been decreed that he was officially a citizen of Babylon, but he would always be a son of Judah. He had countless questions. However, knowing the protocol of the court, he waited for the king to speak.

"You have heard, of course, of the birth of the Princess Nitocris?"

"Yes, your Highness, and I am told she is very beautiful."

"Indeed. She shall be the mother of a great king someday."

Daniel had a few moments with Deborah in the courtyard when she described the baby, and he had a feeling that she was keeping something from him; he had known her too long not to be able to detect her unrest. But right now the moods of a woman, no matter how beloved, were not his chief concern. His heart was heavy over the plight of his people. And yet he felt the Lord had brought him to Babylon for this very purpose: to prepare for a time such as this.

"You are, I suspect, anxious to find out about the captives from Jerusalem." Nebuchadnezzar twirled his empty goblet and signaled the servant to fill it again.

"I have prayed for their safety, your Highness."

"Those who have surrendered willingly are being treated with fairness. They are at this moment on their way from Judah and should arrive in Babylon within a month. Meanwhile, there is much to do. These people must be assimilated into our culture as rapidly as possible." Nebuchadnezzar stroked his long beard and narrowed his eyes. It would be stimulating for Babylon to have some new kinds of arts and music. Granted, the Judeans were not as advanced as the Chaldeans, he thought, but their ways did have a quaint appeal. He especially liked the religious artifacts from their Temple worship.

"And so, Daniel, I want you to see that the Hebrew exiles are housed in a special section of the city, that they are allowed to pursue opportunities in business, and . . ." Nebuchadnezzar paused to allow the next concession to have its full impact on Daniel, ". . . they may practice your religion of one God and assemble freely." He leaned back in his high-back chair, satisfied with his own beneficence. The servant filled his glass once more.

"Furthermore, my friend, you will see that the educated among your former countrymen are given every opportunity to learn in our cultural centers and to tour our palaces and temples. It is my wish that they gain a thorough understanding of Chaldean culture."

Nebuchadnezzar examined Daniel to see how the Hebrew was reacting to his words. Why did he admire this young man so much, and yet feel so disquieted when he was around him? Daniel seemed to possess a knowledge so deep that even the wisest men in his kingdom were puzzled by him.

"Your wishes will be carried out, King." Daniel replied, anxious to get to the subject closest to his heart. "May I ask you about the exiles, your Majesty?"

"Ask."

"Is Arioch in charge of the caravan?" Daniel knew that the fate of his countrymen would depend upon the attitude of those who guarded them. He would never forget their exile journey.

"Arioch suffered a severe gash in his leg as a result of a skirmish with a Hebrew guard. He is returning on a litter, but he is not so weak that he cannot supervise the guards. The Hebrews will receive good treatment as long as they submit." The king emptied his wine goblet with one draught and, steadying himself on the arm of his chair, stood up, signaling the end of the conversation.

"I have much work to do myself, Daniel. We are preparing a great celebration on the Plain of Dura. I have ordered our craftsman to make a magnificent golden statue for the festival. . . . Yes, there is much to be done. You are dismissed, Daniel." Weaving slightly, the king picked up his sword and hit the brass cymbal with its broadside, bringing Ashpenaz scurrying to his side.

"Order the scribes to prepare messages for all the princes, governors, captains, judges—the rulers of all the provinces of the empire. They are to assemble, along with all their subjects, on the Plain of Dura on the day I declare." He belched loudly. "And Ashpenaz, bring the finest musicians in the kingdom to the palace tomorrow. I shall personally choose the music."

A grin spread from one side of Ashpenaz's face to the other. "We're going to have a party, great King?"

"Not a party . . . a feshtival." The king paused, placed his hand on his servant's shoulder, and laughed at his own slurred speech. "No, Ashpenaz, my fat friend, it will be a festival of the new Babylon! This celebration will make history!"

In Daniel's room that night, Shadrach, Meshach, and Abednego gathered with him for their prayer time. Although their daily tasks took them into different areas of Babylonia, the men still met as often as they could for talk and worship. They would recall for each other the stories from the Torah and repeat the psalms and proverbs they had learned as children. The words they had hid in their hearts sustained them as they lived in this pagan land.

Daniel's friends received the news of the great exile with mixed emotions.

"Do you think our families are among the captives?" Shadrach asked the question running through the minds of them all.

Abednego, always the optimist, was sure they would have a great reunion, but Meshach, his usual comic nature subdued, warned that they should not get their hopes up. "The Lord God gives and takes away. Who are we to determine the survivors among our people?"

Daniel looked at his faithful friends. They had taken strength from God and each other during their years of captivity. They had become leaders in the city—derided by some for their devotion to the one God but respected for their integrity and principles. However, their influence had also brought them enemies.

"I am proud of you, my brothers," Daniel said, "I know the temptations of wealth and easy pleasure you have had, and yet you have been faithful."

"Not always with my eyes," admitted Abednego ruefully.

"You speak the truth for all of us," Daniel laughed. "Remember that Solomon said to treasure the commandments . . . to write them on the tablet of your heart . . ."

". . . And they will keep you from the foreigner who flatters with her words," continued Shadrach.

Throughout the years the men had tested themselves in this manner—beginning a proverb or a psalm and then waiting for someone else to finish it. By this game they had kept their minds keen and their memories alive.

Daniel walked over to Deborah, who had been sitting in the corner of the room, embroidering on a small garment for the princess. She had been given some time off by Amytis and had joined the men during their prayer time. However, she seemed to be absorbed in her own thoughts. Daniel, with all of his wisdom, could not understand her introspection. "Is there something you want us to pray for, little one?" he asked quietly.

She did not dare tell him. For days she had been occupied by thoughts about Arioch. She had heard he was injured, and she didn't know if he would return or not. And to her surprise she had realized that his safety was very important to her. She had asked the queen to make further inquiries to the king about his chief guard, but Amytis had become upset over this request. Deborah's heart was in a turmoil, and she had no one she could tell.

"Just pray for my family, Daniel. That's all." Deborah stood up, anxious to change the subject. "I must return to the queen. She wants me to choose the silk for her festival robes." Deborah picked up her embroidery and ran from the room.

An embarrassed silence permeated Daniel's quarters. In the years the young Hebrews had been together, one of the chief topics had been when the king would allow Deborah and Daniel to marry. Daniel had not forgotten that Nebuchadnezzar had said it would be after the next campaign. The time was at hand, but somehow the circumstances had changed. Slowly Shadrach, Meshach, and Abednego moved out of the room, leaving Daniel with a perplexed spirit.

"Lord, you have given me visions of the future. What is your plan for Deborah and me?"

From the depths of his memory came the deep voice of Jeremiah, speaking to him when he was just a boy of sixteen, "I believe, Daniel, that you are going to be used mightily by the Lord. Whether this includes a woman and family, I do not know."

The next few weeks Daniel was involved in the immense task of preparing for the arrival of ten thousand Hebrews. He must supervise the building of new houses in the city, designating an area to be known as the Judean quarter. Rations of food, schools for the children, and places to house the sick had to be planned. He scarcely saw Deborah, except for brief encounters in the halls of the palace compound.

The activity in Babylon was not confined to plans for the new arrivals. Most of the citizens in the streets were indifferent to this news. To them Nebuchadnezzar's conquests were not nearly so interesting as the great festival that was planned. Everyone had been ordered to take a holiday and go to the Plain of Dura, which was about six miles southeast of Babylon. The high officials throughout the entire country had been invited to come for the dedication of a magnificent new statue.

Workmen said that Nebuchadnezzar had ordered sixteen metric tons of gold for his idol. It was reported that the dimensions were six cubits wide and sixty cubits high, which caused the height to be disproportionate to the width.

The queen was displeased about the music the king had commanded. All of those instruments would surely make a discordant sound! The royal band was to be comprised of a cornet, flute, harp, sackbut, psaltry, dulcimer, and many other wind and string instruments. "Have them play what they wish . . . just make it loud," he said. This would be a celebration long remembered, Nebuchadnezzar vowed. Hadn't Daniel said when he interpreted his dream that he was the king over many kings, the head of gold?

"Amytis, I want you to wear your finest robes and bring the little princess in a royal gown. Our people must see you at my side."

"But, my King, the baby is too small. The noise and dirt will disturb her."

"The good genies will protect her. You both will come. I have decreed it."

As the time for the great festival approached, the excitement mounted; a renewed spirit surged throughout the provinces. Soon the elite from the kingdom of Judah would be arriving, and the men had heard that Hebrew women were very beautiful. Many of the nobles in the court, jealous of the favor which Daniel had found with the king, were eager for the captives to arrive, for they would occupy much of Daniel's time and perhaps keep him away from Nebuchadnezzar. If Daniel could not be corrupted, he could at least be distracted.

Before the day of the celebration, Daniel received official orders to visit a neighboring province to supervise some administrative details. It had been reported that the governor was ill and Daniel's advice was needed, although Daniel suspected that the sickness was feigned to prevent his attending the festival. He called his friends together and said, "I shall be praying for your wisdom and strength while I am gone; please do the same for me."

The friends embraced each other, only vaguely guessing that trials lay ahead. Until now their time in Babylon had been lonely, but not dangerous. However, in recent months, as their influence had become more predominant, the number of their enemies had grown. The persecution was subtle, for the king had ordered their protection; nevertheless, there had been several strange incidents. Meshach had discovered a deadly scorpion in his bed one night. Shadrach had barely avoided the spiked wheels of a runaway chariot by ducking into an open doorway. It was becoming evident that they had aroused some jealous passions.

On the day of the festival, the roads leading out of Babylon were filled with chariots festooned with flowers; people were dressed in their finest tunics, the women balancing baskets of fruit upon their heads and the men patting the full wineskins at their sides.

The king and queen rode in their ceremonial chariot, drawn by two ebony-colored horses whose harnesses shone and jingled with gold tassels and bells. A purple and magenta parasol shielded them from the sun. Nebuchadnezzar's dark hair was piled on top of his head and his beard was waved in precise rows; his barber had spent an hour that morning on those curls. Amytis had pulled her long hair back from her face to reveal the massive new sapphire earrings that the king had given her to mark the event. Deborah and Nitocris, with a special nurse for the baby, followed the royal couple in their own chariot.

They went down the wide Processional Way and through the Ishtar gate, passing through the double row of walls and across the great moat which protected the city. Nebuchadnezzar beamed at the security of this fortification; it was so designed that an attacker could be trapped between the two walls, if he were able to approach the city that closely. *Babylon is impregnable,* he thought with pride.

Among the citizens were Shadrach, Meshach, and Abednego. They had dressed in their finest tunics and walked to the Plain of Dura with the others. They tried to keep their eyes upon Deborah, as Daniel had asked them, but soon the royal entourage was out of their sight.

Construction workers had been toiling for months on the great statue. It was an immense image—so tall and thin that it looked like a strong wind across the desert could snap it in two. It stood at one end of the Plain, and at the other end was an ugly cylindrical iron furnace with a perpendicular shaft at the top and a gaping opening in the side, large enough for the workmen to keep it continually stoked to an intense heat. Questioning murmurs ran through the crowd—what was it for? Perhaps it had been used in constructing the king's statue. But why was it still burning?

Deborah was beginning to get a little queasy from the swaying of the chariot. Or was it from the mounting uneasiness about this festival, Daniel's absence, Arioch's injury, and the new crown princess? Why couldn't life be simple, as it had once been in Jerusalem? Daniel kept telling her the Lord would direct her, but He seemed to be pulling her in so many directions!

When the procession reached the destination, a throne was set up for Nebuchadnezzar and Amytis in front of the golden image, and a herald sounded a trumpet call. The crowd quieted down. Even the children stopped their chatter when the king made a proclamation; their mothers threatened them with a severe thrashing if they made a sound.

"O people of all nations and languages, this is the king's command: 'When the band strikes up, you are to fall flat on the ground to worship King Nebuchadnezzar's golden statue.' " The herald paused and pitched his voice higher. "Anyone who refuses to obey will immediately be thrown into the flaming furnace."

The guards shoveled more fuel onto the roaring fire to emphasize the decree.

Deborah lowered her eyes and took the royal princess from the nurse. She held the baby on her lap, looking again at the innocent little face. What had the queen tried to say about this child before the labor pains erased the thought? Deborah was not certain she wanted to know.

The band began to play—loudly, as Nebuchadnezzar had ordered—and the Plain of Dura was the scene of thousands of prostrate bodies, kneeling on the dry ground with heads lowered. But some of the court nobles raised their eyes cautiously and saw a shocking sight.

Three men remained standing!

The king clapped for the people to get up, and leaned back in his throne, pleased with this great act of homage to the gods of the kingdom.

Two of his court nobles were quick to run to the king. "O king, live forever. Your Majesty, you made a law that everyone must fall down and worship the golden statue when the band begins to play, and that anyone who refuses will be thrown into a flaming furnace."

"Of course, get on with it."

"There are some Jews out there—Shadrach, Meshach, and Abednego, whom you have put in charge of Babylonian affairs—who have defied you, refusing to serve your gods or to worship the golden statue you set up."

Nebuchadnezzar pushed the court nobles aside and stood up, his face contorted in anger. He would not be defied this way. "Bring the three men from Judah to me." How had they dared do such a thing, after all he had done for them? He had let them have their one God in private, but now they were inciting others to rebellion by this action. He began to shake with rage.

Amytis put her hand on his arm to quiet him, but he shook it off.

Shadrach, Meshach, and Abednego walked between the rows of

people and stood before the king. Their faces were impassive, neither fearful nor defiant.

"Is it true that you are refusing to serve my gods or to worship the golden statue I set up?" Without waiting for their answer, he continued. Out of respect for Daniel, he should give these men an opportunity to change their defiant attitude.

"I'll give you one more chance. When the music plays, if you will fall down and worship the statue, all will be well. But if you refuse, you will be thrown into a flaming furnace within the hour."

He allowed that threat to sink in. "And what god can deliver you out of my hands then?"

Meshach and Abednego looked at Shadrach and nodded. He said, "O Nebuchadnezzar, we are not worried about what will happen to us. If we are thrown into the flaming furnace, our God is able to deliver us."

Meshach added, "But if he doesn't, please understand, sir, that even then we will never under any circumstance serve your gods or worship the golden statue you have erected."

The Chaldeans who had reported the Judeans smiled. They knew these foreigners had no right to positions of influence in the kingdom. Now their true loyalties were evident, and the gods would demand justice for this flagrant act of defiance.

"Take them away!" roared Nebuchadnezzar. "Heat the furnace seven times hotter! Bind them and throw them in!"

Deborah cried out, "No!" and then pressed her hand over her mouth. Why wasn't Daniel here? He could do something!

Three of the strongest men of the king's guards pulled the arms of the Hebrews back and bound them with heavy ropes. Shadrach, Meshach, and Abednego remained quiet; they did not cry for mercy or pray for deliverance.

With eyes straight ahead, calmly and steadily, the three doomed men walked toward the furnace. The people stepped back, making a path for the prisoners. Terror played upon the faces of the Babylonians, for no sentence aroused more dread than death by fire. Children began to whimper and women moaned.

As they reached the huge iron structure, the guards hesitated. Then two stood on each side of the captives, and with a mighty heave shoved them into the furnace.

At that moment the crowd began to shriek in horror. For they had viewed the terrifying spectacle of searing flames that leaped from the furnace and engulfed the guards. The men were consumed like human torches, the odor of their burning flesh permeating the air.

Nebuchadnezzar stepped down from his throne and walked with long, quick strides through the crowd, ignoring the charred bodies of the guards. His mouth was open and his skin a vivid purplish-red as he stared unbelieving into the furnace opening. He shouted to anyone, "Didn't we throw three men into the furnace?"

In terror, the same nobles who had reported the three Hebrews stammered, "Yes, we did, your Majesty."

The king stood, transfixed by what he saw in front of him. His voice fell as he said faintly, "Look, I see four men, unbound, walking around in the fire. They aren't even hurt by the flames! And the fourth looks like . . ."—the king was afraid to say the word—". . . looks like a god!"

Nebuchadnezzar moved cautiously as close as he dared to the fire and called, "Shadrach . . . Meshach . . . Abednego . . . servants of the Most High God! Come out! Come out of there!"

Shadrach, Meshach, and Abednego, their arms no longer bound, stepped out of the furnace and over the dead soldiers, then walked steadily to the king. Their faces were calm, glowing with a light which was not a reflection from the heat.

The princes, governors, captains, and counselors crowded around them, wanting to touch them to make sure this had not been a hoax.

"Their hair isn't even singed!"

"Look at their coats—unscorched!"

"By the gods, they don't even smell of smoke! Unbelievable!"

Nebuchadnezzar himself led them back to his throne. Tears were flowing down Amytis's cheeks as the king signaled the three Hebrews to take their places beside him. He motioned for the Chaldeans to move away.

Deborah dared not look at them. They had obeyed the Lord God Jehovah and not bowed down to false idols. She had compromised, rationalized that being true to her God was not worth the price of being killed. Could God forgive her sinful heart?

Nebuchadnezzar raised his staff for silence. The murmuring, confused crowd was still. They had seen and experienced something that day that they would never forget. It was a story they would tell over and over again in amazement and awe: three Hebrews had been thrown into the fiery furnace and survived. And an unknown man . . . or god . . . or someone . . . had been in there with them. Some began to doubt that Marduk could have that power. Others said the whole event had been magic from the underworld.

But the king, for the second time in his life, acknowledged a power that was stronger than his. He proclaimed:

"Blessed be the God of Shadrach, Meshach, and Abednego, for He sent His angel to deliver His trusting servants when they defied my commandment, and were willing to die rather than serve or worship any god except their own."

He looked with piercing eyes at the Chaldean nobles and stared at them directly before continuing.

"Therefore, I make this decree, that any person of any nation, language, or religion who speaks a word against the God of Shadrach, Meshach, and Abednego shall be torn limb from limb and his house knocked into a heap of rubble. For no other god can do what this one does."

With that he dismissed the crowd and issued an order that the Hebrews were to be promoted to higher positions in the province of Babylon.

That night, weary from the high emotion of the day, the king reclined on his bed, the image of what he had seen in the furnace imprinted upon his mind. Amytis sat beside him quietly. She fingered some grapes upon the tray, but couldn't eat.

"Did I really see four men?" he asked.

"I'm not sure, my king."

"Yes, I know I did. But where did the fourth one go?"

Ashpenaz burst into the room, stammering with the news he had brought, "The captives are arriving, your Majesty. Thousands and thousands of them. And they are a sorry lot, yes indeed . . ."

Nebuchadnezzar sat up. "They will be housed and fed, Daniel has worked out all the arrangements. Now, where is Arioch? How is he?"

"He is being helped in by the servants. He seems weak, but he is able to report."

"Good, bring him in."

Ashpenaz shuffled out, shaking his head over the amazing events of the day. Life in Babylon was one crisis after another. From the time he had met Daniel, things had never been the same. He must ask the chief wiseman how he kept such a peaceful attitude amidst all of the confusion. But now there was this other situation . . . Arioch. In recent days Ashpenaz had held his ear to doors enough to know that the captain of the guard could have more trouble than just a sword wound in his thigh.

Arioch limped into the royal bedchamber, his clothes soiled and torn, his face lined with exhaustion. He bowed before the king, his eyes taking in the whole scene, including the queen's startled look at his condition.

"What is the state of the captives, Arioch?"

"The king of Judah is safe, and the treasures from the Temple are well protected. Only a few of the older ones died on the trip and one baby who was stillborn."

"You have done well, Arioch. You shall have a promotion and a long rest. And have you heard of the birth of the royal princess, Nitocris?"

"No, your Highness." Arioch looked at Amytis, who turned her face away. The king noticed this exchange with curiosity. Why was there such a strange attitude between his wife and the captain of his guards? He must take an offering to Ishtar; perhaps the goddess of love had the answer. But later. His mind right now was too full of the miracles of that day.

"Sit down, Arioch. I know you are weary, but you must hear this story. If I had not been there myself I would not believe it. But I swear by the God of Israel and Judah, this is what I saw."

Arioch sank into a high-backed, carved bronze chair and stretched his bound leg in front of him. He wanted to leave the room, to escape from the king and queen. If the king knew . . . It might have been better for him to have been slain in Jerusalem. King Nebuchadnezzar's vengeance was notorious, and loyalty or favoritism had no influence. Would the gods . . . or the one God . . . grant him reprieve from any results of the king's jealousy? He wished he could collapse in his own bed and allow his wounds, both of the heart and the body, to heal. What story could possibly be so important that the king would invite him, Arioch, the captain of the guards, to sit in his presence?

"Can you imagine ordering three men to be thrown into a fiery furnace and then seeing them walk around inside, conversing with a fourth person?" Nebuchadnezzar wiped his brow and took another long drink from his silver goblet.

"Listen, Arioch, I know there are none of our gods who could do what the God of Shadrach, Meshach, and Abednego did.

"This one Daniel calls the Lord God Jehovah . . . He is a God of great and wondrous miracles!"

7

THE WILL OF JEHOVAH

As Nebuchadnezzar retold the story of the fiery furnace, Arioch forgot his exhaustion and leaned forward to catch every word. What was the power of this Judean God that He could save men from the flames of a furnace? What hold did this God have over people that they would be willing to sacrifice their lives rather than worship other gods? How could one God be more powerful than all the gods of Babylon put together?

"It's a mystery," Arioch murmured, more as a question than a statement. "But what about the fourth man, your Majesty . . . did he disappear or did you, perhaps, just imagine that you saw him?" Arioch realized that was being audacious. One did not test the views of the king.

But Nebuchadnezzar did not seem to hear. The retelling of the story had upset him and his wine glass had been frequently replenished. "Amytis, speak . . . tell Arioch what you saw that day on the Plain of Dura."

The queen drew her eyes away from the bracelets she had been fingering on her arm. Trying to avoid looking directly at Arioch, she answered in a voice which was scarcely above a whisper. "Yes, I saw him, too . . . the fourth man in the furnace."

"You're sure?" Nebuchadnezzar asked, his speech beginning to slur. He was staring at Arioch; even through his wine-blurred vision he had noticed something which puzzled him. Why, in this land where most people had dark hair, was there one with a head that looked like polished copper? There was something to be considered here, but the meaning of it slipped away from him. . . .

"Arioch, you're dismissed . . . report tomorrow." The king stood up and immediately sat down again, his head swirling with confusion. He reached for his sword, but dropped it with a clatter on the tile floor. "Yes . . . tomorrow . . . we have much to discuss. . . ." His voice trailed off as his head lolled uncomfortably against the winged genie carved on the back of his chair. The headband, embroidered with a purple dragon-peacock, slipped down on his forehead, and his mouth dropped open in a wine-induced stupor.

Without another look at the queen, Arioch limped out of the royal chambers, almost bumped into the ever-watchful Ashpenaz in the outer corridor. "Is there anything I can do for you, noble Arioch?" the chief eunuch asked.

Arioch looked at Ashpenaz and for a brief moment envied his impotency. It would keep him out of a lot of trouble. "Yes, there is. I would like to have you arrange a meeting for me with Deborah."

"She has charge of the royal princess, Nitocris, these days," Ashpenaz said.

"Then I shall see the babe, also," Arioch replied with irritation. "Only you can arrange this, Ashpenaz. I trust few men, but I know you will use discretion."

Outside the royal compound, in a barren field behind the marketplace, Daniel walked among the newly arrived captives. His eyes were wet with tears as he beheld the people from his beloved Jerusalem. They were exhausted, discouraged, and bewildered by this strange country and its dazzling buildings, its maze of streets, its towering ziggurat. Many of them looked at the handsome noble with his fine embroidered tunic and sturdy sandals and were startled when he spoke to them in Hebrew. "Is Abiel, the royal supervisor for King Jehoiakim with you?" he would ask, searching anxiously through the crowd.

A captive spat on the ground in front of Daniel and muttered, "Jehoiakim is dead . . . and we might as well be. Why should you want to know where Abiel is?"

"Because I am Daniel, from the house of Abiel in Jerusalem."

A woman, her long hair matted from the neglect of weeks of weary journey, her robes soiled a mottled grey, held her thin arms out to Daniel and cried, "Daniel, is it really you? Don't you recognize me? I am Rachel, from the house of Barak. Deborah was my sister." She fell to the ground, clutching Daniel's robe with her rough hands and sobbing with pent-up emotion and fatigue.

Gently, Daniel lifted her to her feet, holding her like an injured child while she cried out her anguish. "Rachel, you're going to be all right now. Deborah lives! Hush, my sister, and tell me of your family. Are they here?"

Her skeletal body shook as she told of the arrival of the soldiers, how her father had resisted and had been speared through the chest. She related the horror of the scene that followed: gathering a few personal belongings in a cloth, being herded through the streets of Jerusalem, seeing families separated and shops looted. Even the Temple had been invaded and the holy vessels taken.

Daniel listened, waiting for the news he wanted. "And my father?" he asked, praying silently for her answer.

Choking back the tears, she pointed to an old man huddled against the base of the statue of a goddess, his knees pulled up to his chin like the crippled beggars that used to sit outside the gates of the palace in Jerusalem. Daniel started to turn away, to ask Rachel once more about his father. Then he saw that the old man had only one ear.

Daniel fell on his knees beside his father, taking the gnarled hand in his and crying over and over, "Father, you are alive. Praise the Lord God Jehovah. He has guarded you with His angels and brought you back to me. You are safe now . . . I shall take care of you."

Abiel shook his head in disbelief. Beside him stood a noble dressed in rich clothes—Babylonian clothes. The face was Daniel's, but the old man could not be sure if this was his son or a member of royalty who looked like him. He had thought that he would never see his son again. And yet here he was, praising God and speaking like a true believer. They had not captured his mind or heart! "Daniel, Daniel," he murmured weakly, "the Lord is good."

Father and son embraced, laughing and crying with the joy of being together again. Daniel found some blankets among Abiel's ragged belongings and spread them in the shelter of a merchant's stall. "Just for a time, my father," he said, easing him gently upon the makeshift pallet, "until I find you proper shelter." He gave some shekels to a boy and told him to hasten to the marketplace for some barley bread and dates.

"You will be safe, my father. Do not fear."

"I was close to death at the hands of my enemies, just as King David was," whispered Abiel, weakly, "but the Lord has given me back my life and my son again."

Daniel spent the next hours organizing food and temporary quarters for the captives, grateful for his years of administrative training that had prepared him for a challenge of this magnitude. Then, when Abiel had been given some food and was able to talk, Daniel asked for his father's account of what had happened after this conquest by Nebuchadnezzar's troops. Abiel told him of the siege of the city, how the troops had arrived and selected the nobles, tradesmen, and the most prosperous families to bring to the land of Shinar. "It was all preplanned," Abiel explained, shaking his head. "Just as the prophets foretold, our people are being punished for their sinful ways." Abiel rubbed the side of his head where he once had an ear. "But why, my son, are the good punished with the bad?"

"The Lord sees more than what is happening in the present, my father. He has his plan for all the ages, now and the future." Daniel paused, feeling again the reassurance of the Presence when he uttered statements he did not fully understand.

Abiel told Daniel of the young priest by the name of Ezekiel who had given them spiritual strength during the journey. Then he pulled a scroll from his sack and handed it to Daniel. Jeremiah had slipped into the refugee camp while the caravans were being loaded for the journey and whispered, "Take this with you and have it read at the proper time. The Lord gave me this message."

"Here, Daniel, this is the time. Tell us what it says," Abiel said.

Daniel eagerly read the scroll out loud:

"After Nebuchadnezzar, king of Babylon, had captured and enslaved the king of Judah, and exiled him to Babylon along with the princes of Judah and the skilled tradesmen—the carpenters and blacksmiths—the Lord gave me this vision. I saw two baskets of figs placed in front of the Temple in Jerusalem. In one basket there were fresh, just-ripened figs, but in the other the figs were spoiled and moldy—too rotten to eat. Then the Lord said to me, 'What do you see, Jeremiah?'

"I replied, 'Figs, some very good and some very bad.'

"Then the Lord said: 'The good figs represent the exiles sent to Babylon. I have done it for their good. I will see that they are well treated and I will bring them back here again. I will help them and not hurt them; I will plant them and not pull them up. I will give them hearts that respond to me. They shall be my people and I will be their God, for they shall return to me with great joy.' "

Abiel's wrinkled face relaxed in a smile. "Did you hear that, my son? We shall return . . . we shall return." He leaned back against the pack containing his worldly goods, the only things he had been able to gather from the house which had once contained the finest furnishings in Jerusalem, and closed his eyes, experiencing the greatest peace he had felt since Daniel had been taken from him eight years before. "Praise Jehovah," he murmured before falling into a deep sleep.

Daniel pulled off his white linen cloak and covered his father. He sat down on the pitiful pile of possessions from the house of Abiel and looked at the confusion of the scene around him. Judeans and Chaldeans alike stared at the incongruous figure of a Babylonian noble with the clothing of royalty, his hair to his shoulders but his face clean-shaven as a warrior's, sitting in the dirt and rubble with the captives. He gave them a strange strength by his presence. Perhaps there was still goodness and kindness left in this world of turmoil and slavery.

After a short time he stood up, assigned a guard to watch his father, and once more began giving orders to provide food and temporary shelter for the thousands. He moved among the people, speaking to many and encouraging all that God had not forsaken them. "He has brought you here for a purpose. Don't give up hope," he told them.

One woman reached out and kissed his hand, saying, "You are an angel sent to us." He smiled and looked into her weary eyes, "Not an angel, mother, but a son of Judah who will see that you are safe in Babylon."

"Don't touch him, old woman," a man shouted, his sun-blistered lips drawn in a snarl, "he is contaminated by Nebuchadnezzar's idols. I, for one, could never trust such a dog."

Daniel looked at the man with compassion. What bitterness could fill a man's soul when he had given up hope! Daniel placed his hand upon the man's shoulder and looked into his angry eyes.

"Do you remember, my friend, the words of Isaiah's song we sang in the streets of Jerusalem?

> "Do not fear, for I have redeemed you;
> I have called you by name; you are Mine!
> When you pass through the waters, I will be with you. . . .
> When you walk through fire, you will not be scorched,
> Nor will the flame burn you."*

"Do not forget the Law and prophets, my friend. Jehovah be with you."

The people began to pass the word through the ranks of the captives: "Jehovah be with you . . . fear not . . ." And some were encouraged.

They began to hear from the guards the miraculous story about three of their own countrymen—men who had been taken captive in that first deportation to this land—who had been thrown into a fiery furnace and yet lived. Was that what the prophet Isaiah had meant? And who was this Babylonian noble? Was he a spy from the palace of the king, or was he another prophet sent to them in a foreign land?

Daniel looked among his people and saw that the Lord God Jehovah had given him a mighty task. "Lord, how can I be a part of two worlds and remain your servant?" he prayed as he looked at the contrast of the thousands of bedraggled captives surrounded by the golden luxury of the great city.

Suddenly the noise of streets and the sights of people and pagan shrines faded and Daniel saw a light, diffusing the entire scene with its glow. And he heard Someone say, "You are My man for this time, Daniel. Listen to My voice."

Down a long, statue-lined corridor in the palace, near the chambers of the queen, Deborah had a special room that had been given to her when she first became Amytis's maidservant. Her living quarters were covered with elaborate wall-hangings that were embroidered with brilliant peacocks and bordered with lotus buds. The furnishings, however, were simple: a couch, two small chairs with ivory carved backs, and a round brass table. In contrast to every other room in the palace, there were no idols.

---

* Isaiah 43:1–2, NASB.

Deborah sat on one of her chairs, singing softly to the babe in her arms. It was a joy to her to care for Nitocris whenever she could. The little princess had her own nursemaid, as well as a wet nurse and a special astrologer, whom Deborah tried to avoid as much as possible. Life was confusing enough as it was without confronting that man of evil.

She jumped when she heard a knock. Placing the child in the middle of the couch and covering her with a soft linen square, she ran across the marble floor and opened the heavy door. Ashpenaz, looking more solemn than his usual self, said, "The noble Arioch wishes to see you, Deborah. Do you wish . . . oh my, I mean do you want . . . will you see him?"

She ran her hand nervously through her hair; there was no time to reply, because Arioch was standing behind the chief eunuch, leaning on his staff to ease his injured leg.

Deborah stood aside and Arioch limped in, waving Ashpenaz away. "You are startled to see me, Deborah?" he asked. "Perhaps you had heard that I was dead, as some had begun to spread that word?" Arioch walked painfully to one of the chairs and eased himself down. He saw a wiggling on the couch and heard the beginning cry of a baby.

"This is Nitocris, the princess born to the queen while you were in Judah." Deborah rushed her words together and picked up the baby, embarrassed, yet excited about seeing Arioch. Why did he arouse such strange emotions in her? She must not show her nervousness.

"May I see her?" Arioch asked, gesturing toward the child who was crying with more insistence.

Deborah walked over and lowered the baby so that Arioch could see her without standing. He stared blankly at the pink little creature—all babies looked alike to him—but his expression changed when Deborah pulled back the cloth and revealed the fine fuzz of copper hair. Quickly, she covered the baby's head and carried her to the door, beckoning for the nursemaid to take her.

Arioch watched the hurried little steps she took and the graceful way she held her head, tossing the lustrous hair from her face. She had not changed since the day Daniel had asked to protect her during that first journey with the young Judean captives. How different that had been from this time, returning midst the thousands, borne on a litter and then jostled on a camel, his leg throbbing with pain. But he had returned, just as he had sworn by the gods he would. He could not die in Jerusalem when he had important business in Babylon. He was young, and still the king's favorite, except for Daniel, the one person whom he admired and envied more than any other under the stars.

"Deborah, sit beside me," Arioch said.

She sat stiffly in the other chair, awkward in the presence of this man. She kept her eyes upon the floor and spoke in a barely audible voice. "Do you know anything about my family? Is there any way of finding out about my mother and father and sisters and brother from the house of Barak?" she asked, dreading to hear any answer.

Arioch reached over and lifted her chin so he could see her face. He was a man who wished to look others straight in the eyes; it was the only way to test their feelings. "You will soon know, Deborah, when the total census is taken. If your family was among the nobles and skilled craftsmen, they must be here. Daniel is directing the administration of these details and I'm sure he will tell you."

Arioch paused and breathed deeply. It was not the pain in his thigh which caused him to feel this pressure in his chest. "When I spoke of Daniel, I must know what has happened since I left. Tell me, Deborah." He held her eyes with his in that unflinching gaze.

"The king has said he would allow us to wed after his next campaign. And now that is over," Deborah answered, her own eyes steady.

Arioch pushed himself up with his staff and moved to the back of his chair, leaning on the carved ivory and watching the girl carefully. Her reactions were important. "I once thought Daniel was a man of great bravery, but I wonder about one who would not take the woman he loves for his own."

"You do not know Daniel," Deborah said indignantly, her black eyes snapping. "He is a man of honor and will not take a wife until the one in authority over him grants him that right. You dare not say he is not a man of honor! You, of all people, have no right to say that!"

Arioch began to laugh. "You defend him well, Deborah. I admire you for that."

"Daniel is like the brother I never had and the father I cannot see. Through all of these years, he has prayed for me and kept my hope alive. I believe Jehovah has chosen him for special purposes."

"You say, 'like a brother.' Is that the way you feel about him?" Arioch started toward her, but stopped, realizing he must be cautious about this subject. Mentally, he said, *Lord, what do I do now?* and then was startled to realize he was petitioning the one God, just as the Hebrews did.

Deborah did not answer; instead the tears began to well up and spill down her cheeks. It made her angry to show this weakness; after all she had been through, why should these questions bother her so? Perhaps because they were the very questions she had been asking herself for the past few years. And she had no one who would understand—not even Daniel.

"I believe I understand you, Deborah," Arioch said gently, "just as I am beginning to understand myself." He paused, not sure how to go on. "No one has been able to fill this emptiness I have. I have prayed to the goddess Ishtar, I have consulted the astrologers for what the stars have in mind for me, but I cannot find answers."

"You have asked the queen, perhaps?" Deborah questioned, the rapier edge of that insinuation sharper than the sword which had pierced his body. Did he think she was still the naïve little girl who stumbled across the desert? His very life was at stake if the king knew what she suspected and Ashpenaz had secretly insinuated.

"You know me, Deborah, and I cannot hide my true self from you. Your Jehovah has given you certain laws . . . certain rules to live by. I have seen the results in the lives of many. I had thought when we entered Babylon that you all would fall down before our gods, but that has not happened." Arioch's lips were beginning to get dry. There was so much to explain . . . and so much that he himself couldn't understand. "All I know is that our gods have no such rules. Do you understand what I mean?"

She did understand . . . more than he thought. A woman was born with intuition which a man did not possess. But she did not know how to answer without betraying one who loved her deeply and faithfully. How long could she suppress the way she felt about Arioch?

Arioch started toward the door and then paused. "I am going to talk to Daniel." A trace of sarcasm came into his voice. "He is the chief of the wisemen and should have some answers."

Putting her hand softly on his arm, Deborah said, "Arioch, there is a blessing that I was taught from the words of Moses. I want it for you:

> The Lord bless you, and keep you;
> The Lord make His face shine on you,
> And be gracious to you;
> The Lord lift up His countenance on you,
> And give you peace.*

Arioch's eyes narrowed in thought; he placed his hand briefly over hers and then left the room hastily. Daniel would give him the answers. If he could tell the king's dream and interpret its meaning, he could certainly read the heart of a Babylonian noble.

Arioch leaned heavily upon his staff as he dragged his injured leg through the palace grounds, determined to see Daniel before the night was over. The wound throbbed, but his will was stronger than the pain. He touched the bronze statuette of a standing demon who had goat's horns protruding from the head of a dead man, the body that of a dog and the feet of an eagle, with a pair of man's arms ending in lion's claws. Since his return from Babylon, Arioch's mind had been plagued by the thought that evil spirits, spirits of darkness, were following him. His body felt cold in spite of the warmth of the evening. Which god could take away this terrible oppression? He had offered sacrifices to Marduk, prostrating himself in the temple at the base of the great golden statue. Marduk was the most powerful of all the gods, the prince of the legions of stars. He was a warrior, armed with a spear, bow, and shield to fight off the evil spirits. But Marduk did not seem to help. The demons in his head gave him no rest.

What had Deborah said? ". . . And give you peace"?

"There is no peace for a soldier," Arioch muttered to himself. "We are made for war." He thought of his approaching encounter with Daniel and anger was added to the turmoil within him. This man had everything he, Arioch, had ever wanted: the favor of King Nebuchadnezzar, the respect of his people, and the woman he loved.

Daniel's quarters were in the far end of the palace grounds. There were two simple rooms, one containing an unadorned bed and bol-

* Numbers 6:24–26, NASB.

ster, a few palm-wood chairs, and a low chest; the other holding a table, some plain crockery bowls of varying size, and a brazier for cooking as well as heating. Daniel was kneeling beside the chest in the bedchamber, his head bowed low; Arioch could see him through the one small window beside the door.

"Daniel, open up . . . it's Arioch," he shouted while banging with his fist. "I need to talk to you, open up!"

Daniel opened the door and helped Arioch to a chair. This man, who had befriended him in many ways throughout the years, was more agitated than he had ever seen him. Many times Daniel had prayed for him, but his heart seemed planted in the pervasive Chaldean superstitions and idolatry. This was the first time he had ever admitted a need to talk.

"But why now, when I am so weary?" Daniel prayed silently, knowing in his heart that the timing was not his, but the Lord's.

Arioch stared at Daniel, sparring with his eyes in the manner they had used when they first met. "Did you expect me to return from Judah, O wise Daniel, or did you have a vision which told you exactly what would happen to me?"

Daniel waited for him to continue. With Arioch in such a mood, it would be wise to allow him to vent his feelings before attempting to respond.

"Interpret my mind, wisest of soothsayers; tell me what I am about to say."

"Arioch, my friend, I cannot read minds, and I am not a soothsayer. My Lord has given me the ability to interpret dreams, but it is His will, not mine."

Arioch banged his staff on the floor and raised his voice. "Your Lord, your Lord . . . if your Lord is so wise and powerful, why did He allow us to take His people captive? If He is stronger than our gods, why are you here, rather than in Judah near that crumbling Temple of yours?"

"My people were warned to turn from their sins and they did not obey. Jehovah has His plan, and I, for one, will wait until He reveals it." Daniel sat down beside Arioch, waiting for the captain to reveal the real purpose of the visit.

"Daniel, I have watched you stand for the things you believe in when there were times it could have meant your life. I am a soldier, and I admire that in you. But you are also a coward in other ways." Arioch waited for a reaction. Beads of perspiration stood out on his upper lip; his eyes left Daniel's and stared at the corner of the room. It would be easier to battle physically with this man, Arioch thought, than confront him mentally.

"And why am I a coward?" Daniel asked quietly.

"You leave the woman you have been betrothed to since you were a boy, and allow the king to decree whether you marry or not. You deny yourself what a man needs for fear of Nebuchadnezzar's displeasure. If you were the man of strength so many think you are, you would take your little Judean beauty whenever you wished!" Arioch stopped, his energy spent and his voice unsteady.

For a moment Daniel felt his jaw tighten in anger. How many times had he prayed that the Lord would make it clear to him what his destiny was with Deborah? Those men who took their concubines at will, who used women as vessels for their brief pleasure, could not comprehend his celibacy. "If I explained, I don't believe you would understand, my friend," Daniel said.

"Then try to understand this," Arioch said with a degree of defiance he found it difficult to muster. "I love your Deborah more than any woman I have ever known. I intend to have her, even if it means taking her as my wife."

Arioch stopped, lowered his eyes to the table, and waited for Daniel's reaction. Somehow his mind seemed clearer than it had been in months; the tension that had gripped the back of his neck was gone. Just being around this other man gave him a peace he could not understand. They should be enemies. But somehow, even after dealing such a blow to Daniel, he felt closer to him at that moment than he had to any other man or god in his lifetime.

Daniel stood and turned away from Arioch, his eyes clenched shut in pain. If Arioch had used a sword to pierce his chest, the wound could not have been deeper. And yet it was a pain he had anticipated, feeling it would come but hoping it would be delayed. He walked to the window and looked out at the courtyard. Only a few miles away, his people from Judah would be settling down on their pallets, waiting for work and living assignments to be given the next day. Tomorrow he was to see the king and confer about his duties for the next few months. The work seemed endless—but this was why he had been trained for these past years. For the first time since he had been brought to Babylon he felt a clear sense of his purpose here. Would he be able to devote himself to a wife and a family with all of these other responsibilities?

Arioch stared at Daniel's motionless back. How could he have said this man was a coward? Daniel was the only man he had ever met who could encounter Nebuchadnezzar without compromising his beliefs and his honor. He had the calm, the strength Arioch wanted for himself. The confession about Deborah had been a deliberate stab at Daniel's vulnerable spot, and yet he had taken even that blow without flinching.

Without warning, a desire gripped Arioch's body—stronger than any emotion he had ever experienced; stronger, even, than his love for Deborah. He could contain this deep longing no longer; the words were released like a sudden rain storm.

"Daniel, I want to know more about your Lord God Jehovah."

Daniel's eyes blurred as he turned to speak with the man he had known from the time of that first exile journey would be his friend. His own emotions were ambivalent; he should be angry, but there was no room for anger. He should be hurt, but this was not the time for self-contemplation. Daniel pulled a chair close to Arioch and began to tell him of the Law and the prophets. They talked far into the night, with Daniel relating to him some of the amazing stories from Israel's history. When he heard how the Lord had parted the sea and made a path for Moses to lead the people of Israel away from the Egyptian enemies, and about how the sea had been flooded again and all Pharaoh's army destroyed, Arioch listened in wonder.

"Our gods have never had that kind of power," he said.

Daniel, drawing on his store of scriptures memorized in childhood, related to Arioch part of the song Moses had sung after this great triumph:

> I will sing to the Lord, for he has triumphed gloriously;
> He has thrown both horse and rider into the sea.
> The Lord is my strength, my song, and my salvation."

But the part of the song that impressed Arioch most was:

> Who else is like the Lord among the gods?
> Who is glorious in holiness like Him?
> Who is so awesome in splendor,
> A wonder-working God?

Arioch pushed himself up from his chair, his eyes misted with emotion, and put his arm on Daniel's shoulder. "I have watched the way your wonder-working God has affected your life, Daniel. I would like to have that same strength and power, but if I believed in your Jehovah, it could cost me my life."

"Only you can make that decision, my friend."

"And Deborah?"

"Deborah has been my sister from Judah. We were betrothed as children and I have a special love for her. However . . ." He paused, his eyes narrowing in contemplation. ". . . my life and my times are in the hands of the Lord. Only He has the answer," Daniel replied.

In the following weeks, Daniel was intensely involved in the settlement of the captives. Thousands of the strongest young Judeans were conscripted to repair and strengthen the double wall of the city. Abiel, with his past experience in building, was encouraged that he would be able to use his knowledge in this alien country.

"This Nebuchadnezzar is a man of great vision," he remarked to Daniel. "Surely nothing like this city has ever been seen on earth. But how can we work on the pagan places, my son?"

"It is not where we work, but whom we worship, my father," Daniel answered, knowing that these were questions he had had to settle himself. "The Lord will honor our commitment to Him."

"The land is evil, but there are people within it who are good," Abiel commented. "I only wish to live as long as I can close to you, so I will obey their laws." Abiel had seen some results of breaking Babylonian rules. "Yesterday I passed a temple courtyard and heard a man moaning in pain. I walked in to see if I could help and saw him bathing a raw mark on his forehead with oil. He will have an ugly scar there all of his life. He told me that he had been convicted of forgery upon a clay tablet, and for punishment that tablet had been heated and used to brand his skin." Abiel winced as he remembered the sight.

Daniel put his arms around the thin, stooped shoulders of his father. "As long as I live, no one will harm you, my father," he swore.

One night Ashpenaz pounded on Daniel's door and panted, "The king wants to see you . . . immediately. And he is in a terrible temper."

Daniel laughed at the eunuch's concern. "You have not said anything new, Ashpenaz. If you had said that the king was rocking the princess and singing soft songs, that would be news!"

Ashpenaz looked at him sideways and muttered as he hurried away, "You may be very surprised at the news."

Daniel entered the throne room and saw King Nebuchadnezzar pacing the floor, stopping only to pound his fist on a table or to take another gulp of wine. When he saw Daniel, he tried to bring himself under control, but his anger had built to such a crescendo that his voice cracked.

"You . . . you wisest of the wisemen. You interpreter of dreams . . . how will you explain this?" The veins on his neck stood out and his eyes blazed with fury.

"You have not told me, my king, what the source of your problem is," Daniel answered softly, concern showing in his eyes.

"Daniel, you of great integrity . . . what would you do if you were me?" Nebuchadnezzar paused, realizing that he was asking of this man—younger than he, a man he had ordered to be taken captive in Judah—advice on his, the great king's, personal affairs. But who else could he ask? His other advisors were fools who could not even interpret his dreams.

"I have been filled with doubts since I first beheld the princess Nitocris. Could it be possible that she of the copper hair was fathered by my trusted guard, Arioch?" Nebuchadnezzar spat out the words as though they tasted of poison. "Amtyis only wept when I confronted her with my suspicions. Her tears were the only confession I needed. She is mine, and yet when I was absent, she slept with another. What am I to do?"

The king sunk onto his throne, spent from emotion, and placed his head in his hands. Daniel could scarcely hear the next words. "But she has changed toward me since the birth of Nitocris. She is tender, more devoted . . . and she says she has no love for Arioch, the cursed dog."

Daniel looked out the windows onto the glowing walls of the Temple of Marduk, the moonlight splashing against the white stone. All the riches of Babylon . . . and yet this great king could find no peace.

"You have confided in me, my king, and now I must ask you. Do you love the queen?"

"More than any other woman," he answered. Nebuchadnezzar sat up straight and pointed his sword at Daniel. "Tell me, should I have him killed or sent to slave labor for the rest of his life?"

Daniel prayed silently for the Lord to give him wisdom. He knew that Nebuchadnezzar was hungry for vengeance; he would not be deterred from some punishment. How could he, Daniel, save the life of his friend?

"Arioch is a Babylonian noble," Daniel answered slowly, weighing every word with care. "Why not banish him to live among the Judean captives, to take a Hebrew name and live their life? He would then be a captive among the captives. It would be torture for him to see the public life of the city and yet not take part in it." He held his breath, hoping that this would be an acceptable answer for the king, who had sent men to a fiery death for less reason.

"You have a keen and quick mind, Daniel. That is a punishment which suits the crime. With such a sentence it will be known that I am a just man!"

Nebuchadnezzar spiraled his forefinger through the curls of his carefully coiffed beard. For several minutes the two men, so contrasting in their lives and beliefs, sat in silence. Daniel sensed that the king had more to say, but was reluctant to say it.

"Is there something else, your Majesty, that is bothering you?" Daniel asked, sensing his uneasiness.

"Yes, there is." His temper vented for the time, Nebuchadnezzar relaxed and motioned for Daniel to sit down. "Daniel, you have been here now for eight years. During that time you have excelled at our university, proven your wisdom, and been a loyal magistrate in my kingdom. You have remained true to your one God and shown how He has given you great ability."

The king paused, looking out the window at the ziggurat in the distance. His eyes narrowed thoughtfully. "Daniel, I had promised that you could marry my wife's maidservant, and the time has come. Do you wish to take Deborah as your wife?"

Daniel felt that the king knew more than he was telling. For all of his arrogance and cruelty, Nebuchadnezzar cared for him, perhaps more than he did for any other person on earth except Amytis. Now the moment had arrived that Deborah and Daniel had talked about for almost ten years. He remembered the excitement in their houses when they had been betrothed, the waiting of that first year, the long years of waiting in Babylon. "Lord," he prayed to himself, "give me a certain answer."

And he turned to Nebuchadnezzar and said, "There have been changes in my life in recent days. I must pray and then speak to Deborah, your Majesty. The answer is with the Lord."

The king tapped his fingers impatiently on the arm of his chair. When he asked a question he wanted it answered immediately. There was no time for indecision about matters of love and war. "If your God can rescue men out of a fiery furnace, He must be able to provide you with a simple answer about whether you should marry or not."

"And He will," Daniel laughed. "He is a God of miracles, but He also cares about everything we do. Our lives are in His hands."

The king did not answer. He looked at Daniel with curiosity; he had never known such confidence, such quiet assurance, in a man. If Daniel had cowered before him, as so many did, or begged his favor, as most wanted, it would have been so much easier to understand him. Even the jealous ones in the court found it difficult to find any fault with him.

"Go pray, then . . . and you might include me, too," Nebuchadnezzar finally said with a wave of dismissal.

"I always do, your Majesty," Daniel said gently.

When Daniel returned to his room he found Deborah waiting for him. She was pacing the floor, holding her arms close to her and rubbing them nervously. When she saw Daniel she rushed to him, spilling her words out in a torrent. "Oh, Daniel, I don't know what to do. My mistress has just told me something that is so terrible . . . I mean, I suspected it . . . oh, I don't know what I mean!" She began to cry.

"Come here, little one. The Lord has not forsaken you." Daniel held her in his arms as a father would protect a hurt child. She spent herself with crying and then stepped back and looked up at him. He noticed that she had been using the antimony with which the women blackened their eyelashes, and that her pretty face was streaked with dark smudges.

"But you don't understand! Amytis told me that the princess is really the child of Arioch . . . that the king suspects and will have Arioch killed." Deborah blurted out that statement in one breath.

"I know, Deborah, but Arioch won't be killed. He will be banished from the court and made to live with our people, a captive in Babylon. The king will not harm him."

It was then, seeing the relief in her face, that Daniel knew Deborah felt the same way about Arioch as he did about her. She had never been able to hide her feelings from him. At that moment he felt the stinging pain of regret for the love he knew would never be consummated, the marriage which was not meant to be. The seed of Abraham and the promised Messiah from the line of King David would be from some other son of Judah, but not from him.

Only a few days before, two messengers from Jerusalem had come to the city as ambassadors sent by King Zedekiah, the new ruler in Judah. In their bags they had carried a letter from Jeremiah; Daniel had received it before a gathering of the Judean captives. Many of them had been sitting on their pitiful belongings, refusing to unpack or attempt to establish a household in Babylon. Then Daniel had unrolled the scroll and read in the familiar script the old prophet's words:

> The Lord of Hosts, the God of Israel, sends this message to all the captives he has exiled to Babylon from Jerusalem:
>
> "Build homes and plan to stay; plant vineyards, for you will be there many years. Marry and have children, and then find mates for them and have many grandchildren. Multiply! Don't dwindle away! And work for the peace and prosperity of Babylon. Pray for her, for if Babylon has peace, so will you."

With those words of the prophet echoing in his mind, Daniel took Deborah's small, cold hand in his and led her to the garden courtyard where they had spent so many hours in the past years. "Come, little one, dry your tears. I have news for you about your family . . . and we must seek the Lord's will for our lives."

While the handsome member of the king's court and the fair maidservant to the queen sat beneath a cypress tree and prayed, in a far corner of the city, the section called the Judean Quarter, a soldier with a wounded leg was shoved from a royal chariot and a few pieces of clothing tossed in the road beside him. He had been beaten, whether by order of the king or the vengeance of a jealous soldier, he did not know, but his leg wound had opened and blood oozed from his scalp. An old man with one ear, hearing his moans, hurried to help him, stooping down to give him words of comfort.

"You're going to be all right; have no fear, my friend," the old man said, waving at the same time for someone to bring cloths and ointment to bind the soldier's wounds. "We will take care of you."

Arioch looked up into a kind face he was sure he knew. "The Lord bless you," he mumbled through swollen lips, then lapsed into unconsciousness, his bloody head cradled in the arms of an alien.

Thus Arioch began a new life, among the captives he had taken from Judah . . . an outcast in the land of his birth.

8

I, NEBUCHADNEZZAR

As THE YEARS PASSED, the Judean captives established a new life. They built homes, bore children, started small businesses. The Babylonians allowed the exiles to conduct their lives with a certain independence, and the Hebrews for their part found the new country tolerable; even the new language, Aramaic, was not too difficult to learn. However, they did not believe that their banishment from Judah would last forever. Many kept their hope alive; "We shall return to our homeland soon," they said. Meanwhile, they met in small sanctuaries, houses of Torah study, and called them synagogues.

Time dealt kindly with Daniel's three friends, Shadrach, Meshach, and Abednego. After the miracle of the fiery furnace they found it difficult to pass unnoticed in the streets. However, they knew they had walked with an angel, or, more awesome yet, perhaps the Lord in the guise of a heavenly being. The memory was too humbling for them to take pride in the positions of influence they attained.

Shadrach was made governor of the province of Elam. He did not marry, but enjoyed visiting the families of Abednego and Meshach or joining Daniel for an occasional meal. When the old friends met, they frequently talked and prayed all night, indifferent to the time.

Abednego married Leah, one of the women who had been in the first group of captives. They had three daughters, but Abednego, always optimistic, continued to say that he was sure they would have three sons. Even when his wife was past childbearing age he persisted: "If Sarah could bear a child for Abraham when he was one hundred years old, I guess I can wait for a son, too." And Leah would shake her head in amusement.

Meshach assisted Daniel in overseeing the Judean captives. He listened to their complaints, registered their requests, and acted as a liaison between the Hebrews and the king. He married a Judean woman who had arrived in the second deportation. She was many years younger than Meshach, but his youthful, irrepressible attitude made them an appropriate match.

Every year, no matter where they were, the four friends and their families came together to share the Passover feast, as they had vowed to do many years before when they still lived together in the palace.

In the Judean Quarter, far from the opulence of the palace, was a square mud-brick house roofed with mats set on wooden beams. This was the house of Aaron, headed by the man who had once been known as Arioch, captain of the king's guards. The former Babylonian noble, now a respected tradesman on the Street of Merchants, lived with his beautiful wife, Deborah, and their young son, Jeshua. The child, whose tightly curled copper hair made him stand out among his playmates, was often seen walking to the place of prayer hand in hand with Daniel, the man more trusted by the exiles than anyone in the king's court.

"He is one of us," the people said.

"But he will never carry on the seed of his forefathers," complained Abiel. "His name will be forgotten when he dies." And the old man would hobble to the house of Aaron to tell stories to Jeshua, the boy who became like the grandson he would never have.

For certain exiles, Babylon was a siren song, enticing them away from their traditional worship. They saw the Babylonians carry a lamb to a temple and present it as an offering, getting a receipt on a clay tablet for the animal. "Not much different from our form of sacrifice," some Judeans rationalized.

During the great festivals, the exiles lined the Processional Way and watched the Babylonians bring out the statue of Marduk, an immense golden figure pulled on a cart through the streets by four white horses that were festooned with flowers and harnessed with yokes of brass. Caught in the magnificence of their new environment, drawn by the opulence of the temples and statues of many gods, some of the Hebrews attached themselves to the pagan cults and joined in their rites.

Watching one of these parades, Abiel shook his fist and shouted, "Graven image!" The words sounded like a curse.

However, in the fifth year of their exile, the words of a young priest named Ezekiel began to draw the Hebrews into new understanding of their duties and obligations in the land of their dwelling. From their homes and shops, or after toiling all day in the construction of the city moats and towers, the people gathered to listen to the priest. Ezekiel stood among them, an unimposing man of medium height, but with a face reflecting such wisdom that even the elders among them listened attentively when he spoke.

"The Lord God wants to know whether you are going to pollute yourselves just as your fathers did, and keep on worshiping idols."

Many listened, knowing that the lure of Babylon had drawn them away from Jehovah. It had been so easy to fall into the temptations of this new land.

Ezekiel did not spare them. He strongly proclaimed, "What you have in mind will not be done—to be like the nations all around you, serving gods of wood and stone. I will rule you with an iron fist and in great anger and power."

Nebuchadnezzar knew little of what was happening in the Judean Quarter. He trusted Daniel to those tasks and occupied himself with more important business. He was pleased with himself; his daughter was becoming a beauty; Amytis was a gracious queen who wore her fine linens and jewels with regal style, and she was a willing wife in fulfilling his passions. He had chosen to forget the episode with Arioch, only boasting to Daniel occasionally of his great gesture of humanitarianism. "I could have decreed that he be dragged behind a chariot on the walls of the city, for all the people to see his downfall."

"Arioch is a redeemed man, your Highness. The Lord forgives a sinner if he turns from his wicked ways and repents," Daniel said.

Nebuchadnezzar bristled at the implication in Daniel's statement.

"Daniel, I admire you for your constant belief, but there is more than one way to experience forgiveness." He glanced at Amytis, who lowered her eyes and stared at the floor. "I am providing work for my people, provisions for our captives, and occasional reprieves for my enemies. Surely your Jehovah recognizes such works and will bless my efforts."

"Jehovah accepts those who believe in Him," Daniel replied simply. These discussions never seemed to come to any conclusion. The king persisted in glorifying his own abilities and believing that one God could not satisfy him.

After talking to the king, Daniel would return to his quarters and fall to his knees in prayer. Sometimes he would agonize over the question of the Lord's will for his life. "Lord, how long . . . how long must I have my feet in two kingdoms? How can I serve you and a pagan ruler with the same mind?"

In the Judean Quarter the people gathered to worship and cried, "How long, O Lord, how long must we be separated from our beloved city, Jerusalem?" And Ezekiel, sitting by the river Chebar, the canal that brought water from the Euphrates, was given a vision from God. He was shown a hand holding out a scroll, and as he unrolled it he saw that it was full of warnings and pronouncements. He began to prophesy, and his words were those of doom for Jerusalem, the people left there, and for the Temple.

Deborah and Aaron sat by the canal, their arms around their young son, and listened to the frightening words from the priest: "O Israel, the day of your damnation dawns; the time has come; the day of trouble nears. It is a day of shouts of anguish, not shouts of joy!

"I gave you gold to use in decorating the Temple, and you used it instead to make idols! Therefore I will take it all away from you. I will give it to foreigners and to wicked men as booty. They shall defile my Temple. I will not look when they defile it, nor will I stop them. Like robbers, they will loot the treasures and leave the Temple in ruins."

Aaron listened in awe. He now believed in the Lord God Jehovah of Daniel and Deborah. He had seen His power. Because his lot was now cast with the Judeans, this prophecy of doom was painful for him, too. He must ask Daniel if he believed in this Ezekiel.

Deborah said, "I once heard the prophet Jeremiah warn my people of coming destruction, but they hated him for it. So far, everything he said has come true." And she held her son close to her, knowing that he might never see the land of his forefathers.

Ezekiel looked over the heads of the gathering crowd and saw the tall figure of Daniel, standing in the distance and listening to him intently. He continued, "God has told me, 'Prepare chains for my people, for the land is full of bloody crimes. Jerusalem is filled with violence, so I will enslave her people. I will crush your pride by bringing to Jerusalem the worst of the nations to occupy your homes, break down your fortifications you are so proud of, and defile your Temple.' "

Listening to Ezekiel, Daniel knew the Lord had sent another prophet to Babylon. Weeks before, Nebuchadnezzar had left the city with thousands of his finest troops. At the very moment when Ezekiel was speaking, the siege of Jerusalem was probably beginning. . .

Far to the west, in the struggling, dying Holy City, the prophet Jeremiah sat in his hut, hidden behind the burial place of the kings. He pondered why his people never learned from history, never learned from prophecy, never learned from experience. He had told Zedekiah, the king of Judah, the prophecies the Lord had given him: "The Lord has said that if you want to live, king of Judah, you must submit to the king of Babylon, for otherwise this whole city will be destroyed."

But the king would not listen, and the people scoffed and continued to ignore the warnings of Jehovah's spokesman. As before, a few believed the prophet, but they did not defend him. He was flogged and put into a palace prison in an attempt to silence him. However, when King Zedekiah decided to depend upon Egyptian support and revolted against the orders of the king of Babylon, Jeremiah continued to speak: "Jerusalem will be captured by the king of Babylon unless you surrender."

But the false prophets counseled Zedekiah, "That kind of talk will undermine the morale of the few soldiers we have left . . . and of all the people, too. Jeremiah is a traitor!" So Jeremiah was taken from his cell where he had been imprisoned and put into an empty cistern in the prison yard. There was a thick layer of murky mire at the bottom, and the old prophet sank down into it. However, he had a few friends left in the city, and they lowered a rope and pulled him out before he starved to death.

Once more, the city heard the rumbling of the mighty armies outside the walls and saw hundreds of soldiers from a foreign land, their pointed helmets rising from the mass of bodies like small, sharp mountain peaks. They formed a human barricade around the city so that no provisions could come in. Nebuchadnezzar sat in his tent, waiting for his siege to weaken the defenses of the remaining Hebrews. At times he left the camp to visit other villages in Judah, returning with captives and slaves and food from their fields.

The people of Jerusalem were starving; the dead and dying were sprawled throughout the once-beautiful city. King Zedekiah took his family and remaining troops and fled by night to the plains of Jericho, but the news of their escape reached the Babylonians and they pursued the king, seizing him and all that were with him.

Dragged before King Nebuchadnezzar, the king of Judah fell on his face and begged mercy. But Nebuchadnezzar commanded, "Line up his sons over there, in front of him. Watch, King Zedekiah, what we do in Babylon to traitors!" At the wave of his hand, four soldiers stepped from the ranks and thrust their spears through the hearts of the young princes of Judah. Then Nebuchadnezzar signaled by placing his forefingers upon his eyes; the strongest guard turned and gave two swift thrusts directly into King Zedekiah's eyes, blinding him forever. He was then bound with fetters of brass and thrown in with the other captives. The last sight he ever saw was the slaughter of his sons.

Jerusalem, the city of the great kings, was invaded by the troops from Babylon; the Temple and all of the houses were burned. As the city went up in flames, all of the remaining vessels from the house of the Lord were taken; the survivors were stripped and taken away as slaves.

Nebuchadnezzar, knowing of Jeremiah, told the captain of the guards not to hurt the old prophet. He was taken as far as Ramah with all the exiled people of Jerusalem and Judah, then given his choice. "The Lord your God has brought this disaster on this land, just as you said He would. Now I am going to take off your chains and let you go. If you want to come to Babylon, fine; I will see that you are well cared for. But if you don't want to come, don't. The world is before you—go where you like."

Jeremiah remained in Judah with the remnant of his people, a poor man who had been chosen by God to do His work. And it was through him that God said, "This entire land shall become a desolate wasteland; all the world will be shocked at the disaster that befalls you. Israel and her neighboring lands shall serve the king of Babylon for seventy years. Then after these years of slavery are ended, I will punish the king of Babylon and his people for their sins; I will make the land of Chaldea an everlasting waste."

The word of Jeremiah's prophecy was passed from believer to believer. Daniel heard in Babylon and he began to count the years.

The Holy City lay in rubble, the Temple of Solomon burned to the ground. In Babylon, the people could be heard lamenting: "What terrible news this is! All is gone. The joyous times we used to have when we gathered together to celebrate the Temple feasts will be no more. The city gates, once filled with happy throngs, are silent."

The old men wept. "Our enemies prosper, for the Lord has punished Jerusalem for all her many sins. Even the children have been captured and taken far away as slaves."

Jerusalem had been stripped naked and humiliated.

Before many weeks the survivors came limping into Babylon, broken in body and spirit. With them they brought the lingering hope that someday Jerusalem would be restored and its holy Temple built from the dust of destruction.

Ezekiel, who had prophesied the downfall of Judah, now became the prophet of restoration. His very name meant "God strengthens," and his messages were a call to personal repentance: that each person must be responsible as an individual before God. Some understood and believed, but many refused, just as they had ignored Jeremiah.

Aaron, eager to grow in the knowledge of the Lord God Jehovah, sat at the feet of Ezekiel and listened to his visions of the future. The prophet spoke of a time when a Good Shepherd, the promised Messiah, would rule over all the people. Looking at the condition of the exiles, knowing the tragedy of their fallen kingdom and ruined place of worship, it did not seem possible that their nation would ever be restored. "But the Jehovah is the God of miracles," Aaron told Deborah. And they believed.

As the years passed, Nebuchadnezzar basked in the glory of his land's growing stronger and his royal coffers' becoming fatter. He praised Daniel for his work with the captives and consulted with him frequently on matters of personal concern. Nitocris grew in beauty and wisdom, and often sat in the royal gardens asking questions of the chief wiseman.

"Daniel will draw our daughter away from our gods," Amytis complained.

"Let her choose her path, wife," Nebuchadnezzar answered, satisfied with his own benevolence. He was at ease in his life; the time of conquering was past, and the years of building at hand. His days were filled with surveying the mightiness of his city, and his nights were filled with the pleasures of good wine and food. He gave little thought to the Lord God, but respected Daniel's viewpoint. "Every man to his own pleasure," he would say, as he patted Daniel on the back in a slightly patronizing way. "If your constant prayers help you, Daniel, do not cease. And be sure to include some for me," he would smile. He felt somehow comforted to have this man around.

Then one sultry night, while the perfume from the blossoming citrus trees permeated the palace bedchamber, Nebuchadnezzar sat up in his bed and shouted for his servants. He had another dream, and he was shaking with cold fear in spite of the warmth of the room.

"Bring in all the wisemen of Babylon to tell me the meaning of my dream. Call the magicians, the astrologers, the fortune-tellers, the wizards . . . every one of them."

They gathered in the throne room in the middle of the night, rubbing their hands, wondering what would happen this time if they could not interpret his dream. The life of a Chaldean soothsayer was very precarious!

Nebuchadnezzar spoke in a voice which was scarcely above a whisper; his wisemen, with one notable exception, were all there, perspiring from the heat and the anxiety of the occasion.

Nebuchadnezzar told a strange story: "I saw a very tall tree out in a field, growing higher and higher into the sky until it could be seen by everyone in all the world. Its leaves were fresh and green, and its branches were weighted down with fruit, enough for everyone to eat. Wild animals rested beneath its shade and birds sheltered in its branches, and all the world was fed from it."

A glassy look came into his eyes as he continued. "Then as I lay there dreaming, I saw an angel coming down from heaven. He shouted, 'Cut down the tree; lop off its branches; shake off its leaves, and scatter its fruit. Get the animals out from under it and the birds from its branches, but leave its stump and roots in the ground, banded with a chain of iron and brass, surrounded by the tender grass.' "

Nebuchadnezzar paused, struggling to continue with the description of his dream. "Then the angel said, 'Let the dews of heaven drench him and let him eat grass with the wild animals! For seven years let him have the mind of an animal instead of a man. For this has been decreed by the Watchers, demanded by the Holy Ones.' "

The Chaldean wisemen frowned in concentration, none of them having the slightest idea of what to say. The king continued:

"The holy angel said to me, 'The purpose of this decree is that all the world may understand that the Most High dominates the kingdoms of the world, and gives them to anyone He wants to, even the lowliest of men.' "

The oldest wiseman, his long white beard hanging to his waist, frowned beneath his shaggy eyebrows and protested, "The Holy Ones, whoever they are, speak treason. O King, long may you live, you and only you dominate the kingdoms of the world."

The rest of the Chaldean soothsayers nodded in solemn agreement. But none of them, with their crystal balls, their astrological charts, or their books of incantations, could tell the meaning of the dream.

Ashpenaz, still in the service of the king, stood in the back of the room waiting for his orders. He knew that the king would send for Daniel, for none of these other fools had ever been able to interpret his dreams. He rushed as fast as his gouty old legs would allow him to move and brought Daniel to the throne room.

Daniel was now a man in his early fifties—erect, slightly greying, but still handsome enough to draw the inviting looks of Babylonian and Hebrew women alike. However, he was known as a celibate, and they had learned their enticements were fruitless. ("What a pity," Ashpenaz had been known to comment, "He might as well be like me.")

As the chief magistrate approached his king, he could see that the monarch was more troubled than he had seen him in years. He listened as Nebuchadnezzar repeated the dream, rubbing his hands together to rid himself of the coldness in his body. When he finished the account he looked at his chief wiseman with pleading eyes, begging for relief from his agony. "Tell me what it means. No one else can help me; all the wisest men of my kingdom have failed me. But you can tell me, for the spirit of the holy gods is in you."

Daniel sat on the step leading to the great carved throne, his head in his hands. For one hour he sat silent, the clear revelation of the dream overwhelming his being. The Lord had shown him the meaning in vivid detail and he did not want to tell the king. Whatever Nebuchadnezzar had done, Daniel had been his trusted advisor for too many years not to agonize over what he knew would come to pass. Finally he spoke, his voice choked with compassion for the message he needed to give. "Your Majesty, I wish I could say that the events foreshadowed in this dream were going to happen to your enemies."

Nebuchadnezzar leaned forward. "Don't be afraid to tell me."

Daniel did not want the others to hear, so he walked to the throne and put his hand on the shoulder of the most powerful man in the known world. "Your Majesty," he said in a low voice, "the Most High God has decreed—and it will surely happen—that your people will chase you from your palace, and you will live in the field like an animal, eating grass like a cow, your back wet with dew from heaven. For seven years this will be your life, until you learn that the Most High God dominates the kingdoms of men, and gives power to anyone He chooses."

Nebuchadnezzar sat expressionless, his eyes vacant and unbelieving. Surely this was some hoax . . . some cruel trick of the gods to obtain more homage from his storehouses. "Continue, Daniel, continue," he muttered.

"But in your dream the stump and the roots were left in the ground! This means that you will get your kingdom back again, when you have learned that heaven rules."

Nebuchadnezzar lowered his head and examined his manicured hands. Surely this time Daniel was wrong. But the prophet continued, "Listen to me, O King Nebuchadnezzar—stop sinning; do what you know is right; be merciful to the poor. Perhaps even yet God will spare you."

The king was silent; he looked up at Daniel for a moment and then closed his eyes as if dismissing what he had heard. Daniel hesitated, then, realizing that he could say no more, left the room, burdened with concern and love for this proud man.

For a year Nebuchadnezzar kept the knowledge of Daniel's dream interpretation hidden in his mind. He told no one. Daniel prayed for him every day, that he would repent and know that God was giving him time, a reprieve. If only he would face the truth of his own sinful nature before it was too late!

One day the king was strolling with Amytis and Nitocris on the roof of his royal palace. He scanned the beautiful city beneath him, the intricate streets teaming with commerce. The Hebrews had contributed much to the business life of the city, even though they lacked some of the artistic skills of the Chaldeans. Nebuchadnezzar sighed with pleasure. Yes, the sight spread before him was good. He looked as far as he could see and spread his arms wide, sweeping across the glittering panorama. Then he spoke slowly to impress his wife and daughter and reinforce his own belief in himself:

"I, Nebuchadnezzar, by my own mighty power, have built this beautiful city as my royal residence, and as the capital of my empire."

At that very moment a streak of lightning was seen shooting above the great Temple of Marduk. Every inhabitant of the city was jolted by a clap of thunder so loud that the earth seemed to shake. The sky opened and a biting rain drove men and animals for the nearest shelter. Amytis and Nitocris fled down the stairs to escape the wild storm, shivering more from fear than the cold. Several moments passed before they realized that the king had not followed them. "Nebuchadnezzar, where are you?" cried Amytis, running back up the stairs, Nitocris close behind. And then she saw him and fell back against the stone wall, clutching her daughter's hand and drawing her close to her.

Nebuchadnezzar opened his mouth and bared his teeth; a low, guttural growl came from the depths of his throat. He started toward the women, his hands tensed, aiming at the throat of his wife. He didn't speak, but snarled, as a mad dog would, or . . . a wolf.

Amytis screamed and screamed, shouting for someone to hear her. As he neared her, his arms outstretched, she kicked at his leg as hard as she could. What had happened? What insanity had taken over the man she loved? She thought she would die at that very moment, that her heart would stop from fright. But he drew back and yelped in pain as the point of her hard sandal pierced his shin.

Then two Assyrian guards, chosen personally by the king for

their size and strength, appeared on the roof, alerted by the queen's screams. They grabbed Nebuchadnezzar's arms and pulled him back from the terrified women, although he fought ferociously, with a power far greater than that of his recently overindulged body. He shouted unintelligible words while the guards wrestled to subdue him.

"Mother," cried Nitocris as the guards pinned her father to the floor, "he has gone mad. All the demons of the deep abyss have invaded his body!"

An emergency council of the chief magistrates, governors, captains, judges, and wisemen of all the provinces was assembled. Who would rule in Babylon now? There was no heir, no successor to the throne. The heads of the outlying districts had been administered by Daniel for many years; they respected his wisdom and guidance. And since they outnumbered the magistrates of the city of Babylon, the vote was cast that for the time Daniel would fill the vacuum of leadership.

Some wished to have Nebuchadnezzar banished to a far country, to die in anonymity. However, Daniel insisted that he remain in Babylon, where he could be guarded and cared for compassionately. So it was to be.

For a while, the man who had been king was imprisoned in one of his own palace cells. Soon it was evident that he would starve to death, because he would not eat the food humans ate. The palace advisors wanted to have him killed, but Amytis, who loved him, begged them to listen to the words of Daniel, who said, "Put a chain around his neck and lead him to the palace gardens. There build a strong fence around him and place him in it. Let the people see him so that they may know the Lord God rules heaven and earth. Watch him for seven years, that no one attempts to kill him. The Lord's will be done."

The once proud king became a wild man, eating grass like an animal, looking down at the ground as he crawled on all fours. His hair, once so skillfully kept by his personal barber, became long and matted, sweeping the ground as he groveled for food. His nails grew sharp and claw-like, reaching through the slats in his cage to gash at anyone who would venture close to the compound.

The years passed; the kingdom was ruled by Daniel and the governors and magistrates of the other provinces. Babylon itself was under the jurisdiction of Daniel, and his duties were great. However, he found time every week to visit Abiel, who had grown very feeble, moving slowly from bed to chair, and to spend time at the house of Aaron.

"Somehow I knew, Daniel, from the first moment we met when you were in my charge as a captive, that you would play an important part in my life," Aaron said one evening as they reclined at his table after supper. "You were the only man who would look into my eyes and not look away."

"My brother, the Lord had His hand upon you before we knew each other," Daniel laughed. He enjoyed these times in the house of Aaron. His care for Deborah had never ceased, but his desire for her had been replaced by the kind of love he would have for a sister. They were his family, and their son, Jeshua, was like the boy he would never have. "Be careful, Daniel," his father had warned him as the patriarch of the house, "you must not allow any jealousy to surface with Aaron, either because of Deborah or Jeshua."

"My father," Daniel would say, "you are a wise man in the practical matters of life. I shall always respect your opinion. But have no fear. The Lord has clearly shown me that a wife and family are not to be a part of my life, just as He directed Jeremiah. I have no regrets."

"Well, I have," mumbled the old man. "Your name will never be remembered. It will die with you."

"Our name is not important, my father, only our obedience," Daniel said. But sometimes Daniel looked at the family of Aaron and knew that when Jehovah calls a man to commitment, He does not withhold temptation. The world, its desires and longings, are an ever-present reality. When the burdens became too heavy, Daniel would take off his royal garments, put on the simpler tunics of the tradesmen, and sit by the River Chebar and listen to Ezekiel.

As often as he could, Daniel visited the animal once known as Nebuchadnezzar, sitting by the fenced enclosure and praying. Sometimes Amytis or Nitocris would join him. As the years passed they began to pray, too, as Daniel did. "Would your God accept a Babylonian?" the queen asked one day. Her loneliness was an ache of remorse—weeping because she had not shown the king the extent of her love, empty because all the counselors of the court had no answers for her. Slowly, patiently, Daniel explained the love and forgiveness of the Lord Jehovah, and Amytis and Nitocris believed.

"But what shall I do about that . . . thing . . . who was my husband?" Amytis asked. They looked at the creature groveling in the ground for fresh blades of grass, head down close to the dirt, and had difficulty remembering the handsome, strutting man he once had been.

"Be patient, my queen, and love the Lord God Jehovah with all your heart. Pray for the king . . . pray that some day he will raise his head and look up."

Seven years passed from the time of the terrible storm. No one had ever seen such a fearsome rain or heard such thunder before or since. Abiel died quietly one night, and Daniel wept with his friends in the Judean Quarter. Young Jeshua, stoic with his emotions, said to his father, "I did not know that strong men cried." And Aaron, placing his arm around the shoulders of his son, answered gently, "It is the weak who hide their emotions for fear of what others might think."

One day the queen was sitting by the enclosure that held the animal who had been her husband. As the years passed, she had become braver and had begun talking to him. She had noticed that he became less restless, almost tame, when she spoke to him in a soft voice. Now she began to tell him about her new faith in the one God, for there were few people in the palace with whom she could share this news. As she talked, the animal slowly raised his head and turned so that she saw his face. He looked right at her, and for the first time in seven years she felt no fear, no revulsion. Then she saw it. A tear. She watched that tear roll down the fur on his face and drop to the ground. Gripping the side of the fence, closer than she had ever dared to come, she saw another tear, and then another, bathe his face.

"His face!" she shouted. "He has a face!"

Slowly, he stood up and raised his head. He looked up to heaven, and at that moment a bright light enveloped his body, making him glow like a candle in the dark. Amytis closed her eyes, not able to look at the light. She could not speak. When she opened her eyes again, she looked into the eyes of Nebuchadnezzar. He was whole, a man again, and yet not the same.

When he spoke, his voice was strong and resonant, as it had

been, but at the same time warm and loving. He lifted his arms to heaven and said, "Praise the Most High God, and honor Him who lives forever. His rule is everlasting, His kingdom evermore. Praise Him above all the earth!"

Amytis flew to open the gate of the pen which had been the king's prison for seven years and ran into the circle of his arms. As he led her back to the palace, he saw the faithful Ashpenaz grasping a pillar to support himself, and he said, "Greetings, Ashpenaz, in the name of the King of heaven." And Ashpenaz slowly sunk to the ground in a shocked faint.

The counselors and governors, the officers and wisemen, gathered in the throne room, unable to believe the astonishing transformation of Nebuchadnezzar. Daniel stood in the back, laughing, as he saw one Babylonian after another walk up to the king and touch his garments or his skin to make sure his restoration was no illusion. To see the dramatic results of his prayers was almost more than Daniel could contain.

Nebuchadnezzar raised his arms for silence. Yes, the face had his features, the people of the court thought, but he seemed somehow different.

"My friends, I have been a terrible sinner in the eyes of the Lord God Jehovah. He brought me to my knees in a a judgment which was only just for the crimes I have done. I had exalted myself above Him, and there is no other god before Him.

"All the people of the earth are nothing when compared to Him; He does whatever He thinks best among the hosts of heaven, as well as here among the inhabitants of earth."

An astonished murmur spread through the great hall. The king raised his arms again and continued. "Now, I, Nebuchadnezzar, praise and glorify and honor the King of Heaven, the Judge of all, whose every act is right and good; for He is able to take those who walk proudly and push them into the dust!"

Many of the court wept, others laughed. Joy filled the hearts of Amytis and Nitocris, and there was feasting in the homes along the Street of Merchants in the Judean Quarter.

A great celebration was planned in the palace. Ashpenaz, forgetting his aching legs, rushed to the royal kitchen to instruct the cooks to utilize their best culinary arts. Musicians were called from all corners of the city, so that the sounds of voices and instruments would fill the halls once more.

Nebuchadnezzar called for Daniel to ask him to recline next to him at the banquet table that night. "Our God is great, my friend, Daniel," said Nebuchadnezzar, "His dominion is an everlasting dominion, and His kingdom endures from generation to generation! I want to tell the world about Him! He brought me out of the dust of the earth and gave me life again!"

Amytis was glowing, her beauty never more evident. "And we have you to thank, Daniel, for being faithful to us through all the years."

Daniel knew it was time for him to take leave and allow the king and queen to be alone. He stood up, started for the great bronze door through which he had walked so many times, and looked down at the inscription on the doorstep. He laughed as he read it: "For Nebo, the exalted Lord, who hath lengthened the days of my life, his temple anew have I built."

"Perhaps, my king, you will want these words removed now."

"Send those stones to the museum, Daniel. I want the people to know that I no longer worship many gods. There is only one!"

Daniel returned to his rooms alone, to think and pray. He felt as if an era in his life had ended. The reason he had been brought to Babylon seemed clear, and now his task was over. "What more is there to do, Lord? Have I fulfilled your purpose for me on earth? I have planted and you have harvested. My mission has been accomplished."

He seemed to hear laughter, and he remembered how the psalmist had written that God sits in the heavens and laughs, amused at all our puny plans.

His little room was filled, as he had experienced before in his life, with the Presence he could not see, but knew was there. It communicated to him an amazing message.

"I am not through with you yet, Daniel. Your work has just begun. You will have visions and dreams which will take you far beyond Babylon and into a future you cannot see. This is only the beginning, My faithful son."

Only the beginning.

PART II

I, Daniel

"I Daniel was grieved in my spirit

in the midst of my body,

and the visions of my head troubled me."

Daniel 7:15, KJV

9

THE BEGINNING OF DREAMS AND VISIONS

How can I tell future generations the awesome visions and dreams the Lord God Jehovah has given me? Will they believe me? The vastness, the immensity, of what I have been shown is more than my mind can contain.

I am a prophet. Just saying those words makes me fall to my knees in wonder!

How did God choose a lad from Judah, a captive in an alien land, to speak the mighty truths of His sovereign will? I do not know the answer, except that I know He loves me greatly to entrust me with this knowledge.

These pages may be covered with my tears or dancing with my exaltation. Those who read in generations to come may scoff or believe, but I know that the knowledge of things to come was given to me and I must tell it to the world and the worlds to come.

God has told me the future of mankind. And I will tell you. . . .

In the First Year of Belshazzar:

When King Nebuchadnezzar died there was a void in my life, as well as in Babylon. Understand that I am not apologizing for his cruel behavior in the past. He was a man who ruled without God's love, but a monarch who wanted a city and a land which would exceed all others in wisdom and beauty. He succeeded. The brilliance and evil of Babylon may never be seen again.

Many will remember him as a vain and proud genius who was humbled by the Mighty King but, before he died, became one of Jehovah's followers. May history record him as such.

I knew that I had many enemies in the court. Some of the College of the Magi had tried every sorcerer's trick they knew in attempts to discredit me. How detestable they are in the sight of the Lord! It was quite obvious to me that there were those who wanted to rid the province of this aging prophet who would remind them of Nebuchadnezzar and the God we both worshiped.

For a time, many of the counselors and lords wanted to follow the example of King Nebuchadnezzar. But as the years passed, their zeal lessened. Discipline was replaced by permissiveness. My old friend, Ashpenaz, used to tell me, "I scarcely know who is in charge any more. One king comes in, reigns a time, and then is replaced or assassinated."

Loyal Ashpenaz (I cannot think of him without chuckling) cared for Queen Amytis and Princess Nitocris for several years after the king died. Then, I am happy to write, his overworked heart just stopped as he was kneeling in prayer with me one night. Yes, he, too, rejected the heathen gods of Babylon and believed in the Lord God Jehovah before he died.

A new era has now crept into the kingdom. Kings have come and gone until the present time in which I have begun this account. Nabonidus is in charge now. I do not know him well, for I have been retired (perhaps I should say ignored) for the past few years. However, this king is more interested in trade routes to Arabia than in looking after the internal affairs of Babylon. He seems to be indifferent to the fact that the Medes and Persians are beginning to take over portions of the empire. The crown prince, Nabonidus's son, a dissolute young man by the name of Belshazzar, has been appointed to rule in his absence.

But administration in the kingdom is not my business now. I am growing old, although my mind refuses to accept the fact. Only yesterday, in a chariot race with Jeshua, my nearly threescore years began to tell. However, and the Lord forgive my boast, I did win!

Within me is a mounting tension that the Lord wants more from me. I spend my days in prayer and study, facing toward Jerusalem, as has been my habit these many years.

This diary may be interrupted from time to time. However, I wish to convey the sequence of what the Lord has given me, as events occur and the course of this stylus moves. When it is necessary, I shall attempt to repeat my conversations with others as accurately as I can.

The reports that I hear about Belshazzar have been of great concern to me. The queen mother, Nitocris, is a woman of great character; she has carried the knowledge of her birthright in secret all these years. It has been to her credit that she did not want to humiliate her father, Nebuchadnezzar, but wanted only to be a daughter in whom he could take pride. He always believed she would be the mother of a great king. It is fortunate that he does not have to see the debauchery his grandson, Belshazzar, has brought to the throne.

As I muse over the lives which have intertwined with mine over the past fifty years, I am grateful that the Lord chose Ezekiel to be a priest and a prophet to the exiles. He was too young to be consecrated as a Temple priest in Jerusalem, but his ministry has been more important here. I hope that he, too, is recording what the Lord has shown him.

After my last entry I was interrupted by Jeshua, son of Aaron and Deborah. He comes frequently to my rooms to talk and challenge me with his questions. He has been something of a rebel from the time of his childhood. The old ways brought from Judah were as alien to him as the manners and customs of Babylon were strange to me when I first came as a youth. Jeshua used to say to me, "It is senseless to keep longing for a return to Jerusalem. It must be a heap of rubble by now at the edge of the wilderness. Why do my people sit by the river and lament? We are well fed and have comfortable homes, and there are many things to do in Babylon."

"God has made a covenant with His people Israel and given them the Promised Land," I explained to him. "And He has promised that the royal lineage of the Messiah will come through King David. Our people long for the Holy City and a return to the land of our heritage."

Jeshua loved to argue with me. "But it is not my heritage! I am a part of two worlds. I didn't ask to be born in Babylon but raised in the Judean Quarter," he would complain.

"I believe God has a special purpose for you, Jeshua," I told him. Immediately I remembered a long-ago conversation with the prophet Jeremiah, when he had told me the same thing. Looking at Jeshua, knowing that his mother and father had taken him to the synagogue, that he had listened many times to the prophet-priest Ezekiel, I could understand his personal turmoil. A handsome young man, endowed with his father's muscular physique and copper hair, he looks the part of a Babylonian noble. He speaks Aramaic better than he does Hebrew, and can drive a chariot on the walls of the city as skillfully as any soldier trained in the Chaldean army. (There are, of course, others who challenge his ability as a charioteer.)

When I tried to encourage him with my thoughts about God's will for his life, he rubbed that cursed amulet tied around his throat. Why, I thought, do some of our good Hebrews adopt the habits of their pagan friends? I sometimes think Jeshua does these things to test me. However, ignoring these obvious gestures of rebellion is better than admonishing him.

One of my constant prayers is that this strong-minded young man, the son I shall never have, will know the wisdom of the Lord and His leading for his life. But I must not alienate him with pious preaching. I want him to keep coming to me to talk, even if we disagree. He is a challenging and beloved adversary.

THE DAY OF AGONY:

I do not know how to begin this account. My heart is as heavy as it was the day I left Jerusalem over fifty years ago. How can I express so great an emptiness?

Jeshua came to invite me one evening to a celebration feast at the house of Aaron on the Street of Merchants. The occasion was the announcement of his betrothal to a lovely Hebrew girl named Rachel. We had almost despaired of Jeshua's ever marrying. For many years he resisted making a commitment to one woman, and tales of his exploits were whispered in the Judean Quarter. His mother and father and I have been praying that we would see the day when the Lord would provide a helpmeet for our restless Jeshua.

I was delighted to be a part of such a happy occasion, and I donned a fine cloak that I had not worn since the days of Nebuchadnezzar. (Little did I know that it would be bloodstained within a few hours.)

Deborah greeted me with a kiss. "Daniel, this is a festive day. You have made our family circle complete by being here." Then she darted into the cooking room to see that the food and wine were ready. (Her walk has slowed a bit over the years, but she still has those quick little movements hinted by her name—the bee. Her beauty is now that of a woman secure in the love of her family.)

Aaron should have been a happy, satisfied man. But I immediately sensed his unrest. "What is wrong, my old friend?" I asked.

He drew me outside; the street was deserted at that hour of the night. In the dim light from the oil lamp in the window I could see that he was deeply troubled. He looked up and down the road, then spoke to me in a low tone.

"I have been told, Daniel, that Belshazzar has sent his spies throughout the province to find me," Aaron said. He was one of the bravest men I have ever known, but his face in the lamplight was frightened.

"It is not for myself that I fear," he added, "but for my family. I have worked hard and tried to protect them from the evils of Babylon all these years."

"But why should the king want you, Aaron?" I asked.

His answer startled me. "I believe he has found out that his mother, Nitocris, was not the true daughter of Nebuchadnezzar. If he knows this, he would not want it discovered, because it could threaten his right to the throne." Aaron buried his face in his hands and moaned. "It was so long ago . . . but some of the elders say that children are punished for their father's sins. I do not want my children to suffer because of what I did."

"That is not true, Arioch." (I lapsed into his old name.) "Each individual is judged for himself. God will be just with anyone who turns to Him in repentance and faith, regardless of the past. You are forgiven."

I can scarcely write. Those were the last words Aaron ever heard. At that moment we heard the horrible clatter of a war chariot in the street. I fell into the doorway, narrowly escaping its lethal wheels.

Aaron was not so swift. A spear pierced his chest, and the spikes of iron on the wheels tore his flesh as he fell.

I dropped to my knees and covered his bleeding body with my cloak, but he was dead before Deborah and Jeshua ran out the door. The day that began in rejoicing ended in weeping.

"I'll kill them . . . I'll kill them!" Jeshua shouted over and over again.

"No, no, Jeshua," I cried, "vengeance is the Lord's."

But at that moment I could see the hatred in his heart begin to grow.

I can write no more. The memory of that terrible night is too painful.

In the past few months I have visited Deborah every day, watching the lines of mourning deepen on her face, and her dark hair turn to white. She speaks very little of Aaron; her mind has returned to Jerusalem and she tells the same stories over and over about her childhood. She remembers details about the house of Barak, but sometimes asks me, "Now who are you?" when I come to her door. Jeshua's wedding, of course, has been postponed.

Jeshua has asked me many times to repeat every word of my conversation with his father on that fateful evening. "The evil live and prosper and the good die," he says. "God has abandoned His people. What's the use of praying and longing for a return to Israel? Israel has no future!"

I have been acutely aware during these months that God has not finished with me yet. Jeshua needs me, and my people need me.

Lord God Jehovah, how can I give them hope?

MY DREAM:

I have been depressed for days. Even now it is difficult for me to hold this stylus and record what I have seen. Outside my window the commerce of Babylon is continuing: people are working, babies are being born, love and hatred weave the pattern of lives. But nothing will ever be the same for me.

I had a dream in which God gave me a vision of the world to come.

In my dream I saw a storm upon a great sea. Winds were blowing from every direction, and the scene was one of turmoil.

As I watched, four great beasts arose from the waves. Each one was distinctive from the other. (It is not my purpose here to interpret their meaning, but to describe what my eyes beheld.)

The first beast was like a lion, but had eagle's wings. I watched and saw the wings pulled off so that the beast could not fly. It was left standing on the ground, on two feet, like a man. A man's mind was given to it.

The second beast looked like a bear; it had its paw raised, ready to strike, and in its teeth were three ribs. I heard a voice shout, "Get up! Eat the flesh of many people!"

The third beast looked like a leopard, with wings like a bird and four heads! This beast had great power over all mankind.

Then, as I watched in my dream, a fourth beast rose out of the great sea, its appearance so dreadful I grow cold when I describe it. It devoured its victims by tearing them apart with huge teeth of iron or crushing them beneath its feet; it was far more vicious than the other beasts. Upon its head were ten horns.

I stared at those horns and saw a small horn appearing among them. Three of the other horns were yanked out by the roots to make room for it. The little horn had the piercing, intelligent eyes of a man and a mouth that continually bragged of great accomplishments.

Then I watched as thrones were put in place and the Ancient of Days—the Almighty God—sat down to judge. (My body quakes in describing Him.)

His clothing was purest white, like snow, His hair like the purest wool. He sat upon a fiery throne brought in on flaming wheels. A river of fire flowed from before Him. Surrounding Him were millions of angels serving Him, and hundreds of millions of people stood before Him, waiting to be judged.

Then court opened session and the books were opened.

As I watched this scene, the brutal fourth beast was killed, its body handed over to be burned. The power of the other three beasts was taken from them, but they were allowed to live a short time longer.

Next I saw a Man arrive, coming on clouds from heaven; he was presented before the Almighty God. And he was given the power to rule in a kingdom which shall never be destroyed, over the nations of the world, for all eternity.

I have reported this exactly as I saw it. However, in my dream, I was confused by all that I had seen. And I dared to approach someone standing beside the throne and say, "Can you explain to me the meaning of all these things?" And the angel I spoke to gave me more understanding of my dream.

He said, "These four animals represent four kings who will rule the earth. But in the end the people of the Most High God shall rule the governments of the world forever and forever."

Although I did not know what those governments or kingdoms would be, I was most curious about the fourth animal. The image of this brutal beast—with its cruel iron teeth and brass claws—was so shocking that it literally made me ill. Surely there was significance in the ten horns, and particularly in the little horn with the eyes and the loud, bragging mouth.

"Tell me," I begged of the angel, "about the hideous fourth animal."

"This fourth animal," he told me, "is the fourth world power that will rule the earth. It will be more brutal than any of the others; it will devour the whole world, destroying everything before it."

"But what are the ten horns?" I asked.

"They are ten kings who will rise from this empire. But then another king will arise, more brutal than the other ten, and will destroy three of them. He will defy the Most High God and persecute His followers, trying to change all laws and morals and customs. God's people will be helpless in his hands for three-and-a-half years."

Before my eyes grew a picture of persecution which was too terrible to believe. I did not want it to happen. And yet the final interpretation of my dream by this angel was so filled with hope!

"At the end of those three-and-a-half years the Ancient of Days will come and open His court of justice and take all power from this brutal king. His kingdom will be completely destroyed for all eternity."

The angel paused so that I could clearly understand and be able to record his last statement:

"Then every nation under heaven, and all their power, shall be given to the people of God; they shall rule all things forever, and all rulers shall serve and obey them."

And that was the end of my dream.

What Does It All Mean?

For the many days since I had my dream, I have remained in my rooms, pacing the floor, wondering about my own reason for existence. I have been thinking about the many years I served Nebuchadnezzar. (I still believe that I was given my position in his kingdom to be a witness for Jehovah.)

Nebuchadnezzar was a man who was able to recognize his own errors. I am convinced that late in his life he realized that the great image he built upon the Plain of Dura was a vain tribute to himself. But perhaps he had forgotten his dream of the fourfold statue with the head of gold and the weak feet of part iron and part clay. I have often wondered if he remembered the warning in that dream of the inevitable triumph of the kingdom of God.

But what about me? Have I lived in Babylon for so long that my own eyes have become clouded by pride of accomplishments and blinded by the affluence of my surroundings?

Have I become so anxious to live my moral convictions before men that I have failed to allow God to use me for His purpose? Perhaps this is the reason I have been ignored for so long in the administrative affairs of the province.

Even as I write, however, with the magnificent dream so fresh in my mind, I thank God that He has allowed me these years to study and pray. Daily, moment by moment, I have prayed for Him to use me. Forgive me, but there have been times when I have thought that He, too, was ignoring me. Now, I have begun to realize that my own pride has been separating me from serving the Lord God Jehovah with all my heart, soul, and mind.

Yesterday evening Jeshua came by to find out why I have not visited them. He found me weak from lack of food, but stronger than ever in my resolve to be a servant of the Lord, not a leader of men.

My attitude must have been puzzling to him.

"Daniel, you look terrible. What have you been eating? Why have you made yourself a recluse?" he said.

I tried to stand tall, the way I felt inside, but my body would not cooperate. "Jeshua, the Lord has shown me through a dream some astounding things. I have been spending my time writing them down, so I beg your forgiveness for not coming out."

He looked at me with curiosity. I was not sure whether he thought I was growing feeble-minded or whether what I said rang true to him. It seemed very important for me to make him understand.

"Whatever you have written can wait," Jeshua said. "Now you must have something to eat and change your clothes. There will be time then to hear about your dream."

His manner was a little patronizing, and I could not help chuckling. He could be my son, and he was treating me like a child. If he thought that my age had loosened my mind, he was wrong. I have never been more filled with spiritual hunger and eager for knowledge.

He brought me some bread and a broth made of lentils; it was like a feast, and I must admit it was easier to stand tall after partaking. We went outside to the garden of the courtyard where I had spent so many hours with my friends in years gone by. My simple living quarters have never changed since the days of Nebuchadnezzar. However, it has been sad to see the gardens go untended and the walls crumble.

"These gardens were once so lush and fragrant, Jeshua," I said. "What a pity that no one cares for them any more."

"Belshazzar is too busy collecting taxes and buying jewels for his women to appoint anyone to care for the gardens. The whole city is beginning to look shabby," Jeshua commented.

I sat on a marble bench, the very one where Deborah and I had spoken of love so many years ago. I lowered my head into my hands, and Jeshua respected the silence of the moment. But I could not contain my dream any longer.

"Jeshua," I said. "Sit beside me. I want this for your ears only. Please listen until I am finished, and then your questions may come."

Slowly, carefully, I told him the dream. I described each of the four beasts in detail, and when I came to the fourth beast Jeshua stood up and began to pace. He stooped and picked up an idol that had fallen from its niche in the wall and began to replace it. Then, almost compulsively, he flung it to the ground, cracking the stone into a dozen pieces.

"Stop!" he shouted. "This is too grotesque. How can you expect me to understand or interpret such a scene? You will be called a madman if you tell it to anyone else."

"I know, my young friend, but wait until I finish," I urged him.

"And then I saw something else," I continued. "It was not a view of earthly powers, but of the Ancient of Days, the Almighty God." My voice grew weak, I know, as I described the fiery throne brought in on flaming wheels, and the millions of angels surrounding Him.

As I told about the arrival of the one like a Man, coming in the clouds of heaven—the one who was given ruling power over all the nations—Jeshua interrupted me.

"Daniel," he said hurriedly, "how is it that you and Ezekiel see visions which are so similar? I have sat beside the Chebar Canal and heard him speak. He said that he saw someone who appeared to be a man, and that he was dazzling like fire and there was a glowing halo like a rainbow all around him."

"Ezekiel is a prophet, my son," I said.

"But the four beasts, what do they mean?"

"In my dream I approached one of the angels standing beside the throne and he explained them to me. They are four kingdoms who will rule the earth. But in the end the Most High God shall rule forever."

"I want to understand more," Jeshua said.

I smiled at his change. His manner had become no longer impatient and doubting, but eager.

"Ah, so you do not think I am a madman, then," I teased.

"Not me, but others may," he answered truthfully. "But go on. Who do you think the beasts may be?"

"I believe that the first beast may be Babylon, where we are right now. You have seen the winged lions that guard the gates of the royal palaces. Perhaps the man's heart given to the lion is that of Nebuchadnezzar."

"And the bear and the leopard?" he asked.

"I do not know. But they will arise to be powerful for a time, then be destroyed."

Jeshua leaned toward me eagerly. "Daniel, the fourth kingdom, what will that be?"

This is the kingdom I find agonizing to describe. It is so brutal, so unhuman, and yet so clever.

"This fourth world power will be on earth at the time of the end. It will produce a series of kings, but will ultimately be ruled by one who is different from all the others."

"Who is this king?" Jeshua asked.

"I don't know. But I was told what he would be like. He will be more cunning and clever than any evil ruler the world has ever known. He will be a great orator and will present a figure of great strength. But he will also be brutal, and for three-and-a-half years will establish a government that defies the Lord."

I had to stop there for a time. My very being mourned for the evil which can overpower God's great creation. I must have moaned, because Jeshua put his arms on my shoulders. "Are you ill?" he asked.

"I am ill with the realism of my dream. When I see the demonic forces that have invaded life—look around us—and know what destruction they can work in men and nations, I do become ill."

"But you said the Ancient of Days would overpower the vicious king and his kingdom. Does that not give us hope?"

"Yes, of course. But if we are the servants of the Lord God Jehovah, we must know what He wants us to do now—in this our present time."

Jeshua shook his head and patted my shoulder. The hint of the condescension had returned to his manner, and I began to wonder if I should have told him my dream.

He left me to go out into the dark. I promised that I would come to see his mother the next day. I needed to rest and allow sleep to give me clarity of thought. I needed to think and to write what you have just read.

But the night was not over.

I returned to my room and fell to my knees at the side of the bed. The floor was damp and I felt an ache in my bones. I am not young any longer, no matter how my mind wishes to ignore the fact. I prayed for what may have been hours. And the longer I prayed, the more insignificant I felt in the presence of the Most High God.

The night became colder and I continued to pray. Then from my childhood study of the great prophet Isaiah came the words of a great promise. I stumbled through the verses, repeating them out loud to the silent walls:

> Comfort, oh, comfort my people, says your God. . . . Shout that man is like the grass that dies away, and all his beauty fades like dying flowers. . . . The grass withers, the flowers fade, but the Word of our God shall stand forever.
>
> O Crier of Good News, shout to Jerusalem from the mountain tops! Shout louder—don't be afraid—tell the cities of Judah, "Your God is coming!" Yes, the Lord God is coming with mighty power.

I could feel the tears on my face. I wanted to shout myself, "Yes, I have been told in my dream. . . . Do not despair, my people; God has not forsaken you."

I pushed myself to my feet. More words from Isaiah swept my memory: "He gives power to the tired and worn out, and strength to the weak."

In spite of the hours in a cramped position, my body surged with new energy. I must tell them, I thought; I must tell my people of my dream, of the final triumph of the Mighty God and the Son of Man. I must tell them now!

My lamp had long since burned out; my room was as dark as a starless night in the desert. But then I felt the Presence, the Light, and heard the Voice. He spoke to me as He had before, not in audible tones, but with unmistakable clarity.

"Daniel, Daniel, My beloved son, there is more I shall reveal to you. You are not able to record everything at once. You are My prophet and will speak of great things to come. In My timing. But for now, tell no one what you have seen."

"But, Jeshua, Lord, I have told Jeshua."

"He will not be able to recall the dream. He has forgotten, Daniel, until the right season. And you shall be used to influence his future."

The Light faded and the Voice was silent. I fell upon my bed in a deep sleep.

I have recorded in this book what I have seen, so I will not forget. However, now I must go forth, to visit Deborah, to take care of my business in the city. But I will obey the Word of the Lord; I will tell no one in Babylon about my dream.

10

A VISIT FROM GABRIEL

THE DAYS OF MY YEARS are passing swiftly, as they did when I was a boy. Although I am willing to continue in the service of King Belshazzar, the assignments I am given are menial. In many ways I am grateful, for these tasks leave me more time to visit my people, and particularly to be of service to Deborah. She is weakening so rapidly.

My life seems suspended, waiting for I know not what. The older I get, the more I remember of what my father taught me. He used to tell me, "Solomon said, 'Listen, and grow wise.' Many times you are too anxious to question and not quiet enough to wait upon the Lord for answers."

I am waiting, Lord.

The Street of Merchants is a bustling place, filled with small shops and stalls of goods from the caravans of the merchants. The cloth woven by the craftsmen of Babylon is known for its beauty and intricate design throughout the Fertile Crescent, and our people have learned how to become sellers as well as buyers of many of the artistic achievements of the province. Rugs, tapestries, fine cloth for the garments of the rich are bought and traded in lively—sometimes heated—bargaining.

At the far end of this road is the house of Aaron, the place of warmth and happiness that I have visited for so many years. However, it is very quiet these days. The voices of laughter have been silenced, and even the one servant left in the household walks softly through the rooms.

Yesterday I took a basket of figs and apricots to tempt Deborah's appetite. She has never recovered from Aaron's death, and bitterness toward Belshazzar has poisoned her soul. I knocked on her door and Ramach, a Chaldean girl Jeshua hired to care for his mother, showed me in. (How much the Hebrews have advanced to be able to hire a Babylonian as a servant!) Ramach led me to the room of her mistress, who was stretched on her bed with her eyes closed, although it was early in the evening. She is so frail, lying on her bed for most of the day, without the energy to leave the house.

Deborah stirred when I came in and opened her eyes, looking at me with little recognition. "Jeshua?" she said weakly.

"It's Daniel, Deborah," I said, taking her thin hand and rubbing warmth into it.

"Of course, it's Daniel. Do you know where Jeshua is? I am worried about him. Ever since he decided not to marry Rachel, I fear"—and at this point Deborah became quite upset—"that he has been consorting with women who practice fortune-telling." She pressed her hand against her head and groaned. "He told me the other day that he believed the sign under which he was born determined his destiny. Signs . . . omens . . . they surround us."

Deborah leaned back in her pillow, spent with emotion.

Most of our conversations these days center around her concern for her son. She gestured for me to sit closer, and spoke in a conspiratorial tone. "Daniel, tell me the truth," she whispered, asking again the question which has plagued her conscience for so long, "Have I been right in not telling Jeshua the reason for his father's banishment?"

I answered, as I always have, "Deborah, the Lord has forgiven Aaron for his sins; you have forgiven him. What purpose would be accomplished by telling his son? It would only add more plague to his soul."

She seemed to relax, but it was unfortunate that Jeshua took that moment to make his appearance. I noticed that his eyes lingered too long on the servant girl. He came to Deborah's bedside, resplendent in a new purple tunic, looking more than ever like the Arioch

I knew many years ago. He sat down on the edge of the bed and stroked his mother's head.

"Do you have pain, good mother?" he asked. "Your eyes look so troubled."

Deborah nodded her head, and Jeshua said the very words that could not have been more inappropriate at that moment. He put his hand upon her forehead and began to speak—or rather I should say chant: "Let the evil demon leave. Let the demons strike at each other. May the good spirit enter your body."

Those are the words used by the Chaldean priests in rites of exorcism.

Oh, Jeshua, I thought, *if you wanted to soothe your mother, you said the worst thing.*

Poor little Deborah began to cough and could not stop. Jeshua ran for some water, and after she had quieted she waved us away. Her strength had ebbed.

Jeshua and I stepped into the next room to speak in hushed tones, so we would not disturb her.

"Jeshua," I said. "Your mother has been telling me of her concern for you. She believes you have grown away from your Hebrew upbringing."

He turned his face from me and watched Ramach, who was shaping barley bread loaves on a low table near the clay stove. He had quickly become defensive, as we are prone to do when confronted with a truth. But I knew I had to speak to him, regardless of his reaction. I love this young man as I would my own son.

Jeshua kicked a stone with the toe of his gold sandal and avoided my eyes. Obviously, he did not want to answer.

"Tell me, Jeshua, did you not hear the warnings God gave to Ezekiel about polluting ourselves like the nations that serve gods of wood and stone?"

"I heard," he muttered, while looking outside to the street where his father had been killed.

I continued, not knowing whether what I said would penetrate his attitude. I prayed that Jehovah would give me the right words. "Ezekiel said that the Lord God will bring His people out from the lands where they are scattered . . . and into the desert judgment hall. There He will judge them, just as He did in the wilderness after He brought His people out of Egypt. He will purge the rebels, and they will not enter Israel from the land of exile."

"Ezekiel said a lot of things that cannot be proven. There are many who believe the Jews will never be returned from exile." Jeshua frowned and rubbed his hand through his copper hair. (I could not help smiling at that gesture—it reminded me so of his father.)

"What about you, Daniel; are you beginning to doubt?" Jeshua asked. He folded his arms and watched me carefully.

"God's people will return to Jerusalem," I said. "All that Ezekiel has said will come true, because he is a prophet of God. And everything, my son, whether the present generation understands or not, will happen as the prophets say."

"I need proof, here and now—not some vague future happening," Jeshua said. "I heard Ezekiel talk about a valley full of old, dry bones that would live and breathe again. He said that the bones represented the tribes of Israel and Judah—joined together to make one nation and back in their land. Can you believe that?"

I could see that argument, even reason, would not touch Jeshua at this time. He is too full of doubt, of anger against the injustice of the world. And yet I feel that God will use my young friend for His purposes. Although there are many who see the wrath of God against evil or experience the love of God in His forgiveness, there are only a few who realize that He has a sense of humor. He chooses the most unlikely people for His great plans.

"Jeshua," I said. "Someday you may understand the reasons why things occur as they do. Trust in God and He will direct you."

He threw his cloak around him and walked to the doorway, his face a mask of defiance. "I respect you, Daniel, for all you have meant to our family, but I think your ideas are for times past," he said. "This is not ancient Israel; we are living in modern Babylon. It is a new era, and the old ways are no longer practical."

He left the house with an attitude of urgency—for what purposes, I do not know.

I watched him leave and remembered the proverbs of Solomon. What was that one? . . . oh yes: "Young man, do not resent it when God chastens and corrects you, for His punishment is proof of his love. Just as a father punishes a son he delights in to make him better, so the Lord corrects you."

But then, I must not tell an ancient proverb to Jeshua. That, after all, was written hundreds of years ago, and this is modern Babylon!

I made sure the servant girl was watching Deborah, then returned to my rooms. I was tired and needed to rest before going about some meaningless task which had been assigned to me for today.

But there was no rest for me last night.

A Vision of Horror:

There is no way to thoroughly interpret what I am to record here—except in future times, when those who read my journal will understand what the Lord meant.

It has been two years since my dream of the four beasts and the four kingdoms. Already I can see that the first great kingdom, Babylon, is beginning to crumble. A great king of Persia, Cyrus, has formed an alliance with a king of the Medians and their combined armies are ravishing nations surrounding Babylon. Perhaps even now my dream is being fulfilled.

And then yesterday afternoon, after returning from the house of Aaron, I had this vision, which I record with quaking hand.

I had returned to my room and sat upon my bed to remove my sandals. I cannot remember any physical or emotional warning, but suddenly everything around me changed! I was in a strange palace beside a river. I looked about and recognized the location, for many years before I had been sent to the province of Elam, about two hundred miles east of Babylon, on an assignment for Nebuchadnezzar. Later, my friend Shadrach had been made governor there. *I must be in Susa, the capital of the province,* I thought.

The architecture of the palace I saw was not Babylonian, however, but built upon a more open scale of courtyards and rooms than the security-minded Babylonians would build.

I stood looking around with curiosity at these strange surroundings, and then I saw a ram with two long horns standing on the river bank. As I watched, fascinated by this animal, one of the horns began to grow and became longer than the other.

Other animals appeared and the ram butted them out of his way, leaving them dead and bleeding on the ground.

(Our Hebrew word for ram means "to be in front," and a flock of sheep moves with the strongest male in front. So the ram in the dream could represent human leaders or kings.)

While I was wondering what this meant, a buck goat appeared from the west. It moved so fast its feet did not touch the ground, and had one very large horn between its eyes. This goat charged furiously at the ram and broke off both its horns. The ram fell to the ground, helpless, and the buck goat trampled upon him triumphantly.

There seemed to be nothing to challenge that goat. I stood, transfixed by this scene before my eyes, mentally storing every detail.

The buck goat pranced around, its head high and arrogant, proud of his strength and power. But suddenly, his horn broke off; it fell to the ground and turned to dust, and in its place grew four more horns pointing in four directions. Again, one of these horns grew stronger than the others. It attacked the south and the east and warred against the land of Israel.

(At this point in my vision the appearance of these domestic creatures became more human than animal.)

The horn which had grown stronger fought the people of God and defeated some of their leaders. He was despicable, attacking the center of Hebrew worship and canceling the ritual worship of daily sacrifices. He polluted and defiled God's holy sanctuary.

How could this be? I wondered. If God allowed this to happen, it appeared to me that evil had triumphed.

Then I saw that standing nearby were some angels I had not noticed before. Evidently they had been viewing this same scene, for I heard one say to the other with great concern, "How long will it be until the daily sacrifice is restored again? How long until the destruction of the Temple is avenged and God's people triumph?"

The other answered, "Twenty-three hundred days must first go by."

I listened, but did not understand the meaning of this vision. I wanted to speak with the angels, but in this vision I didn't have the same boldness that I had two years before, when I asked the angel in my dream about the meaning of the four beasts from the sea.

Perhaps I have learned something in all my years about waiting for God to speak to me in His time. However, I did not expect to meet the next holy visitor as quickly as I did.

But suddenly he was standing in front me. He looked like a man, but I could not be sure. Then I heard a voice calling from across the river. It was deep and resonant; the sound carried across the distance like a whisper in a silent room.

"Gabriel," the Voice said, "tell Daniel the meaning of his dream."

I looked for the Voice, but saw no one. Then I looked at Gabriel, whose very name means "hero of God," and I was speechless, in awe before one of such holiness. He started to walk toward me, and his presence was too much for me to bear. How could I, a mere mortal, dare to stand before a holy angel?

I fell down with my face to the ground. Gabriel came closer, and I could feel a touch upon my head—so light, and yet so real. My entire body began to tremble.

The angel Gabriel said, "Son of man, you must understand that the events you have seen in your vision will not take place until the end times come."

Then my head swirled in confusion and everything became black; I must have lost consciousness.

The next thing I knew, a gentle, firm hand was shaking me lightly and helping me to my feet. Gabriel stood a pace apart from me, his face serious but compassionate. "I am here, Daniel," he said, "to tell you what is going to happen in the last days of the coming time of terror—for what you have seen pertains to that final event in history."

It is awesome to record that I was given another view of God's plan. I pray that every detail will remain precise in my memory.

Then he told me that the two horns of the ram represent the kings of Media and Persia; the haired goat represents the nation of Greece and its long horn is a picture of the first great king of that country. I think he will be very fast in establishing his leadership, because the buck goat seemed to fly upon the scene.

Gabriel explained that the long horn's breaking off represented the death of that first great king of Greece, who will be replaced by four kings, none of them as great as he.

Next, I knew, the angel would tell me of the one who would attack my people, who would war against the land of Israel. I did not want to hear. But Gabriel continued, his voice steady and sure, making the announcement, as he had been told by the Voice, in language most precise.

"Toward the end of their kingdoms," he said, "when they have decayed morally a king of fierce countenance shall rise in power. He will be a shrewd man, of astounding intelligence. He will gain power by trickery and diplomacy, but his rise will not come by his own power and strength, but by satanic force.

"For a time, this fierce king will prosper and advance. Everyone who opposes him will be destroyed, no matter how strong their armies may be. He will destroy the mighty and the holy people; he will devastate God's people."

My mind tried to comprehend this man; the immensity of his evil turned my flesh to cold marble.

"He will be a master of deception, causing many to bask in false security. Then he will destroy them without warning."

While Gabriel spoke, I stood facing him, immobile and silent. He went on, "This evil king will believe he is so great that he will even take on the Prince of Princes in battle. However, by so doing he will seal his own doom, for he shall be broken by the hand of God, though no human means could overpower him."

I remembered the Rock cut from the mountain without human hands which, in Nebuchadnezzar's dream, had crushed the kingdoms represented by the statue of gold, silver, brass, and iron. This wild and angry ruler, driven by demonic forces, and yet so clever that he could deceive people into a peaceful lull, could not be brought to an end by human means. Only a nonhuman hand will be able to break his power.

Gabriel finished and stood looking at me. He seemed to be listening to something, although this time I heard nothing. I looked across the river but saw no one. The entire scene was one of grandeur, with the palace resplendent beside the river, the sky cloudless and clear. Even the birds and the animals were silent.

When Gabriel finally spoke, he said, "None of these things will happen for a long time, so do not tell anyone about them yet."

And then he was gone.

Once more I was standing in my room. Everything was the same. My chest was against the wall, holding the few clothes I own. The brazier was lit, throwing warmth and light into the corners. My sandals were on the floor, where I had discarded them a few minutes (or was it hours or days) before. The sounds of the voices of Babylon outside my simple quarters were deafening to my ears—I heard the crier calling news of a runaway slave, people arguing, children playing. The yelp of a dog and the clatter of hooves upon stones blended in with the chant of a priest. Voices.

But I had heard a voice from one of the hosts of heaven. And he had told me to tell no one.

I felt the room swirl around me and staggered to my bed, growing faint and weak. Why did I feel so depressed?

Since then I have stayed in my room, praying, thinking of what I had seen in this vision, contemplating the state of my life. I have developed over my lifetime in Babylon a superficial sense of well-being and happiness. I have been honored, respected, and—yes—hated, too. My friends have been many, and my enemies have been silenced by influence in high places. However, now I have deep, unanswered questions that are making me more sensitive to the rights and wrongs of history and giving me a greater burden for the victims of life's tragedies.

Even as I write this, I can relate to the writer of Ecclesiastes, who said: "So I worked hard to be wise instead of foolish—but now I realize that even this was like chasing the wind. For the more my wisdom, the more my grief; to increase knowledge only increases distress."

I feel I am near a greater truth, and it frightens me.

No Time to Waste:

Since I last wrote in this journal, I have been up and back to the king's business. Brooding is for old men, and I have not yet reached fourscore years. There is much to be done.

Belshazzar has need of me, although my services go unnoticed by him. My duties remain assignments of inconsequence, but I perform them to the best of my ability.

Yesterday evening, when the heat of the day had softened—a time when the people of our faith were beginning to prepare for Passover—I hastened to the house of Aaron to be with Deborah. It is fortunate that my job is not too taxing upon my brain, for I have much to contemplate, and these times of being with Deborah are important. She enjoys my sitting by her bedside and talking of Jerusalem. Sometimes she opens her eyes and smiles a bit, patting my hand to let me know that she understands what I am saying.

"Why do you bother to talk to her of returning to Jerusalem?" Jeshua asks when he overhears my rambling remembrances.

"Because it gives her pleasure . . . and hope, my son," I tell him. "And we must keep alive the promises of God." I knew when I said these things that Jeshua would bristle. He is stubborn, like his father was.

"No one will see Jerusalem again . . . and why would they want to? Do we want to leave all this and go to a pile of rubble?"

How I want to reach him, to break his hardness and make him see the glory of the Lord God Jehovah. But I cannot. I have been hearing more and more of his activities, and they grieve me, as I know they would grieve his mother if she were alert enough to know.

"Yes, my son," I answered him. "Most of our people would gladly give up the pleasures of Babylon to return."

He shrugged his shoulders, and I knew he did not want this conversation to continue. I tried to hold his eyes, to look into his thoughts with the unwavering gaze which Arioch—I mean Aaron—used to turn on me. However, he would not look directly at me. He has enough conscience to know guilt, but not enough faith to understand God's love.

He sat down beside me, staring at the frail form of his mother. His face had begun to look florid—puffy with too much drink and rich foods. His flesh was no longer taut as a charioteer's. How ravaging the ways of loose living can be on the mind and body!

"Tell me, Jeshua," I said, trying to find a common ground of communication, "is there any more news of the seizure of merchants coming into the city? I have heard that the Medes and Persians have many troops surrounding Babylon."

He reached for the wine goblet we keep beside Deborah's bed to give her occasional sips for stimulation, and drank it dry.

"The fools. They camp about our walls and harass the caravans. They are but puny before our fortress." He stopped and walked to the window, staring toward the gigantic walls with their taller towers, manned by the king's army of strongest youths. "No weapon can fly that high. It would take sixty tall men, all standing on each other's shoulders, to reach the top." He laughed at his own conjecture. "No ladder could be used to scale that wall; nor is there a battering ram with the power to break in."

And I remembered the words of the prophet Isaiah: "He dooms the great men of the world and brings them all to naught. They hardly get started, barely take root, when he blows on them and their work withers and the wind carries them off like straw."

"Like straw houses in the wind," I muttered.

"What did you say?" Jeshua asked.

"I was just thinking that if He chooses the Lord could bring those walls down like straw houses," I said.

Jeshua sighed, as if placating an old man. "Even now the Persians parade around with their huge banners that have pictures of rams on them. And I am told that the king of Persia, instead of the diadem, wears the head of a ram."

I saw again in my mind's eye the vision of the ram beside the river. The time for Babylon was short, and I was anxious to know what the Lord wanted me to do.

I amuse myself. How can one be so old, so long in His service, and still be impatient? How often I have to say to myself, "Wait upon the Lord, Daniel . . . wait!"

The mixture of beauty and sadness in the next few moments I shall record are like honey and bitter herbs in my mouth.

Deborah opened her eyes and let out a cry. Jeshua and I rushed to her side to hear her say, "It is so beautiful. Yes, Lord, yes, I am coming. Aaron, wait for me."

She closed her eyes, her face relaxed . . . the lines of pain faded, and in their place was serenity and joy.

How can I explain the loss of my first love . . . the woman I know could never be mine? The Lord had shown me clearly His way for me, and I have no regrets. In her place He gave me a family: Aaron, my friend and my brother; Jeshua, the son I would never have; Deborah, my sister, my confidante, my dear and cherished one.

Jeshua and I allowed our tears to mix. For all of his rebellion, he is a man who loved and respected his family. We sat by her bed for a long time. He leaned his head against my chest and gave way to low sobs. I remembered a small boy many years ago, in the hills of Judah, listening to his father cry in the still of the night. Strange that remembrances of childhood return when we are old. I embraced Jeshua, my son, and shared the grief of earthly loss.

The bodies of Deborah and Aaron have been buried in a common tomb. She was a woman greatly beloved throughout the Judean Quarter for her sweet and generous spirit. But the days of mourning must end, and I must be on with my work.

It is difficult to go about my daily tasks these days. I keep remembering the vision at Susa. It would seem that the Lord God Jehovah keeps directing His prophecies toward this great, evil ruler who will arise in the time of the end.

I do not understand the vision. Even the interpretation of angels is to no avail. I know I am not meant to completely understand now. I must write these things for future generations, for those He knows before they are born, and has scheduled each day of their lives before they begin to breathe.

Let me be known now as the Recorder.

I had just finished the above words when my door was shaken by a loud banging. A messenger, his face covered with sweat and panting from the urgency of his orders, rushed through his words.

"Daniel, hurry, you are wanted at once. King Belshazzar, long may he live, has sent me to summon you to the hall of the great feast."

Why was I being invited? I did not want to go to the feast of Belshazzar, but was in his service and would obey his summons.

I prayed for God's wisdom and strength, pulled my cloak around me, noticing how thin and shabby it had become—hardly befitting a visit to the king.

But it did not matter. No one in the palace that night had any interest in what I was wearing.

11

FEAST OF DISASTER

LATE AT NIGHT, after receiving the summons from the king, I rushed along the familiar corridors of the palace, guided in the dark by a slave holding an oil lamp to guide me. I knew that at that very hour Darius, king of the Medes and general of the combined forces, was in charge of the army outside the gates. Cyrus, king of Persia, was close behind, not knowing that he and his ally were fulfilling the prophecies of Isaiah made over two hundred years ago. Jeremiah had foretold the same events—and also I, Daniel, through whom God first spoke of these things over sixty years ago.

Will people continue to ignore the words the Lord gives to His prophets?

At the time when I was approaching the great hall, which was ominously quiet behind its heavy bronze door, the soldiers of the Medes and Persians were diverting the waters of the Euphrates and walking along the dry river bed toward the river gate.

No barrier erected by man can restrain God's timing of events.

The great celebration had been in progress at the palace for many hours before I arrived. I had chosen not to accept the first invitation, which had gone out to every official in the kingdom, for it was a time when all the sons and daughters of Israel were preparing for our most important feast—the Feast of the Passover. The day was just before the fourteenth of Nisan, and we were praying and fasting. Except for Jeshua, unfortunately. He was at the despicable Feast of Pleasure.

However, I am grateful for his presence there, because those hours changed his life. He has described for me what took place before I arrived. Let his account stand as the record until the time I entered the banquet hall:

JESHUA'S STORY:

As I write down what I saw in the great throne room on the night of the thirteenth of Nisan, my guilt and shame must be poured out on these pages. However, I shall not ask for sympathy from the readers of Daniel's journal. Whatever they may think of me and my involvement in the happenings of that evening, I deserve their scorn.

From the time of my father's death—and I believe he was deliberately murdered—my hatred of the Babylonians was like the festering sores of leprosy. At first it was just barely noticeable, but as the months went by I became more and more poisoned with hate. I plotted for revenge, but I did not know what form it could take. Before my dear mother closed her eyes for eternal sleep she would say, "You are becoming hard, Jeshua. Do not hate."

She knew me well.

I began to be more and more involved with Babylonian society—drinking with the nobles of the court and indulging in their pleasures. I ate their food, paid lip service to their gods, and slept with their women. My soul had become so twisted that I thought by becoming one of them I would find the way to destroy them.

Instead, I was destroying myself.

When I was invited to the king's celebration, I accepted readily. Although it was a time when good Hebrews were preparing for the Passover, I ignored those preparations. Leaving the house of Aaron, which was my inheritance, and drawing my cloak about my face so the elders might not recognize me, I hastened to the palace.

It was early in the evening when I arrived. The smells of the immense hall were the first to assault my senses. Hundreds of bowls of incense burned, producing an odor so strong that at first my throat hurt. It was not the spicy-sweet scent of myrtle that my people use at feast time, but the heavy, mind-changing gall, juice of the poppy flower.

Row after row of low tables were heaped with meat and food of every kind and surrounded by cushions, upon which hundreds of the Babylonian men from every province of the land lounged amidst lavish splendor. Slaves brought in trays faster than the food could be consumed; soon it was spilling on the floor to be trampled by the constantly moving crowd. No one cared. The wine was plentiful and the jugs were refilled before they had been emptied.

Someone grabbed my arm and pulled me to a cushion. "You are standing in the way, whoever you are."

An old man, his speech slurred and his watery eyes darting around the room, shoved a goblet in my hand. "Here, fill your belly."

"I am Jeshua, from the house of Aaron," I said, not wishing to be "whoever you are."

The old man squinted at me and let out a cackling laugh. Wine stained his dirty grey beard. "House of Arioch," he said scornfully. "I am not too drunk to forget him. I was an overseer in the court of Nebuchadnezzar when he was exiled."

I stared at him in disbelief. Could this wine-sopped imbecile give me a clue to the mysteries which had plagued my life? Why had my father been banished from the court of Babylon? Why did he live in the Judean Quarter, as an exile among the Hebrews? I blamed him for giving me the heritage of two worlds, not knowing where I belonged.

I did not feel that I had to pay respect to this man, although he was my elder. I took him by the shoulders and began to shake him. "Tell me what you know," I shouted.

He shrieked for help, and I believe in the state I was in I might have killed him except that two muscular Syrian slaves grabbed my arms and pinned them behind me. I knew that it was useless to question the old man then, because he had lost consciousness and was dragged to the side of the room and shoved against a wall. I watched his exit with pleasure, trying to keep my eyes upon his form in case he regained his senses.

My arms were released and I fell back on the cushion. Then I had a chance to observe Belshazzar. He sat on an elaborate golden throne, with massive carved arms which bore the heads of the lion, symbol of Babylon. His robe was brocaded with gold and purple peacocks, and over his head was a canopy of rich silks, which I am sure must have cost thousands of shekels. He looked around the room with eyes which were beginning to narrow, his head swiveling about like that of a snake turning side to side to look for his victims. Then he raised his hand, and a hush fell over the room.

"My honored guests," he began. He pushed himself up, holding his goblet high above his head. "A toast to Babylon the great!" he shouted, and brought his drink to his mouth, its red liquid pouring down his black, waved beard and beginning to stain the front of his tunic.

"To Babylon the great!" echoed hundreds of voices in response.

He raised his hand again and the men quieted once more. But Belshazzar just grinned lopsidedly and lolled back on his throne. The celebration resumed.

We had been eating and drinking for more than three hours when the king signaled for more entertainment. He clapped his hands three times; all the side doors were flung open and hundreds of women poured into the hall.

The men shouted and laughed. It was not customary for their wives and concubines to be allowed at such parties. However, there was no objection to their arrival—nor to the presence of certain women who were neither wives nor concubines. It was then that the orgy began.

Musicians played enticing strains, some as soft as winds in the woods, and others as shrill as fifes. Singers sang songs of the might and power of the kingly host under his shimmering canopy, while Belshazzar clapped his hands like a child playing a game.

Dancers appeared, men and women, weaving back and forth, body pressed against body, until their sexual gestures reached a fever pitch and they fell to the floor, writhing sensually.

Hours passed; there seemed to be no end to the erotic pleasures offered to the guests. Soon men and women lost all inhibitions. Kisses turned to caresses as their forms melted together. Few were bothered with watching Belshazzar until a cymbal was hit and he stood once more. This time he was difficult to understand. But then we saw what he was doing and understood the shocking significance of this profane act. . . .

Nebuchadnezzar had decreed that no one should desecrate the holy vessels taken from the Temple in Jerusalem. They had been stored in the great museum behind the palace and never touched for over forty-eight years. But now, at the sound of the gong, ten servants, each carrying a tray laden with the holy vessels, approached the throne and laid the treasures at Belshazzar's feet. Two great golden lampstands with seven branches were placed behind him at each side, fitted with candles, and lit. I sucked in my breath, knowing that these might have been the very ones that had stood in front of the Holy of Holies in the Temple.

Then Belshazzar had the slaves spread the flagons, chargers, basins, goblets, trays, and dishes in front of him. The dust of years had been washed off, and all the vessels were piled high with food or filled with wine. These sacred treasures had been honored by all the monarchs of Babylon since Nebuchadnezzar. That Belshazzar would dare to use them in such a degrading fashion was beyond imagining.

Belshazzar made another toast. He said, "Tonight I am honoring myself, Belshazzar, king of Babylon. Long may I live!" He laughed hysterically and raised the wine to his lips. The people gasped. This was the ultimate in blasphemy!

He drank from a golden goblet, that a high priest in the Temple would have used. And he laughed again like a drunken clown, looking around with a smirk which seemed to say, "Look, I've done it!" No one had ever dared such an act before!

"Such boldness! Praise Belshazzar," someone shouted.

The crowd broke into cheers, the music began, and the feasting continued. Soon flesh blurred into flesh. Many lost consciousness and were pushed into the corners to collapse like corpses or gag in their own vomit.

I knew I was defiling the name of the house of Aaron by remaining, but I was drawn by the licentious atmosphere like a moth to a candle. I watched this wild scene, allowing myself to condone the evil around me by my presence, without an objection.

But then something snapped in the depths of my soul. I pushed a woman from my lap and stood up, sick with what I was doing and crying to God to take me out of this hell. I knew how King David must have felt when he said, "I am a worm, and not a man."

I began to stagger through the crowd, stepping around the prostrate forms and the filth. No words can describe the obscenity of that scene; I was desperate to escape.

Suddenly all sounds in the hall were hushed. The music stopped, the voices ceased. It was as if the rush of an angry river had turned immediately into a frozen mass of ice. I had been walking away from the direction of the throne, heading for the nearest bronze door, when I stopped, turned around, and saw it.

Behind Belshazzar the flames from the candles had blackened the plaster. And against that wall floated the immense fingers of a man's hand, writing bold, high letters. Those eerie fingers moved slowly, methodically, spelling out four strange words.

As that great bodiless hand floated in midair, the silence was like a paralysis. We watched, frozen into a bizarre tableau. Then gasps were heard and moans of fear. I felt the chords of my throat tighten.

The king's face was white; he fell against the back of the throne, staring at the moving fingers. His arms were outstretched at his sides and all signs of drunkenness were gone. The silence was shattered with his scream. Swaying in his golden robes, bracelets rattling on his wrists, he began to shriek, "Bring the magicians and astrologers! Bring the wisemen and the soothsayers!" The hand vanished as quickly as it had appeared, and wild noises of fright filled the hall.

In recounting this story after the fact, I am now able to smile at the irony of that command. The magicians Belshazzar summoned had never been able to interpret dreams and visions before, so what made him think they could do it now? However, he believed—as do most men in power—that the proper inducement would bring forth the desired results.

He made the prize very desirable. He said, "Whoever reads the writing on the wall . . . and tells me what it means . . . will be dressed in purple robes of royal honor with a gold chain around his neck." Then he paused and searched for a greater reward. Then he added, "And he will be made third ruler in the kingdom!"

(His father, Nabonidus, his coregent, was the first in the kingdom. Belshazzar was second. And whoever interpreted the writing would be next in command after these two. What a promotion that would be!)

I wanted to leave, but I could not. Whether it was morbid curiosity, fear, or the will of Jehovah that held me there, I do not know.

The wisemen clustered around the king, staring at the wall and babbling. They shook their heads, rubbed their hands together, and looked at each other helplessly.

The king became frenzied, beating on the chests of his soothsayers and astrologers and shouting, "You are fools . . . idiots . . . your minds are empty. I swear by Anu and Enlil and Ishtar and Marduk that I will have your tongues on a platter. Demons will possess your souls and turn your children to animals!"

He raved until he could think of no more obscenities and then sank to the floor, weeping and banging his fists.

Wine and fear overtaking their emotions, desperate to escape from the scene, the guests at the feast seemed ready to break into mob violence. They pushed each other, stepped on bodies, scrambled to reach the doors.

Then the queen mother arrived. She swept into the great hall, holding her head high and lifting her tunic so it would not touch the filthy floor. Her eyes took in the sight and her face reflected disgust. As she stood before the giant letters on the wall, her veil fell from her head and the copper color of her hair shone against the blackened wall. Her arrival provided the calming influence needed at that moment. Most of the people began to quiet, waiting to see what she would do.

I moved closer. I wanted to hear what this woman would say. I had admired her for a long time; she was a woman of honor, one who had been present when her father had become a believer in the Lord God Jehovah. Daniel respected her and had told me about her secret devotion to the one God. At times, when I had seen her from afar riding in her royal chariot, copper hair flying, I had felt a strange bond with her—that of two humans with a physical trait so unlike most others.

What a pity that this magnificent woman should have a son like Belshazzar.

I was close enough to hear her say to Belshazzar, in tones of authority tinged with scorn, "Calm yourself, your Majesty. Stand up and conduct yourself like a king."

Belshazzar looked at his mother, wiped his face with the back of his hand, and was silent.

Queen Nitocris continued, "There is a man in your kingdom who has within him the spirit of the holy gods. In the days of your grandfather this man was found to be as full of wisdom and understanding as though he were himself a god. Nebuchadnezzar made him chief of all the magicians, astrologers, and soothsayers."

The king nodded. He knew whom she was describing, although he had chosen to ignore his advice during his reign.

"Call for this man, Daniel," the queen continued. "His mind is filled with divine knowledge. He can interpret dreams, explain riddles, and solve knotty problems." She paused to look again at the wall. "He will tell you what the writing means," she said with assurance.

Oh, no, I thought, Daniel will see me here. I was sick with guilt, but nevertheless I lingered in the hall. When the people heard that Daniel was summoned, they stayed. Like me, they wanted to know the meaning of the handwriting. We waited and spoke few words. The supernatural evidence of the moving fingers was too mysterious and frightening even to discuss.

It seemed like an eternity before Daniel came.

SCENE OF SHAME:

When I, Daniel, arrived at the great hall, I was chilled from the walk through the palace compound so late at night. It was difficult to follow the messenger, for my step was not as fast as his, and he was urging me to hurry.

I wanted to hold my hand over my nose and mouth when we entered the great hall. It was a human picture of the depths of Sheol. Men and women were partially dressed, standing or sitting in a stupor, their eyes glazed and frightened. A way was cleared for me to approach the king, and I looked neither to the right nor the left as I made my way toward the throne. Belshazzar seized my arm as I stepped up on the platform; I could feel his hand shaking as he gripped me.

The king looked at me through reddened eyes and asked, "Are you the Daniel that King Nebuchadnezzar brought from Israel as a Jewish captive?"

I nodded.

He chose his words carefully, trying not to slur them. Queen Nitocris stood close by, and as she looked at me I caught the glance of understanding which said she remembered when I taught her the things of the Lord. Her eyes were filled with love. We had shared the secret of her birth for many years.

"I have heard that you have the spirit of the gods within you," Belshazzar said, "and that you are filled with enlightenment and wisdom." He hesitated, his eyes grew wild, and he gestured to the wall behind him.

"Look at it, Daniel . . . a bodiless hand wrote those words." He paused, licked his lips, and continued. "My wisemen and astrologers, sniveling fools, cannot read the writing. But I am told that you can solve all kinds of mysteries."

He pulled at his matted beard and said to me, "If you can tell me the meaning of those words, you shall have purple robes and a golden chain around your neck." Then he paused, wanting to offer the even greater bribe. "And you, Daniel, shall be made third ruler in the kingdom."

I did not want his gifts . . . nor the position. I told him so and he seemed astonished. However, this was the opportunity I had wanted for years. Perhaps in this entire, doomed place there would be some repentant hearts.

I spoke loud enough so all would hear. But I did not have to be concerned; the revelers were either quiet or unconscious. "Your Majesty, the Most High God gave Nebuchadnezzar a kingdom and majesty, glory, and honor. He gave him such majesty that all the nations of the world trembled before him in fear. He killed any who offended him, and spared any he liked. At his whim they rose or fell."

The queen mother stood with her head lowered, her eyes upon the floor, probably remembering the injustices of her father.

No one interrupted me. I continued with my story of the rise and fall of one who was the greatest ruler of his time.

"But when his heart and mind were hardened in pride, God removed him from his royal throne and took away his glory, and he was chased out of his palace into the fields."

The remembrance of those seven horrible years is still etched indelibly in my mind. There were many in that banquet room that night who had wanted the beast Nebuchadnezzar had become to be killed, but God had stayed their hands. For a reason.

"The thoughts and feelings of your grandfather, Nebuchadnezzar, became those of an animal; he ate grass like the cows and his body was wet with the dew of heaven, until at last he knew that the Most High overrules the kingdoms of men, and that He appoints anyone he desires to reign over them."

Belshazzar scowled as I spoke. He did not want to hear my sermon, but he could not avoid it. And now I spoke directly to him.

"And you, Belshazzar . . . Nebuchadnezzar's successor . . . you knew all this, yet you have not been humble."

I looked at the holy vessels from the Temple strewn about the platform. All these years they had been carefully stored. How dare he defile them in such a revolting way!

"Look at what you have done!" I swept my arm over the royal platform. "You brought here these cups from His Temple; and you and your officers and wives and concubines have been drinking wine from them while praising gods of silver, gold, brass, iron, wood, and stone—gods that neither see nor hear, nor know anything at all. But you have not praised the God who gives you the breath of life and controls your destiny!"

There was no shame upon Belshazzar's face; it was as hard as the marble of the floor and as immobile as the statues he worshiped. The muscles about his mouth began to twitch as he stared again at the handwriting on the wall.

"But what does it mean?" he said weakly.

My words had been sharp, but he had not heard them. Telling him again of the harsh discipline Nebuchadnezzar received from God had fallen upon deaf ears. Neither had he understood that his grandfather had been restored to his kingly power only when he had learned his lesson and humbled himself before God.

Belshazzar was not a young man. He might have profited by the experience of his years. But pride had blinded him and sin eroded his conscience.

I looked around at the human degradation surrounding me. God had judged His own people with destruction of their nation because they had mixed idolatry with their worship of Him. Could He be expected to spare this gentile reprobate for committing the same sin on a larger scale?

What is the true purpose of every man's existence? It is to glorify God. Belshazzar ignored me when I told him that truth.

"The words . . . the handwriting . . . what does it mean?" he repeated like a child asking, "Why?"

The words stood out boldly. I read them out loud. "MENE. MENE. TEKEL. PARSIN." They were Aramaic, the common language on the streets and courts of Babylon, and yet as written they were meaningless.

With the interpretation of each word, however, Belshazzar's face became more ashen.

"MENE means 'numbered'—God has numbered the days of your reign, and they are ended."

For the first time since I had arrived, the king sat down.

"TEKEL means 'weighed'—you have been weighed in God's balances and have failed the test.

"PARSIN means 'divided'—your kingdom will be divided and given to the Medes and the Persians."

I waited for the king to understand the significance of what I had said. He shrugged his shoulders and snapped his fingers for a servant. Within moments a purple robe was placed upon my shoulders, and a golden chain fastened around my neck. Belshazzar made a pronouncement, ironic and useless as it was:

"This man, Daniel, is the wisest man in Babylon. I proclaim him third ruler in the kingdom." He waved his scepter over my head and signaled for the music to resume.

Belshazzar was a condemned man in a doomed kingdom. I do not know of others in the room who believed what the Lord God Jehovah had revealed to me. But I do know of one. Jeshua.

Oh Jeshua, Jeshua! I knew you were in the room; I had seen you when I first entered, although you had averted your head and would not look at me. How I have prayed for you, Jeshua—loved you, felt the pain of your anguish. I knew, as your mother and father did, the secret they carried to their graves—the secret of why your father was banished. They didn't want you to know, believing as they did that this knowledge would not help your rebellious heart. They were your parents and I respected their wishes. But very soon, I sensed, you would know.

Slowly, as in a death march, the revelers left the great banquet hall. Some stopped to drag or half-carry their friends with them. Others covered their nakedness and slunk away in shame. Their hours, too, as free Babylonians, were numbered.

Jeshua stood before me, his face wet with unceasing tears. He fell to his knees on the steps leading to the throne, throwing his arms about my knees and pulling off the purple robe as he sobbed.

"Daniel, I have been wrong. Forgive me. I have known about your prophecy to King Nebuchadnezzar of the world power which would conquer Babylon. My father told me that you are a man chosen by God to be His Revealer. Oh, I believe it. I believe it. I have been a fool."

I pulled him to his feet and we embraced. At that moment I realized that there was someone else remaining in that room besides the unconscious ones on the floor. I turned and saw the queen mother, Nitocris, watching us.

Nitocris stared at Jeshua and he at her. They stood, face to face, on the night of that scene of human destruction, and discovered a truth they must have both suspected but dared not acknowledge. Now it did not matter. Babylon the great was broken.

I released Jeshua and he walked over to the queen. He, the son of a daughter of Judah and a banished son of Babylon; she, the illegitimate daughter of a queen and a court noble. Half brother and sister.

The hair, the bearing, the rumors and stories pieced together from whispers and lowered eyes—all resulted in this glad meeting on the eve of destruction.

"You are my brother," Nitocris said softly.

"My sister," murmured Jeshua, holding out his hands to her.

She reached out with her slender fingers, heavy with the rings of royalty, unstained by physical labor. Within moments, without shame, they embraced and cried and laughed with the recognition of the strange and mysterious ways in which God works in the lives of His children.

WITHIN THE GATES:

At that moment the troops of Cyrus and Darius were coming into the city, just as the Prophet Isaiah had said they would.

The conquest was without parallel in the military practice of conquerors. No columns of smoke rose behind shattered walls, no temples or palaces were razed to the ground, no houses were plundered, no men butchered or impaled. Later King Cyrus was to write:

"As I entered Babylon in peace and established my royal residence in the palace of the princes, Marduk, the great Lord, warmed the hearts of the Babylonians towards me."

On that fateful night, Belshazzar's scepter fell from his hand and broke upon the mosaic pavement; he collapsed near the shattered rod, a forlorn heap in golden cloth. One groan and he was gone, smitten by an unknown, but foreordained hand.

Belshazzar died in shame, and the glories of the Babylonian empire crumpled with him.

Jeshua and I walked into the darkness of the courtyard arm in arm . . . too exhausted to talk, too full of what we had seen and experienced to comment. We heard the rumbling of hundreds of feet upon the Processional Way. We stopped, not knowing whether to watch the march of the conquerors or not. "It is just as God has foretold, Jeshua. The world power which would conquer Babylon is at our doorsteps. The Medes and Persians are arriving to take the kingdom."

"Daniel, there is so much I must confess. Your prophecies have been accurate . . . and I thought Babylon would never fall!" Jeshua's words were those of a man with a contrite heart. But I knew there was more he must say, and I waited for him to tell me. I had not watched him grow to manhood without being sensitive to his spirit.

We touched the mezuzah at my entryway and entered my home. How long would this place where I had lived for scores of years be mine, I wondered.

"Daniel, I know of my father's sin. I have suspected for years the reason Nebuchadnezzar banished him, but I loved both my mother and father too much to tell them. Tonight, when I saw the queen mother Nitrocris, I knew my secret burden would be lifted."

"King David sinned greatly, Jeshua, and yet was able to say that the Lord was his light and his salvation. He was the same to your father, my son, and He is the same to you."

Jeshua sat on my reed chair, where he had spent so many hours as a youth, asking questions about life. It had been so long since he had asked my advice or confided in me, but this fateful night seemed to have changed that. He put his elbows on the table and held his head for a few moments. When he looked up it was with pleading eyes. Then he revealed to me an astounding secret.

"Daniel, I have a son. He is now five years old. His mother is Ramach, the servant girl. She bore me this boy before I hired her to care for my mother. He has been living with Ramach's relatives in a village on the outskirts of the city." He paused to see my reaction. I have lived too long and seen too much to be surprised by anything, but I must admit that this revelation left me speechless.

"I wish to have my son raised to know the Lord God Jehovah and learn from the wisest man I know, just as I learned as a child." Jeshua reached across the table and put his hand upon mine. "Daniel, so much has happened on this night. Are you able to take one more challenge upon your shoulders?"

"If the Lord chooses, Jeshua," I said, feeling younger than my four score and two years.

"May I bring Mishael to you to listen to your wisdom?"

My eyes grow misty so easily these days. I had not heard that name in years. "Mishael?" I said.

"I named him that after hearing my mother tell of your three friends. I did not want him to have a Babylonian name." Jeshua looked relieved, almost refreshed, although the night had been the most difficult one of his life.

I had been unprepared for this astounding confession, but knew that Jehovah had given me many circumstances in my life for which there was no warning. Now my family had expanded again. I was to have a grandson!

"Bring Mishael to me as soon as you can. We must get acquainted," I said. "I do not know how much longer the Lord will leave me here."

Even as I finish this part of my journal, I know there are some who are plotting for my demise. I am visible once more, with my interpretation of the handwriting on the wall, and a potential threat to those who would court the favors of the new ruler of Babylon.

I laugh as I write this. That this old man, growing more feeble in body each day, should be looked upon as a danger to anyone!

However, I have no time to muse over my personal popularity. My time, I believe, is growing short, and there is still much to do.

Tonight, as I come to the end of the story about the Feast of Disaster, there is joy in my heart. How I wish I could write with the eloquence of the psalmist:

> Praise the Lord! Yes, really praise Him! I will praise Him as long as I live, yes, even with my dying breath. Don't look to men for help; their

greatest leaders fail; for every man must die. His breathing stops, life ends, and in a moment all he planned for himself is ended. But happy is the man who has the God of Jacob as his helper, whose hope is in the Lord his God. . . . He is the God who keeps every promise.*

Yes, He keeps every promise. And fulfills every prophecy.

* Psalm 146:1–6, LB.

12

JAWS OF DEATH

My people prepared for the Feast of the Passover this year with new hope for the future. As families and friends gathered to commemorate God's deliverance of His people from bondage in Egypt, they talked about what might happen to them now that Babylon had fallen to the Medes and the Persians. Moses had pleaded with Pharaoh, "Let my people go." Would the new rulers heed this cry from the exiled Jews, so long held from returning to the Holy City?

Lambs were slain and their blood placed upon the lintels over the doors and on the side-frames, just as the Lord had told Moses and Aaron many generations ago. Unleavened bread and bitter herbs were prepared for our time of worship together.

Outside our closed doors were new conquerors, new masters preparing to establish their rules of the kingdom. But within our separate sanctuaries we were obeying Jehovah, who told my people that the blood of the lamb is a sign of divine protection and preservation from death.

Although my years are many, at Passover time my thoughts return to the house of Abiel. The warmth of the rooms, the glow of the lamps, the carefully prepared food for the ceremony—what cherished memories there are for children who know they are loved. I can still recall the feeling of wonder when toward the end of the Seder the front door of our house was opened to demonstrate that this was a "night of watching," a night in which the children of Israel would know no fear. I would stand beside my father, holding his big hand, and stare into the blackness of Jerusalem, but I was never afraid. My father always held me tightly.

And I am not afraid now, although tomorrow our lives may change.

Jeshua was very quiet during the Passover Feast, partaking mechanically of the food and singing the beloved psalms by rote—without feeling. I did not press him to speak. He must settle for himself the turmoil which has beset his heart within the past days. The revulsion of Belshazzar's feast and the significance of the handwriting on the wall must be resolved within his mind. I cannot do this for him.

We had a new member at our table, a solemn little boy by the name of Mishael. He greeted me with respect—or, perhaps it was fear—and addressed me as "Prophet Daniel." The ritual of Passover was strange to my new little friend, but he loved the singing and even joined in searching for the hidden half of matzah.

I find it is refreshing to have a child at my feet. He has his father's hair, although his dark curls are only lightly tinged with copper. He follows me with his eyes, as his grandfather did. Perhaps in time to come we shall have a match to see who can keep his eyes steady the longest.

I must admit there is a revival of excitement in this old body. Mishael makes me feel young again, as only a lively, curious boy can do. And the arrival of the Persians is a prophetic fulfillment which gives me a sense of anticipation. How will they rule? Are we approaching the time of the end of exile?

The king of Persia, one Cyrus by name, is a man whose fame has preceded him. It has been told that his grandfather, Astyages, king of the Medes, had a vision that his daughter would have a child who would conquer all of Asia. This worried Astyages so much that he commanded a servant to slay the babe as soon as his daughter gave birth. The servant exposed the child, Cyrus, but a shepherd found the infant and raised him. When Cyrus became a man, he overcame the Medes, and in so doing took away the power of his own grandfather, the man who had wanted him murdered.

The boy Mishael listened attentively as I told him about the new rulers of Babylon. (He will be an eager audience for my teachings, I can see.) I told him that the Medes and the Persians came from a land east of the Tigris, where the snow-tipped Zagros Mountains gleam against the sky. To the north of Susa, where I had my vision of the four beasts rising out of the sea, the Persians rose from obscurity to dominance within the lifetime of one man. For a time the Medes and Persians formed a weak alliance, but when Cyrus captured the Median capital of Ecbatana he won control over the whole empire.

Cyrus has had a brilliant rise to power. And now, with the capture of Babylon, he is the undisputed king of the four corners of the earth. If we can believe the reports we have of him, he will be a tolerant ruler, one who may be able to bring some order out of chaos. We shall see.

I have been told that the religion of the Persians is called Zoroastrianism and that fire is sacred to them. They do not execute by using the furnace, as the Babylonians have done, because the flames would be contaminated by corpses. I wonder what their method of execution is? (A gruesome thought which I should not allow my mind to contemplate.)

I am anxious to meet Cyrus, if the Lord wills. Meanwhile, I have been summoned by his appointed viceroy, King Darius. Now, I must go find myself a new tunic and robe. I am very shabby, and a royal summons should be treated with respect. I shall have to ask Jeshua where to obtain my garments, since it has been many years since I required anything new.

My New Job:

It seemed strange to walk around the palace and see the repair work which is being done. It looks cleaner, more polished. The standards of excellence promoted by Nebuchadnezzar are being revived, although I do not believe the grandeur and opulence of his reign can be duplicated. Instead of the destruction we saw under Belshazzar, the new regime is initiating improvements.

I was shown into the throne room, which has been wonderfully restored. The great hall was filled with distinguished-looking men, most of whom were, as far as I could tell, much younger than I, and dressed in garments of more elaborate quality. Perhaps Jeshua did not advise me well.

I found it interesting to view this familiar hall now filled with unfamiliar faces and customs.

The Persians used pages with wands to usher us to the throne. These are young boys who prance like well-groomed colts. They have loose scarves around their mouths, and I was told that it is the custom for the servants to muffle their breath lest it touch the nostrils of the monarch. (I wondered if the leeks I had for my supper would be noticeable.)

I had also been informed that when I approached the king I should keep my hands in my sleeves. Obeisance to man does take strange forms!

Darius does not have a cruel face. He must have been chosen by King Cyrus for his ability to rule with compassion for the conquered, for the mood of the governors in the room was cooperative.

I approached him (my arms in my sleeves) when my name was announced. Darius was a colorful figure to behold. He wore a long purple overmantle, embroidered with designs in gold, on top of a striped tunic and crimson trousers. His head was adorned by a high flat-topped cap (called the "kidaris"), with blue and white ribbons hanging from it. Dangling from his ears and around his neck and wrists were massive amounts of jewelry. I wished Mishael could be with me to see how the king jangled as he moved.

Darius addressed me with respect, which was something I had not heard during the entire reign of Belshazzar, and said, "Daniel, I have been told of your long service to previous monarchs. It has also been reported to me that you are one of the wisest men in the kingdom."

(He may have doubted my wisdom if he had smelled the leeks!)

"And I have called all of you together," Darius continued, "to appoint governors over all of the one hundred twenty provinces of Babylonia. In this room, not counting myself and my servants, there are one hundred twenty-three invited men of influence and ability."

There was a murmur of appreciation from the assemblage. However, it did not take extraordinary intelligence to surmise that there had been three more invited than there were provinces to rule.

King Darius answered the unspoken question. "Three of you I have chosen to be presidents and to administer the kingdom efficiently. The governors will report to these three, who will in turn report to me. Those three . . ." and he paused to look around the room . . . "will be Shanabi, Nabubalitt, and Daniel."

I bowed with appreciation at such an honor, but had to chuckle to myself. Many have been saying that a man of my age has lost his usefulness. However, perhaps more than sixty years in public service has given me the required experience for such an exalted position.

Now that the proper introductions have been made to the governors under my jurisdiction, I have begun my administrative duties.

It is necessary to meet with forty governors (or satraps, as they are called by the Persians) and help them plan the ruling bodies of their provinces. Some of these governors are unfamiliar with Hammurabi's law codes, which have regulated the commercial, social, and domestic life of Babylon for over six centuries. I have always marveled at the similarity between these codes and the Mosaic Law. It is a consuming task to see that these men administer with wisdom and fairness. Some of them do not even understand our system of canals. My work is not light. But I thank the Lord God Jehovah for this new responsibility. Although it is by the decree of King Darius, I know it is by design of the one God I serve.

OPENING THE BOOKS:

How grateful I am to the Lord God Jehovah that through all these years of exile my people have had the written words of our prophets and holy men to turn to for guidance and instruction. Only today, in reading the scrolls of Jeremiah, I made a discovery that has stirred my soul and increased my understanding of where we are in the Lord's appointed time.

During all the years of exile it has been very difficult for my people to be denied the opportunity to worship at their Temple. The Lord has been gracious in providing us with the scrolls, some brought across the mountains and deserts with great care by the exiles, others received from merchant caravans. (How desolate we would be without them!) But my people have missed the Temple, for it was there they believed they were coming into the very presence of the Lord. At first they felt cruelly cut off from access to Him in Babylon. But then, as the priests comforted them and they listened and read in their homes and small gatherings, they discovered that they could encounter the Lord without entering the Temple in Jerusalem.

I believe that, when my people are allowed to return to Jerusalem (and I am revealing a hint of my exciting discovery), a new manner of worship will have been established by the use of the small sanctuaries, houses of study, and synagogues for prayer.

I had been sitting by my table with the scrolls of Jeremiah spread before me when Jeshua entered, Mishael following his footsteps. The boy was frequently with his father these days, and I was grateful for every opportunity I had to see him. I slipped a sesame cake into his hand and gave him a wink. He winked back. His sober young face is beginning to relax as he becomes less fearful of my grey hair and beard.

Jeshua was flushed and very upset over something; he told me he had bad news. But then, Jeshua is frequently agitated; I have become accustomed to it. I invited them to sit down, for I was anxious to share my excitement. Also, I believed that, whatever was bothering Jeshua, my good news would overshadow his concern.

I spread the scroll before them and said, "I have been reading from the words of my old friend, the prophet Jeremiah, and listen to what he has to say . . ."

They had no choice. They had to listen.

"Jeremiah said, 'Israel and her neighboring lands shall serve the king of Babylon for seventy years. Then, after these years of slavery are ended, I will punish the king of Babylon and his people for their sins; I will make the land of Chaldea an everlasting waste.' "

Jeshua was paying attention. He had seen for himself the punishment of the king of Babylon.

"But there is more," I continued. "The Lord gave Jeremiah this prophecy: *after* the seventy years in Babylon, our people will be released from bondage and allowed to return to Jerusalem." I paused to allow the impact of that prophecy to reach Jeshua. Mishael didn't understand, but watched me intently. (I am looking forward to the day he begins his studies.)

Jeshua did not respond. "Don't you realize what that means?" I said. "Listen . . . the time has almost come. We have been in exile for sixty-seven years. Can you understand what you may see in your lifetime? The return to Jerusalem!"

If I had expected some sort of a dance around my room, or even a hearty smile, I was sorely disappointed. Jeshua shook his copper hair and stood up, spilling my goblet of palm wine on the table.

"Daniel, you sit there reading from a dusty scroll, telling me of these prophecies, and yet right now there are powerful men plotting for your death. Isn't my news more important than the words of an old man—even a prophet?"

"Nothing is more important than the word of God," I said, a little pompously, I must admit. "Furthermore, I believe the Lord will plan my death when He is finished with me." I was curious about this death plot, however.

Jeshua began to pace the room, and Mishael's little face again grew very somber. "When King Darius appointed you as one of the presidents, it was an insult to most of the Medes and Persians in that room," Jeshua said.

I was not totally ignorant of that fact.

"You are a Judean; you have served under Babylonian kings; and to be recognized as an equal, or superior, is an outrage to them," Jeshua's words spilled out in a torrent.

I listened.

"They have been asking questions all through the city, trying to find moral or intellectual weaknesses to condemn you." For the first time, Jeshua broke into a rueful smile. "But, my dear friend Daniel, no one can find anything to criticize." He paused, then became more serious, "Except your religion."

So be it, I thought, but wanted him to continue. For Jeshua to come to my defense was gratifying; my old heart was warmed.

"I have my spies in the court," Jeshua said, "and I have learned that this morning there was a gathering of the other two presidents, all the governors, the counselors and deputies, who went to the king with a petition."

"But I was not invited," I protested.

"So," said Jeshua, "I have your attention at last!

"These men bowed before the king, flattering him to satisfy his vanity, and told him it had been decided unanimously that King

Darius should make an irrevocable law that for the next thirty days anyone who asks a petition of any god or man except from King Darius himself would be thrown to the lions. He was handed his official seal and pressed it upon the document, signing it into law.

Jeshua laid his hand upon my shoulder. "They have tricked you, Daniel. These unprincipled men know you would not be disloyal to your Lord. You must leave the city for the next thirty days where they cannot find you."

Mishael spoke for the first time, raising his eyes to mine with a pleading look. "Will you take me with you, Prophet Daniel?" he asked.

I placed my hand on Mishael's shoulder and turned to Jeshua. "My son," I said, "the Lord has placed me as one of the presidents for a reason. I cannot run from my responsibilities or change my commitments. I am staying here." I looked at Mishael, pleased that he would want to be with me.

"Responsibility! Commitment! By all the gods of Babylon, we are talking about your life!" Jeshua shouted. "Have you seen a pit of lions? They are so hungry and vicious that when some poor soul is thrown to them they leap up and rip him to shreds before he hits the ground. I have been close enough to hear the cries of those condemned to such a death!"

Jeshua's distress was growing even as he spoke. "I saw my father murdered," he said, "I don't want to see you slaughtered like a sacrificial lamb!"

At this Mishael began to cry. I wanted to comfort him, but I also wanted him to understand that a man did not deny the Lord for reasons of personal safety.

"I shall continue to pray three times a day, as I have done all my life," I told Jeshua. Did he think I would do otherwise?

The temper I used to see in his father flared in Jeshua. He knew there was no dissuading me, so he grabbed his son's hand and stalked out, slamming the door as he left.

Jeshua, how I love him. And in love, he has warned me as I did the prophet Jeremiah more than sixty years ago.

I do not know when I shall have time to continue my journal, since my duties are pressing, and I must spend more time in worship.

My prayers have never ceased to be directed toward Jerusalem. The roof-chamber of my house, added in recent years, gives me a free view toward the holy city, and yet this corner of my housetop is private enough for meditation, in case someone enters my door from below.

It is time for me to ascend to my place of prayer. Each year the rungs of my ladder seem to be more steep.

THE PLOT:

It was several days after Jeshua brought me the news about Darius's decree that I had my first official "visitors.". . .

I was on the roof as usual, praying. Whenever I fall upon my knees these days, I thank the Lord for the words He has given me through Jeremiah concerning my people's return to Jerusalem. When that will be, I am not yet sure; there are several possible ways to calculate the seventy years. But I have felt the reassurance of the Presence that it will be soon, and my heart rejoices at the prospect.

At any rate, I must have been praying for an hour before I realized that there were loud voices in the street below and a pounding upon my door.

I pulled myself to my feet, a simple movement that has become more difficult for me in recent years, and was thankful, again, that although my physical ability is dwindling, my mental capacities are still intact. (I thought with amusement that my dear Jeshua might not agree with that!)

"I'm coming," I called as loudly as I could.

When I opened my door I was greeted by the other two presidents and several of the governors of nearby provinces. One of them, Shanabi, evidently had been chosen as spokesman. And it was clear they were not there on a friendly visit.

Shanabi scowled at me and said, "Daniel, did we see you praying on your rooftop?"

"You did," I answered.

"And were you praying to your God you call 'Jehovah'?"

"I was."

It was quite evident that they had been watching me, just as Jeshua had said they would. How I wanted to reassure them that I had no desire for position or power, but they would not give me that opportunity! These men had deliberately placed my life in jeopardy by tricking King Darius with their clever scheme.

They asked no more questions, but turned and left, and I thought

I detected some satisfied smiles on their faces. I returned to make another slow ascent up the ladder to continue my prayers.

The following day I had another caller, this time with an order for my arrest! No questions were asked this time. My hands were bound behind me, like a common criminal, and I was led through the streets where I had spent more than threescore years of my life like a slave going to the place of auction. Citizens of conquered Babylon and my Hebrew friends gasped as I passed, escorted by four stalwart Persian soldiers. Somehow, even during such a humbling experience, I was amused by the scene. Two of the guards were armed with short spears, and two had slung quivers and cane arrows over their shoulders, with daggers hanging over their right thighs. They clanked as they walked; their iron trousers, which looked like fish scales, protecting the lower part of their bodies.

Such a formidable group to accompany an old man with a long grey beard wearing a robe and open sandals! What did they expect me to do? I had trouble just keeping up with their long strides!

When we arrived at the palace, I was shown in without the usual ceremony. King Darius was not sitting upon his throne, but pacing back and forth on the royal platform. The two presidents and many of the governors were lining the aisle in front of the dais. I walked through the center of this stern assembly; not a man looked at me favorably.

The king spoke, his voice was unsteady and his face showed concern. He was not an unjust man.

"Daniel," he said, "I am a representative of Ahura-mazda, the greatest of the gods. By his favor, and the appointment of Cyrus, I have been established as viceroy in this kingdom. Ahura-mazda and Cyrus have bestowed upon me divine powers."

His bracelets and other pieces of jewelry tinkled as he paced. He was rubbing his hands nervously and twisting the rings upon his fingers.

"All my appointed leaders advised me to issue a decree and sign into law that for a period of thirty days anyone who would ask a favor of any god or any man except from me, Darius, would be thrown into the den of lions." He paused, cleared his throat, and continued. "I signed that decree in good faith. The law of the Medes and Persians cannot be revoked. It is a matter of honor."

Not all the appointed leaders were there, I thought, but said nothing.

"I have been informed that you were seen praying on your rooftop to your Hebrew God. Is that true?"

"It is," I answered.

He suddenly pounded the arm of his throne with his fist. "I have been tricked," he said. "It has been told to me that you are a man who has been loyal to the one you call the Lord God Jehovah all the years you have been in Babylon. I have heard the stories of your prophecies to King Nebuchadnezzar, and the commitment to your God that he honored."

I thought for a moment he might weep. "I wish I could release you from this judgment, Daniel, for you are a man of integrity."

Shanabi stepped forward and said, "Your Majesty, there is nothing you can do. You signed the law and it cannot be altered."

Darius held his head and paced some more. The great room was very quiet. Finally he said, "Is there anything you can say in your defense?"

I answered. "I shall worship and praise the Lord all the days of my life, your Majesty."

I was sorry for King Darius. As the new ruler of the kingdom, he felt it necessary to establish his authority. He had been placed in an untenable position. I remembered how King Nebuchadnezzar had reacted many years ago to my three courageous friends who would not bow down and worship him; he had vented his wrath upon them by having them thrown into the fiery furnace. Darius, however, realized his own mistake in signing that decree, and was turning his anger upon himself.

How many times in my long life had I been called to this throne room? I could not count them. Monarchs had changed, kingdoms had risen and fallen. I had come as a prisoner when I was just a boy. And now I was a prisoner again.

Darius gave the command in a voice trembling with emotion: "I, Darius, appointed by Cyrus the Great, under special protection of the great god Ahura-mazda, according to the law of the Medes and Persians, order this man, Daniel, to be thrown into the den of lions before the dawn of a new day."

A murmur of approval was heard in the room. No one came forth to offer any objections, or give me any support.

I was accompanied by my four bodyguards to a cell within hearing distance of the den. The room was scarcely large enough for one person; there was no chair, no accommodations for my personal needs. I was left alone without food or water, and the only sound I heard was the growling of the lions. The intensity of their roars indicated the increase in their hunger.

Over and over again, the psalm I had learned at my father's knee came into my prayers: "Even though I walk through the valley of the shadow of death, I fear no evil; for Thou art with me."*

As I was praying, there was a tap on the door of my cell, and a face appeared at the small, barred window. It was King Darius. His face was distraught, the furrows in his brow deep with anguish. I wanted to reach out and comfort him, but there was a strong barricade between us with no room for a hand to be extended.

He said, "Daniel, I am so sorry for all of this. May your God, whom you worship continually, deliver you. I am going to spend tonight in fasting for you."

With those words he disappeared. It was gratifying to think that this new ruler would even acknowledge that my Lord was able to save me.

At that point I had no assurance what the hours before the dawn would hold for me. There were no visions, no visits from angels, only the quiet peace that my life was in Jehovah's hands.

However, that is not to say that I did not pray for protection! I was very tired by the time the guards came to lead me to the den. The cell was not large enough for me to recline and the tension of the past hours had left me in a state of exhaustion.

The roar of the hungry lions became almost deafening as we approached the large square cavern which had been dug deep below the surface of the earth. It was open from above, wide enough for several victims to be thrown in at a time, deep enough that the lions could not climb out. Surrounding this hole was a wall about as high as my chest. One could stand there and look far down into the den.

We stood for a moment, my four stalwart guards and I, and peered into the caverns. Below, about ten beasts were pacing, shaking their mighty bodies restlessly, growling, and baring their sharp teeth at the humans staring at them from above. An overwhelming gamy odor rose to meet our nostrils.

---

* Psalm 23:4, NASB.

I thought I had never seen such huge animals in my life. A blow from one powerful paw could down a fully armed man. Those jaws could snap off an arm like a twig on a tree.

The guards were anxious to finish their unpleasant duty and leave the scene. They stared down for a few moments, then picked me up and threw me over the side.

In a split second I thought, "My old bones will break before the lions touch me."

However, at that very moment I felt the softness of gentle arms surrounding my body. I saw nothing except a light that blinded me with its brilliance.

When I opened my eyes again, I was resting upon the reclining body of a lion, its shaggy fur providing me with all the soft comfort of a royal pillow. The same animals who just moments before had been ready to devour me now lay about me like oversized house cats contented in front of a warm fire. One huge animal stood in front of me, cocking his head to one side and then another. Evidently satisfied with what he saw—one harmless old man—he rubbed the broad side of his enormous head against my leg, stirring the circulation in my body with the motion. The others looked at me for a while, and then retired to their corners to sprawl in contented slumber. I reached out and ran my fingers through their tangled manes; what had been growls a moment before were now loud purrs. They licked my arms and hands with their rough tongues and gently placed their massive paws in my lap. I've never seen friendlier creatures.

"Lord, Lord," I laughed, "thank you for the decree of Darius and for sending your angels to guard me." What a story I would have to tell Mishael! But how will anyone ever believe this?

And with that, I fell asleep.

The next morning I was awakened by a voice calling to me from the opening above the den. It was Darius. He said, "O Daniel, servant of the living God, was your God able to deliver you from the lions?"

I stood up, rested after one of the best night's sleep I had enjoyed in a long time, and called back, "Your Majesty, live forever!" (It was, after all, my duty to answer him with the respect due his position.) "My God has sent his angel to shut the lions' mouths, for I am innocent before God, nor, sir, have I wronged you."

I could hear him laugh and clap his hands. In a few moments a basket was lowered. I said goodbye to my animal friends and was lifted out of the den.

The king embraced me with tears rolling down his cheeks. He kept saying, "You haven't a scratch upon you. Your God is a powerful God!"

The king did not delay in his orders. He commanded that all the men who had accused me, along with their wives, concubines, and children, be thrown into the lion's den.

It is with great sorrow that I record this manner of vengeance. It was reported throughout the city that the victims did not reach the bottom of the pit alive. The lions leaped up and tore them apart before they fell. It was hard for me to believe that these were the same gentle beasts who had provided me with rest and companionship.

Then Darius issued another decree. This time he ordered that everyone should tremble and fear before the God of Daniel in every part of the kingdom. Here are the remarkable words of that pronouncement, written by a pagan king:

"For his God is the living, unchanging God whose kingdom shall never be destroyed and whose power shall never end. He delivers His people, preserving them from harm; He does great miracles in heaven and earth; it is He who delivered Daniel from the power of the lions."

I, Daniel, now face my tomorrows with eager anticipation. I do not know how one lifetime can contain so many blessings. However, there is a stirring within me that there is more to be revealed.

I long to know more of the coming of the Rock cut from the mountain without human hands, of the one called the Prince of Princes. Am I to receive a revelation about the Messiah? How long, Lord, oh how long will it be before His coming?

I feel like I am on the brink of a great canyon which is covered with a hazy mist. Soon the cloudiness will evaporate, and a magnificent panorama will be unveiled.

My life is a question mark. What is it, Lord, you would have me do?

And He answers, "Wait."

13

PRAYER AND PROPHECY

My journal has lain idle for three years. Now, however, I have a new sense of urgency to resume my writing, hoping that these words will be preserved by the miraculous hand of the Lord who has called me to be His servant. I feel I cannot delay my recording in these scrolls. For the Lord has given me new revelations which must not be lost to future generations.

It is a quiet life I lead these days in Babylon. So many who were my friends are gone now; that is one of the hazards of living to an old age. The two members of my adopted family, Jeshua and Mishael, are a paradox. Jeshua is working as a superintendent of the palace repair and is frequently away; he does not often attend the gatherings in the synagogue. He lives alone with Mishael, since the boy's mother left the province to be wed to a Persian in Susa.

But Mishael is my joy. He visits frequently and sits on the floor at my feet asking questions about the Law and the prophets until I am too weary to answer.

The kingdom itself has changed since the time when I had my night with the lions. (Mishael asks me to tell that story over and over again; it seems to have great appeal to children.) Cyrus the Great has taken over the throne from his viceroy, Darius. He has been a fair-minded ruler and has reestablished, for a time, a reign of tolerance.

But I am growing impatient. The Lord has told me "wait" so many times that I sometimes feel as if I have iron boots upon my feet. I long to gain new strength, to walk and not become weary, as Isaiah the prophet has said.

My people have served the kings of Babylon for seventy years. They have built temples in this land; they have married and had children; many have died. Some have given up hope, as Jeshua has, but others still believe that someday, as their fathers and grandfathers have told them, they will return to Jerusalem.

Lord, when? When will you release your children from bondage?

I have searched the books, and as I have read over and over the words of Jeremiah, I am more convinced than ever that the exile is to end after seventy years. But when does the date of that time begin? Did it begin from the time I, Daniel, first came with the little group of young people on that unforgettable journey led by Arioch? Or does the time start when the Temple was completely destroyed?

So many questions have been plaguing my spirit in the past few weeks; so many burdens for my people have weighed upon me. In the past few days they became too heavy for me to carry, so I carried them before the Lord. I bolted my door from any intrusion and knelt before the Lord God Jehovah wearing the rough garments of sackcloth and sprinkling myself with ashes. I felt I could not adequately confess my sins and the sins of my people without these outward symbols of grief.

"O Lord," I prayed, "you are a great and awesome God; you always fulfill your promises of mercy to those who love you and who keep your laws.

"But we have sinned so much; we have rebelled against you and scorned your commands."

I could do nothing but weep when I thought of the rebellion of my people. Over and over they have refused to believe the prophets the Lord has sent them down through the years. I carried shame for all the men of Judah, the people of Jerusalem and all Israel, who have been disloyal to Jehovah.

My voice was choked with the agony of confession.

"O Lord our God, we have disobeyed you. We have turned away

from you and haven't listened to your voice. And you have done exactly as you warned us you would do . . . never in all history has there been a disaster like what happened at Jerusalem to us and our rulers.

"Every curse against us written in the law of Moses has come true; all the evils he predicted.

"O Lord our God, you brought lasting honor to your name by removing your people from Egypt in a great display of power. Lord, do it again! Though we have sinned so much and are full of wickedness, yet because of all your faithful mercies, Lord, please turn away your furious anger from Jerusalem, your own city, your holy mountain. For the heathen mock at you because your city lies in ruins for our sins."

I find it hard to record my prayer. My tears stain the scroll. I know the power and the love of the Lord. He has given me interpretations of the dreams of kings and visions of kingdoms to come. He has brought the mightiest king of Babylon back from a living death to praise Him and be His servant. He has sent His angel to bring my friends out of the midst of fire and quieted the beasts who might have devoured me. And yet thousands in this very city say, "If your God is so powerful, why does he leave the sons and daughters of Judah in bondage?"

"O our God, hear your servant's prayer! Listen as I plead! Let your face shine again with peace and joy upon your desolate sanctuary—for your own glory, Lord. . . . See our wretchedness, how your city lies in ruins. . . . We don't ask because we merit help, but because you are so merciful despite our grievous sins."

I had been praying for many hours—I don't know how long. The day had turned to night, and I had eaten nothing since dawn. Every part of my mind and body was sharpened in a manner which belied the calendar of my earthly years. Except for the difficulty I had in standing after being in a kneeling position for so long, I felt like a youth.

It was the time of the evening sacrifice. For many years that sacrifice had been interrupted. How my people longed for a return to the Temple, where the guilty worshiper, after he had committed sin, could bring his animal to the altar and have it slain as expiation for his sin.

For our God requires a sacrifice to atone for sin. I remember when my father first told me the story of Abraham and Isaac—how God commanded Abraham to take his beloved son to a high mountain, to build an altar there and gather wood for a fire. When Isaac saw this he asked, as any curious lad would, "But where is the lamb for the burnt offering?" And his father answered—it must have been with great agony—"God will provide himself a lamb for a burnt offering."

Abraham knew that God had told him to bind his own son and lay him on the altar. And his devotion to the Lord God Jehovah was so great that he was willing to do that.

But God intervened because Abraham was true to Him, and saved Isaac. He provided another sacrificial lamb.

"Lord, how can our sins be forgiven without a sacrifice? When will we return to your holy mountain?"

The Prophecy of Seventy Weeks:

My prayers were interrupted by a visitor. No locked door could keep him out, for walls built by man are no obstacles to him. I wish that more men could be honored with a visitor of such holiness. (Perhaps there will be a time in the Lord's eternal kingdom when all people who believe in Him will meet angels—or be angels!)

It was the second time the angel Gabriel, the one known as the "hero of God," had appeared to me. The first time had been in Susa by the riverbank; he had told me the meaning of my dream about the ram and the goat. And already some of his explanations have come true, for the two horns of the ram—Darius and Cyrus, the kings of Medea and Persia—were even now ruling Babylon.

When I first met Gabriel, I had fainted in his presence. Awed, I prayed that I would be more alert this time. What more was he going to reveal to me?

I recognized the angel immediately, but could not speak his name. He surrounded my being with pure light, and yet he had the visage of a man. His robes held no ornament and contained no color, but they were the most beautiful raiment my eyes have beheld. His face was kind, his eyes piercing with an intelligence which seemed to see beyond my earthbound being into a realm I could not comprehend. I longed to touch him, but my arms were incapable of movement. When he spoke, his voice was clear and resonant, like the sound of the shofar that the priests blow to begin the religious ceremonies.

When Joshua gave the order to the priests to sound the shofar, the walls of Jericho fell. And so I fell before Gabriel, the angel of the Lord.

He revealed to me a prophecy infinitely more than that of seventy years. It is of a time so far in the future that to think of it stretches human comprehension to the limits. If ever I have felt that the Lord has greatly blessed me with important positions in Babylon, these prophecies of things to come have humbled me in their majesty.

I wanted to confess my unworthiness to Gabriel, but he did not give me the opportunity to open my mouth. My tongue was silenced, although my thoughts may be recorded in this humble journal.

"Daniel," he said, "I am here to help you understand God's plans. The moment you began praying, a command was given. I am here to tell you what it was, for God loves you very much."

(My every wish through the years of my life has been to do the will of the Lord God Jehovah. My life is His. There is no greater honor that I desire than what the angel Gabriel gave me . . . to know that I am greatly beloved by God.)

"Listen, Daniel, and try to understand the meaning of the vision you saw.

"Whereas the prophet Jeremiah predicted seventy years of desolation for Jerusalem, and you, Daniel, know that time is coming to a close, God has another prophetic period in mind to tell to you.

"The Lord has commanded seventy weeks of further punishment upon Jerusalem and your people."

Gabriel did not say "seventy weeks of days," so I knew he was referring to "seventy weeks of years," which has been the meaning from the days of the Law. I did not need an abacus to know that seventy weeks of years would be seventy times seven, or four hundred ninety years. But why, I thought, is so long a time being revealed to me? On the other hand, I knew that even within this prophecy there may be mysteries that would not be revealed until the very end of time.

Gabriel did not rush his words. I knew that he wanted me to understand as much as I could, and to be able to accurately record what I heard.

He told what God would do in that coming period of four hundred ninety years, and how these things would come to pass. Gabriel told me that the disobedience of Judah—indeed of all Israel—will cease, and an age of obedience will be ushered in. He said that Israel will make things right with God when they are again in their land, and that all my people will have their guilt cleansed.

Gabriel said there will be a kingdom of everlasting righteousness and a new Temple would be rededicated on Mount Zion.

I could not understand these words, for I remembered that Jeremiah had said that a Righteous Branch would come from the lineage of King David. This great King would bring justice to the earth, and in those days all Judah would be saved from their sins. So how could this kingdom of righteousness of which the angel Gabriel spoke be brought in before the great King appeared?

Gabriel thrilled my soul and then destroyed my hopes with his next prophecy.

"Now listen!" he said, as if knowing my unspoken thoughts. "It will be forty-nine years plus four hundred thirty-four years from the time the command is given to rebuild Jerusalem, until the Anointed One, the Messiah the Prince comes! Jerusalem's streets and walls will be rebuilt despite the perilous times.

"After this period of four hundred thirty-four years, the Anointed One will be killed, his kingdom still unrealized."

(I do not pretend to understand how Messiah the Prince will be killed. However, I did do some speculation about this revelation which was given to me by Gabriel. If there are four hundred ninety years of prophecy before the kingdom of everlasting righteousness will begin . . . and the Anointed One will be killed after a period of four hundred eighty-three years from the time of the decree to rebuild Jerusalem, then there are seven years which are unaccounted for at the time of the death of the Anointed One. In the timing of the Lord, I am not able to understand what will happen during that seven-year period.)

Gabriel continued giving his account in such a precise, detailed manner that only the One who has the entire course of world events in His hand could have given him the message. He said, "After Messiah the Prince is killed, a king will arise whose armies will destroy the city and the Temple."

Then Gabriel told of an Evil One who will make a seven-year

treaty with the people of Israel; after three-and-a-half years he will break his word, stopping my people from all their worship and entering the sanctuary of God to completely defile it. My body grows cold when I hear of this man of such immense iniquity. I have had glimpses of his character in years gone by, especially in the little horn of the fourth beast which was revealed to me in my first dream. I was told then that he will be the master of deception—shrewd, clever, and able to astound the world with his intelligence. Now Gabriel was telling me of him again.

"Daniel, Daniel, listen to these words," Gabriel proclaimed, his voice a trumpet sounding over the cacophony of my troubled thoughts, "Fear not, in God's time and plan, His judgment will be poured out upon this Evil One."

God will triumph! Although evil will reign, the ultimate victory belongs to the Jehovah. May I never forget this great and ultimate hope!

And that was all. It seemed that I heard a banging upon my door, like the fist of an insistent caller. There was no light in my room; Gabriel was gone. I groped for a lamp, but finding none I called through the darkness, "Who is it?"

"Daniel, are you there?"

How could I have answered if I had not been there? (I praise God that through visions and dreams, through lions' dens and kings' palaces, he has not taken my humor from me.)

"Jeshua, come in; I cannot see," I said.

I could not tell him of my visit from Gabriel. If he could not understand those things he could see, how could he begin to comprehend those which are unseen?

But perhaps I underestimated Jeshua. He stumbled into the room, holding a light that cast dancing shadows upon the wall. "Bring me your lamp, Daniel, that I may light the oil." His voice was quick, excited. I had not heard such enthusiasm in him for many years.

As the room brightened, I was able to see his face. He looked so much like his father that I almost called him Aaron. His words tumbled out in the manner in which his dear mother used to speak—rapid and breathless.

"Daniel, it has happened at last! Cyrus has decreed that our people can return to Jerusalem. The period of exile is over; we may go back to our land. I have a copy of the proclamation here. Let me read it."

He pulled a scroll from beneath his cloak and laid it upon the table, moving the lamp close so he could read.

"I, Cyrus, king of Persia, hereby announce that Jehovah, the God of heaven who gave me my vast empire, has now given me the responsibility of building Him a Temple in Jerusalem, in the land of Judah. All Jews throughout the kingdom may now return to Jerusalem to rebuild this Temple of Jehovah, who is the God of Israel and of Jerusalem. May His blessings rest upon you. Those Jews who do not go should contribute toward the expenses of those who do, and also supply them with clothing, transportation, supplies for the journey, and a freewill offering for the Temple."

I wanted to shout with joy—my prayers had been answered! Yes, I had expected the decree; Jeremiah had prophesied it. But it was Jeshua's reaction I was not prepared for.

He placed his arms on the proclamation and covered his face with his hands, and his entire body began to shake with sobs. I had not heard him cry since the night of Belshazzar's feast. I put my hand upon his shoulder until his emotions were spent. In my heart I was rejoicing, because I believed these were tears of repentance.

When he raised his head, I saw that the bitterness had gone from his face. He said, "Daniel, I have been so wrong. My heart has been so filled with hatred that there was no room for the Lord. I hated my mother and father for making me a part of two worlds, Babylon and Judah. I hated the idol worship and debauchery of this city, but found myself pulled into it. I hated myself for my relationship with Ramach, and even found it difficult to accept my own son."

"I know, Jeshua, I know," I replied. I had not been so blind all these years!

"Just before I heard of the decree of King Cyrus, I found a copy of the writings of Ezekiel; my mother had preserved them in a jar in her house. I read this: '. . . When I have brought you home to the land I promised your fathers, you will know I am the Lord. Then you will look back at all your sins and loathe yourselves because of the evil you have done. And when I have honored my name by blessing you despite your wickedness, then, O Israel, you will know I am the Lord.' "

I was not able to reach him, and yet the man the Lord sent to be a priest to the exiles had touched Jeshua's heart with his writings. I wonder if someone will someday read my journal and be touched by the power of the Lord in the same way.

Then Jeshua said the words for which I had been praying these many years.

"My old friend, Daniel, I want the Lord God Jehovah of Judah to be my God. I am going to Jerusalem and want you to come with me."

I walked to my small window and looked out at the courtyard which had been my garden for more than threescore years. There I had met with my three friends, Shadrach, Meshach, and Abednego—discussed our studies and prayed together. They are gone now, but some of their children might go to Jerusalem.

I could almost see Ashpenaz waddling along the path, puffing toward my door with some message from Nebuchadnezzar. Beneath that orange tree over there I had kissed Deborah. Then I remembered the night years later when Arioch had walked across that garden and told me of his love for Deborah.

None of these friends would see Jerusalem again. But here was Jeshua, this one who was like my son, wanting to return to the land he had never seen.

Some people believe that life is just a game of chance; they are like the ones who cast lots to gain a prize. Solomon had a proverb, however, which said, "We toss the coin, but it is the Lord who controls its decision."

I did not need to toss a coin.

"Jeshua, you must go. And I shall provide you with the supplies you need. But I cannot go with you. The Lord has given me more light upon things to come and I do not believe He is finished with me yet. I must stay here and study and pray. I am old, and the strength I have left must be used in His service in Babylon."

Jeshua pleaded with me, but it was to no avail. I know where I should be.

The next few months were filled with plans and activity, as some prepared for the return from exile. However, I was burdened that more were not going; not everyone wished to go back to Jerusalem. Life in Babylon had become comfortable for many, and they chose to remain. However, over forty-two thousand persons did return to Judah; in addition to seven thousand slaves, two hundred singers, and more than eight thousand donkeys, mules, camels, and horses.

King Cyrus was generous in donating all the gold bowls and other valuable items which Nebuchadnezzar had taken from the Temple at Jerusalem. Jeshua was given the task of counting all the holy vessels, and he told me that more than five thousand valuable pieces were turned over to Sheshbazzar, the leader of the returning exiles.

Jeshua and Mishael came to say goodbye before they packed their mules and began the long journey to Judah. Mishael has grown tall and has gained in knowledge in the past few years. I am proud of him. He is almost as old as I was when I came to Babylon; now he is retracing that trek and returning to Jerusalem in my place.

"When will I see you again, Prophet Daniel?" he asked, biting his lower lip to keep it from quivering.

My own voice was not much steadier. How I would miss them! "In the Lord's timing, my grandson. But I shall send you my journal when I am finished. It will be your inheritance from me. When the time comes, I will find a trusted caravan leader and give it to him. When you receive it, take it to the Temple and have the priest preserve it in a safe place."

We prayed together and I sent them off with the benediction the Lord had given to Moses almost nine centuries ago:

> The Lord bless you and keep you;
> The Lord make His face shine on you,
> And be gracious to you;
> The Lord lift up His countenance on you,
> And give you peace.*

If I had a voice to sing, I would sing with those who are returning! However, that is not one of the gifts the Lord gave me. I face each new day with anticipation, and also fear: I anticipate more prophetic visions, and yet I fear the responsibility of what these prophecies may mean. They must be preserved, not only for Mishael, but for all the generations to come!

Within me there is a mounting tension that the knowledge He has given me is only a foretaste of what is to come.

* Numbers 6:24, NASB.

14

BOOK OF THE FUTURE

JESHUA AND MISHAEL have been gone for two years now. I miss them, and so many of my friends who have returned to Jerusalem. Today I went to the Judean Quarter and visited with some of my people who have chosen to remain in Babylon. I am deeply troubled by what I have seen.

Abigail, the beautiful child whose sweet voice used to sing the psalms like an angel, is now practicing astrology and telling fortunes. As I passed the stall of Shelemiah, the merchant, I noticed that he was using the pressure of his thumb to hold down the balance scale and cheat his neighbor out of a fair price for his fruit. The synagogues are almost empty, except for the very old.

I spoke to many, urging them to return to reading the scrolls and praying, and to forsake the ways of Babylon. But most of them nodded and smiled, treating me with condescending tolerance.

Also, I was brought some news from Jerusalem which is very upsetting. I heard that Jeshua was in charge of supervising the rebuilding of the Temple, but that when the foundation had been laid and the priests had blown their trumpets and praised the Lord, enemies of Judah had begun stirring up dissension. Their deceit and trickery have caused the entire construction work to cease.

I have never had children, but I am old enough to feel that these, my people, are my children. Oh, my people, my people, you stay in Babylon and forget the Lord; you return to Jerusalem and are not able to build your Temple.

Lord, what will happen to my people?

I left the Judean Quarter and wearily made my way back to my rooms. With the affairs of the Hebrews in such a low state, I needed to pray.

For three weeks I prayed and fasted. I ate and drank only enough to sustain my life, and I saw no one. Finally, one day early in spring, two of my old friends persuaded me to go out in the sunshine and take a walk beside the Tigris River.

The following account of what happened to me is the most startling and significant of anything that I have recorded heretofore.

I pray, as the years of my life grow short, that I shall be able to finish the telling of the revelation I have been given before my body turns cold in death.

We were standing beside the river, watching the slow movement of the barges bringing goods to the market. The day hinted of the first warmth of the season to come, and the air held the faint perfume of fruit blossoms about to burst open. My senses were especially keen after the prolonged time of prayer.

I had been looking at the ripples in the water when I sensed that Someone was standing nearby. I looked up and saw before me a Person robed in linen, with a belt of purest gold. His skin was glowing, lustrous, and from his face came blinding flashes like lightning. His eyes were pools of fire. His arms and feet shone like polished brass, and his voice was like the roaring of a vast multitude of people. He was more than an Angel, He was a Person I dare not name because of His majesty.

My two friends saw nothing, yet they ran away, their countenances filled with terror, and hid.

I was left alone.

Then the Person spoke to me. All my strength left; I felt the ground come up and hit me and I lost consciousness.

Then a hand touched me. Gently, yet firmly, I was lifted to my hands and knees. My entire body was trembling. I heard a voice like that of the angel Gabriel, which said, "O Daniel, greatly beloved of God, stand up and listen carefully to what I have to say to you, for God has sent me to you."

I stood up, but I was trembling so much my legs found it difficult to support me. I could not see the other Person, the one who looked like a man. But somehow, I knew He was still there; I could feel His Presence.

The voice of the angel was soothing. He said, "Don't be frightened, Daniel, for your request has been heard in heaven and was answered the very first day you began to fast before the Lord and pray for understanding."

Even in my weakened condition, I could not help wondering why the Lord had not answered my prayer sooner. However, I had no idea the warfare that went on in the heavens when a man of God prays fervently.

Gabriel told me of the mighty battle he had with one of Satan's evil spirits. He said, "For twenty-one days the mighty Evil Spirit who overrules the kingdom of Persia blocked my way. Then Michael, one of the top officers of the heavenly army, came to help me, so that I was able to break through these spirit rulers of Persia. Now I am here to tell you what will happen to your people, the Jews, at the end times—for the fulfillment of this prophecy is many years away."

While the angel was speaking I was looking down, unable to speak a word. Then someone—he looked like a man—touched my lips, and I could talk again. I said to Gabriel, "Sir, I am terrified by your appearance and have no strength. How can such a person as I even talk to you? For my strength is gone and I can hardly breathe."

My voice was a whisper. I thought I was going to die beside the Tigris River that afternoon. However, I desired with all my soul to live to hear the prophecy for my people.

Then the one who seemed to be a man touched me again, and I felt my strength returning. The voice said, "God loves you very much. Don't be afraid! Calm yourself; be strong."

I felt energy flow through my body. My voice was restored and I said, "Please speak, sir, for I have been revived."

He sat down upon a rock beside the riverbank and motioned

for me to do the same. He spoke to me in clear language, although there were times when the Voice of the One who seemed to be a man sounded through the words of Gabriel.

The angel said, "Do you know why I have come, Daniel?"

I could only shake my head.

"I am here to tell you what is written in the 'Book of the Future.' Then, when I leave, I will go again to fight my way back, past the prince of Persia; and after him, the prince of Greece. Only Michael, the angel who guards your people Israel, will be there to help me."

And these are the prophecies he gave me for the future of my people, and for all people on earth.

THE MARCH OF KINGS:

In a manner so explicit that only the Lord God could know the fine details, the angel revealed to me prophecies concerning Israel and the nations that would rule the world.

I listened carefully, and the Lord allowed the exact circumstances of each reign of kings to stay in my memory, in order that I might relate them accurately.

First, he told me of the rise and fall of the empires of the Medes and the Persians. Then he told me of a mighty king who will rise in Greece, and who will rule a vast kingdom.

These are the same prophecies that have been given to me since the time of Nebuchadnezzar's first dream. However, now they were given with greater exactness; I was told of the kings of the north and of the south, Syria and Egypt, and of their conflict with one another and with my people.

I cringed again as I was told of a very evil man who will persecute my people with the worst of inhuman cruelties. However, he seems to be only a forerunner of the one who will be the most Evil One of all time. I had received descriptions of this person in the prophecy of seventy weeks—also in the little horn of the fourth beast.

And now I was told of him again. But this time the angel said this Evil One would be known at the time of the end.

The end? How can my finite mind comprehend what the end is

to be? Our God existed before time began and created all the creatures and the earth. He will exist for all time beyond. But what does the end time mean?

THE KING OF THE END TIME:

This Evil One will be the greatest blasphemer the world has known, for he will boast that he is greater than God. He will honor the god of force and make the winning of wars his god.

He will have fortunes at his command to bribe men to do his bidding, and he will appoint whom he chooses to rule over lands.

However, his reign will come to a catastrophic end, with a war which will make all previous wars pale in contrast.

First, the King of the South, the leader of a political and military force that comes from the south of Judah and Israel—from the land we know as Egypt—will attack the Evil One. At the same time, the King of the North—the King of Syria and other countries which may come into power to the north of Israel—will attack the military forces of the Evil One.

However, the Evil One will counterattack and invade Israel, as well as Egypt and the countries of the Libyans and Ethiopians. Then he will hear of further armies about to attack him from the east and the north. He will establish his tent-palace between the seas in the glorious holy mountain, which would be in our Holy City of Jerusalem.

The angel paused, seeing that I was greatly troubled and added, "But while the Evil One is there his time will suddenly run out and there will be no one to help him."

I was stunned by the impact of this prophecy. In a short time, while sitting by the great river, an angel of the Lord had told me what would happen in the generations to come with the kings of our world, and then of the far distant future, when the forces of the one king who would set him up as a world ruler and the head of a world religion would prevail.

This cannot be the end. The Lord God Jehovah is in command. His children will disobey and follow other gods, as they have since time beginning, but His kingdom shall rule forever.

"My people . . . what will happen to the chosen people?" I pleaded with Gabriel.

"At the time of the end," the angel said, "Michael, the mighty angelic prince who stands guard over your nation, will stand up and fight for you in heaven against satanic forces, and there will be a time of anguish for the Jews greater than any previous suffering in Jewish history."

How the Jews have already suffered throughout the ages! Now I am told there is more to come.

"And yet, Daniel," said the heavenly messenger, "every one of your people whose name is written in the Book will endure it."

To have one's name in the Book of Life is the most reassuring hope for all people of this age and ages to come.

He closed the prophecy with these words:

"Many of those whose bodies lie dead and buried will rise up, some to everlasting life and some to shame and everlasting contempt.

"And those who are wise—the people of God—shall shine as brightly as the sun's brilliance, and those who turn many to righteousness will glitter like stars forever."

The tears began to flow down these wrinkled cheeks. I have not been one who is prone to high emotions, like Jeremiah, but I knew then that the Lord God had given me the hope that I prayed for my people. I do not know when it will be, but I do know that during that time when the Evil One reigns in Jerusalem, many of God's chosen people will realize the truth as never before. They will awaken to "everlasting life," as the angel said.

Now, I shall continue to pray for everyone to believe in the one God. I do not know how they can continue with their worldly pleasures and pursuits of other gods, when the Lord God Jehovah offers such a shining hope!

SEAL THE PROPHECY:

How will my readers of the future understand these miracles and prophecies?

Will these scrolls be preserved and read?

The angel spoke to me and said: "Daniel, keep this prophecy a secret; seal it up so that it will not be understood until the end times, when travel and education shall be vastly increased!"

I knew then that as the time approaches for the period of great tribulation, many will begin to read these prophecies, as well as the words of the other Hebrew prophets, and they will begin to search for answers from the books.

Then the seal will be broken, and many will understand.

As I stood meditating on these revelations, I saw two angels on each bank of the river, and one of them asked Gabriel, "How long will it be until all these terrors end?"

He replied that the time of great tribulation will end three-and-a-half years after the power of God's people has been crushed; the Evil One will have his terrible reign for that length of time. Then he will be defeated, abolished forever by the God in heaven, who will set up a kingdom that will never be destroyed.

I longed to know more. I asked, "Sir, how will this all come out?"

But he said, "Go now, Daniel, for what I have said is not to be understood until the time of the end. Many shall be purified by great trials and persecutions. But the wicked shall continue in their wickedness, and none of them will understand. Only those who are willing to learn will know what it means."

The Light which has been present so many times in my long life shone upon the river, reflecting from the water with the brilliance of a thousand gems. Oh, Lord, I see the meaning of my life! My arms are uplifted in praise and glory! If I could stand on a mountain and shout Your praises to the world, I would do it. From the time I was bruised by the Chaldean guard and carried to Babylon by the order of Nebuchadnezzar, You were in charge. When Shadrach, Meshach, and Abednego walked through the fiery furnace, You were in charge. In the lions' den and the hall of kings, You were always in charge. Through three different rulers, You have placed me in leadership for Your purposes.

You have given me dreams and visions to tell all peoples of all nations. You are in charge!

Listen, my people, listen! The Lord God Jehovah is in charge! Out of Zion will come the Redeemer, the Messiah. He is the Rock, not made with human hands. And His name will be called Wonderful Counselor, Mighty God, Eternal Father, Prince of Peace!

Then the heavenly messenger gave me my final instructions, which caused my heart to sing with the greatest joy I have ever known. He said:

"But go on now to the end of your life and your rest; for you will rise again and have your full share of those last days."

So I close this journal on a note of triumph. May I give to all in generations to come who read these words the same wish:

"May you rise again with me, and may we share all the glorious tomorrows of eternity together."

Now I understand why I have been called upon to be the messenger of the Lord. It is to proclaim His power and glory! When my book is opened, God will provide His interpreters. Listen to them, for the word of Jehovah is sure and His plan for the future is certain.

Until God's great tomorrow . . .

Selah.

About the Author:

CAROLE C. CARLSON is a prolific writer and coauthor with more than a dozen books to her credit. Perhaps the best known is *The Late Great Planet Earth*—the bestselling nonfiction book of the 1970s—coauthored with Hal Lindsey, with whom Carole also wrote *Satan Is Alive and Well on Planet Earth* and *The Terminal Generation.* Other books include *Corrie Ten Boom—Her Life, Her Faith; Established in Eden;* and the autobiographical *Straw Houses in the Wind;* as well as collaborative efforts with Dale Evans Rogers (*Woman* and *Grandparents Can*), Corrie Ten Boom (*In My Father's House*), Bob Vernon (*The Married Man*), Skip Ross (*Say Yes to Your Potential*), and Billy Graham.

Carole and her husband, Ward, a management consultant, are partners in an Amway distributorship in southern California. They are parents of two grown children and have two grandchildren.